Beet Fields

ROBIN SOMERS

Contact @somers_r

Printed in the United States of America

ISBN 978-1-7349572-0-4

First Edition

14 13 12 11 10 / 10 9 8 7 6 5 4 3 2 1

This is a work of fiction. Names, characters, businesses, places, events, locales, and incidents are either the products of the author's imagination or used in a fictitious manner. Any resemblance to actual persons, living or dead, or actual events is purely coincidental.

For Dennis

Beet Fields

1

February, 2015

In normal years, the soil would be wet. But this wasn't a normal year. It was a year of records. Record drought and record heat. Record anchovy die-off, record humpback whales, and pelicans so numerous they drove the seagulls inland.

It was the gulls that woke her. Their screech pierced the morning and drew her to the balcony. The rising sun cast stunted shadows over the land, and the land prostrated herself to the coming heat and light. Meanwhile, the gulls foraged the bells beans. The beans should have been waist high by now but had failed to germinate for lack of rain.

Olive yelled at the gulls, and when her shouts failed to scare them, she ran barefoot from the house, down the narrow road, dodging potholes and loose gravel until she reached the fields. She entered at a row of beets. They reminded her of skulls. Underfoot, they felt like cobbles. The yellowed leaves had wilted to the ground and the vermillion roots rose from the dirt, calloused and rotting. Olive grabbed a loose beet—large as a softball—and threw it into the flock. One gull flew up and settled a few yards downfield. She threw another and another until the birds lifted in a complaining cloud of bone and feather.

That's when she saw him. A man, sprawled on his back and stark naked. She approached him cautiously, thinking he might have come down from the forest and passed out on her farm. His eyes were wide open and blue as the dull sky, the right one pecked by the gulls. A grayscale tattoo of a jellyfish spanned his torso. Tentacles trailed down to the right wrist. She stared at his hand, which she judged delicate for his size, and familiar. She knew this man. Cris Villalobos, her neighbor who lived across the road.

Olive knelt in the dirt and pressed his wrist. Unable to find a pulse, her fingers probed deeper, aching to find some current of life. She put her ear to his chest, listened for a heartbeat and detected a faint scent of chlorine. The only sign of blood was a nick under his left ear, as if he'd cut himself shaving, and a thread of blood in the crease of his neck. Not far from his head, she saw an indent in the dirt that could be a large boot print.

Her mind raced. Cris's wife Thea would still be working the night shift at the bakery. Her husband Cal was in Berkeley at the Farmers Market. She called 911 and began spewing too much information to the dispatcher—I was on my balcony … the gulls … the man … I couldn't get a pulse—until the dispatcher asked for her name and address.

"Olive Post. 111 Shell Bean Way."

"Are you alone?" the dispatcher asked.

Olive scanned the twenty acres of row crops and fledgling apple orchard. To the north, coastal redwood forest rose for miles up mountain. An old narrow gauge railroad hemmed in the property to the east. Behind her, a bramble-choked creek drained into the San Lorenzo River, and to the west backed into the coastal foothills was her home. Something caught her eye—a deer, coyote or human—and quickly vanished into the woods.

"I'm alone," she answered. "But my children are home asleep." She'd left in such a hurry, she hadn't locked the front door. Byrd was only four and Augusta had turned one last summer. They could wake up anytime.

"Ma'am," the dispatcher said, "we need you to remain on the scene until the police arrive."

"I can't stay here," she said. "My kids are at home." Then she called Cal. He'd left before dawn to rescue their broken-down box truck and its driver from the freeway outside of Oakland. He'd wound up taking the truck to market. The call went to voice mail. She had to tell Thea. When Thea didn't pick up, Olive called Little Bee Bakery.

"Thea," Olive said. "I found Cris in the field and he looks really bad. The ambulance is on its way and you have to come home."

Cal was calling back. She accepted the call and updated him in as few words as possible.

"I found Cris Villalobos in our field. He looks dead."

"Breathe," Cal said.

She didn't feel like breathing.

"Go home," he said. "Lock the doors and stay inside. I'll be there as soon as I can."

Olive stared down at Cris, strewn across the rotten beets and stunted bell beans. His gruesome blue eyes that she remembered being brown, his naked vulnerability, flaccid penis. She pulled off her sweatshirt, intending to cover his genitals before the onlookers arrived.

"Don't do that."

She whirled around to find Johnny Pogonip standing at the edge of the field, prancing side to side like a wolf on a rope. The neighborhood branded Johnny as one more in a growing population of transients. Olive considered him taproot, a man who lived in the forest above their farm because he preferred sleep under the redwoods to a roof over his head.

"Don't you watch TV?" He pressed his fingers to his temples and leaned toward her, bent at the waist, careful not to step off the asphalt into the dirt. "Put away the shirt and stand back unless you want the cops on your ass."

Olive wasn't afraid of the police, but she was having second thoughts about Johnny. She glanced back at the boot print then checked Johnny's feet. Tennis shoes, and his feet were small like the rest of him.

She stayed until the sirens grew into a deafening cacophony. The red paramedic engine with surf boards on top raced across the railroad tracks, the only entrance to the farm. The medics in navy blue uniforms lugged their equipment into the field. One knelt in the dirt and, as she placed white discs on both sides of Cris's groin to begin checking his vitals, a glimmer of hope raced through Olive that Cris might not be dead.

A female cop pushed into Olive and backed her away as two others strung a perimeter of yellow police tape around the scene. Olive, surprised, lost her footing and fell. As she got up, she noticed the sliding door to the greenhouse twenty yards away was open. They always kept the door shut to keep out feral cats and whatever else preferred a warm interior to a chilly night.

No one seemed to notice as she walked away from the scene toward the greenhouse. Inside, it looked like bobcats had used the seedling trays as litter boxes. Potting soil was scattered everywhere. Precious tomato seedlings littered the ground, their delicate roots exposed. Olive had spent hours in the greenhouse thinning and pricking out these seedlings. In spring they'd be transplanted to the field and become the cash crop that she and Cal counted on to deliver them from debt so they could farm another year.

She tucked a wilted seedling back into its cell and sprinkled a pinch of spilt dirt around its stem. Just as she wondered if the wreckage was linked to Cris, a voice ordered her to turn around. When the silhouette that hulked in the greenhouse entrance moved his hand to the gun on his right hip, she froze.

"Stand up."

She rose, brushing dirt from her hands onto her sweatpants.

"What are you doing here?"

"This is my farm. I live here."

"Ma'am. Answer the question."

The cop stared at her thin white T-shirt. She pulled back her shoulders. "This is my greenhouse. It's been vandalized."

"Your name."

"Olive Post. I'm the person who discovered Cris and called 911."

"What's your address?"

Clearly, they were not on the same side. At this point, he probably considered her a suspect. She told him her address and waved her arm around the damage.

"Whoever hurt Cris could be responsible for this." It seemed so obvious she almost didn't mention it.

"If that's true, ma'am, you've spoiled the evidence. What time did you find the victim?"

"Roughly seven."

"Did you hear anything. Dogs barking?"

Her two Australian shepherds had died last year, Pancho first and Pixie a few weeks later.

"I didn't hear anything until early this morning when one of my husband's employees woke us up with a phone call." Kat Granger had called at five in the morning to tell Cal that she'd run out of gas on the freeway outside of Oakland. Cal had left in the dark and when he located the box truck on the shoulder of the road, Kat had already abandoned it without a note or a text. Olive had told Cal that she should have checked the gas tank before she left town. But he'd defended Kat, saying the gas gauge was broken. "Even more reason to check the gas," Olive had replied.

"What's your husband's name?"

"California Post. Cal." She hugged herself and asked, "Is Cris dead?" The cop deflected her question and asked if she'd noticed anyone hanging around the area. She had. Johnny Pogonip, but she knew what would happen if she mentioned him.

"Johnny something." Pogonip was a nickname. "He camps in the park."

The cop spoke into his shoulder mic as he turned and abruptly left the greenhouse. Olive decided to leave through the backdoor next to the wash area.

She stepped outside, about to jump over a mud puddle, when she saw tire tracks. The crew, on principle, never parked this close to the greenhouse. The structure wouldn't hold up to a careless vehicle bumping into the glass siding.

As she held out her cell phone to take a picture of the track, she heard a cry. Byrd. She jogged to the road. Emergency vehicles were parked at all angles. Thea's yellow VW was nowhere in sight.

She saw Byrd standing on a rocking chair and leaning over the balcony, wailing, as a man pushed a microphone in her face. She recognized him. The reporter from the local television station.

"Just a few questions."

"I can't talk. My son," she said, as the reporter walked briskly to keep up and his sidekick lifted a camera onto his shoulder. Meanwhile, Byrd leaned over the balcony, bawling, and god only knew what Augusta was up to. Olive had left her asleep, but with the sirens and Byrd, she could have climbed out of the crib by now.

"How do you feel about what's happened here?" the reporter asked.

"What is wrong with you?" Olive pushed him aside and pointed her finger at her four-year-old, shouting, "Byrd, you sit down on that chair, now. One, two, three …" By four, he was down from the railing, his butt in the chair.

"What was he like?" asked the reporter.

She stopped and glared. "Seriously?"

"Just doing my job, ma'am."

Olive had been a reporter before she married Cal, and she'd been assertive in that role, but she'd never stood in the way of a mother trying to prevent her child from falling from a second story balcony. This one, she knew, wouldn't stop badgering her until she gave him something. "Cris Villalobos was the nicest person you could ever meet. He was the mayor of Shell Bean Way."

"What did you see?" His sheepish expression revealed he knew he'd crossed the line.

"I'm done here" she said. "Do not follow me."

Ahead, a black and white patrol car rounded the last curve of the forest road and proceeded through the open metal gate as Olive reached her driveway. The same cop who'd questioned her in the greenhouse drove past without a glance, while the man in the back seat looked up in defeat. Johnny. He leaned forward in a way that indicated he'd been cuffed. Johnny could not have killed Cris. He was no match in size or strength. He had no motive that she knew of. Then again, she knew very little about Johnny or, for that matter, Cris, outside of passing him on her daily walks on Shell Bean Way.

Olive opened the front door and saw Augusta teetering at the top of the staircase.

"Gus. Stop." Olive took the stairs two at a time, swept the girl up, and headed for the bedroom porch. Byrd was at the railing again. She grabbed him by his pajama top and pulled him back. The three of them collapsed into the old porch swing. Byrd whined of being hungry. He asked for the French toast she'd promised him last night before he'd gone to bed.

"A lot has happened this morning, sweetheart," Olive said. "I can't make French toast right now."

His round brown eyes narrowed and a crease deepened between his eyebrows. His father had that same crease when he was upset.

"You lied," he said.

"I didn't lie, Byrd. I intended to make French toast, but there's been an emergency and you need to be a big boy."

"I'm not a big boy." He stomped a foot and crossed his arms. "I'm a kid." He buried his eyes in his pajama sleeve and started to cry. "Where's my dad?"

"On his way home from the market," she said, pushing down his elbow and tipping his chin up for eye contact. He allowed her to wipe his tears with the hem of her T-shirt. "You can have some box cereal for a treat."

Byrd's crestfallen expression meant surrender, she hoped. A tantrum would topple her efforts at appearing calm and bury her focus. "You said French toast." He allowed her to wipe his tears with the hem of her T-shirt.

Cal picked up on first ring. Olive lowered her voice. She spelled it out for Byrd's sake. "Cris is d-e-a-d. And the greenhouse has been ransacked. Seedlings all over the place. I couldn't put them back in their cells because of the kids." She felt a painful lump in her throat and pushed it down. She couldn't add tears to the chaos.

"Did you tell the police?"

"About the plants? They weren't interested." From the balcony, she watched the ambulance leave. Cris remained on the ground.

"What's d-e-a-d?" Byrd asked.

"Cal, would you talk to your son? He was standing on the rocking chair leaning over the railing. Byrd, Daddy wants to talk to you." She handed the phone to Byrd, whose lower lip puckered and quivered.

"She counted on me," said Byrd. Pause. "No, like one, two, three ..." Byrd threw the cell phone across the balcony and stomped inside.

Gus started to paw her T-shirt. Olive suspended her efforts to wean the child and lifted her shirt, surrendering her waning breast milk to comfort her daughter as she watched the paramedics load the body into the Coroner's van. She didn't want that. She wanted the police to remain and the medics to stand around Cris a while longer. Cris was dead, but she didn't want him dead and gone. Especially before Thea arrived. The red paramedic fire engine was the last to leave, and in its wake, the wintered farm offered no sign that Cris had ever lived.

As the engine drove across the railroad tracks and brake lights flared, Olive heard the tourist train approach from the beach and boardwalk. She imagined how they would view from their open-air cars a pastoral landscape and become filled with awe at the otherworldly beauty they were passing through, oblivious to what had gone very wrong on this farm.

Cirrus clouds hovered as Gus continued pulsing Olive's breast with feathery fingers. The wispy cloud to the east did likewise—coaxing moisture from the dry air. Olive's feet throbbed. She turned her ankles inward and saw the bloody, dirt-filled cuts on the soles of her feet.

2

Olive pulled out her bag of flour and a sack of assorted apples. She was too distracted to bake an apple pie, but the aroma of a fresh apple cobbler might mask some of the day's wretchedness, at least for Gus and Byrd. It might help her to focus on something other than the dead body of Cris Villalobos.

As she pressed crumbs into a buttered glass baking dish, Byrd stood beside her on a small kitchen stool. Gus sat on the linoleum, banging wooden spoons on steel mixing bowls that Olive had placed on the floor upside down. The racket didn't bother Olive. Rather, it muffled the mental cacophony. Until she started slicing the apples and imagined a knife cutting flesh. Her hands shook as she layered Pippins in the bottom of the dish and Jonagolds on top to caramelize the juice.

"Let's give our cobbler to Thea," Byrd said, as Olive zested lemon rind.

"Wonderful idea." The scent of lemon eased her nerves and she decided a cobbler might comfort Thea, especially if Byrd presented it. Thea didn't have children, but she had a way with Byrd and Gus. Olive showed her son how to sprinkle the mixture of butter, zest, hazelnuts, and sesame seeds evenly over the apples.

"I want to do that by myself," Byrd said.

The thud of boots hit the patio bricks. Cal was finally home. He was in the mudroom, sitting on the bench as he removed his shoes. The elongated pause between the first and second boot hitting the ground signified exhaustion. Olive shoved the cobbler onto the oven's middle rack as Cal opened the porch door, and Byrd barreled into him. Gus raised a wooden spoon and shrieked.

"How are you holding up, babe?" He drew Olive close and brushed crumbs from her cheek while she studied his eyes, blood-shot from waking up so early and driving so many hours. "I'm really sorry you had to see this," he whispered into her ear.

"What did she see?" Byrd asked.

After a few moments of looking into each other's eyes, figuring out how to answer their son, Cal tussled his son's hair. "Time for a nap, Buddy. I'll tell you a story."

Sometimes kids are so in tune with family crisis that they co-operate. This was one of those remarkable times. While Cal herd-ed them upstairs, she took refuge on the living room futon, their meeting place. She checked her phone and text messages. A voice mail from Detective Henry Rogers asked her to call him. She'd known Rogers when he was a rookie cop. He hadn't been on the scene today. But she wanted to talk to him, wanted to know what the police were thinking about Cris's death. And Brody Hamilton, the farmer who'd helped Cal set up this morning at the Berkeley Farmers Market, had called.

"Hope you're doing okay," Brody's message said. "If there's anything I can do for you or Cal, let me know. You looked good on U-Tube."

She cringed. A comment on how she looked on television when someone had died was incongruous. Cal's footsteps down the stair-case were slow and steady compared to the frantic trips she'd made up and down those same steps since finding Cris. He sat down and snugged one arm around her shoulders and the other across her lap, hugging her thigh in a buffer zone of safety.

"How's Thea?"

She recalled Thea's VW finally driving up the road shortly after Byrd had thrown the phone. The way she'd sunk to the floor when Olive had gone to check on her. Thea's home—a fixed up log cabin that Cal and Olive had lived in before moving to this house—so neat and tidy, a home without children. Why had she been so long getting here? Olive had asked, kindly. I couldn't drive, Thea had explained. She'd sat in her car, hands frozen to the steering wheel, her vision skewed until a Highway Patrol pulled over to see if she was alright. She was not alright.

Olive shook her head. "She's in shock."

"They're saying Cris caught a drug addict rifling through our recycle bin for aluminum cans and the guy turned on him?"

"Who's saying this?"

"It's on Facebook."

"Herd mentality. How can they possibly know that?"

Cal wrapped his arms around her and moved a wisp of hair from her eyes. "I'll make us a fire."

When he knelt before the hearth, setting aside the screen, she gazed at the heels of his socked feet, recalling the boot print she'd seen. He crushed newspaper into balls, stuffed them under the grate. Laid on a few pieces of kindling and eucalyptus bark before setting down logs. Soon, his fire would ease her innermost craving for warmth and light. When he sat back down beside her, his thigh pressed against hers.

"Want to start from the beginning?" he asked.

She nodded and took a deep breath. "I heard the seagulls screeching and got out of bed. When I went out to the balcony they were foraging the bell beans. I shouted, but they didn't move, so I ran outside to scare them off, and that's when I saw Cris on the ground."

She turned to Cal. "It didn't look like Cris. Blue eyes. The gulls had pecked one. I'm sure he has brown eyes. Then I registered the tattoo. And his hands. Something about those hands, just," she snapped her fingers, "clicked. I called 911 and the dispatcher, I called you, no answer, called Thea, no answer. Felt like slogging through mud. Then Johnny Pogonip got weird on me and I saw the greenhouse door was wide open. A tire track near the back door. I took a picture of the tire track."

She'd already told all of this to Cal during their phone calls, but she needed to repeat it, and she knew she'd need to repeat it many more times before she could make sense of it. Cal dropped back down on his knees and placed an oak log on the flame, sending up sparks. He reached for another. "Babe, you're staring at my feet."

"I'm thinking of the boot print I saw near Cris. I didn't have my wits about me to take a picture."

Cal leaned back on his haunches. "Are you serious?"

"What?"

"You're wondering if it was my print."

"No," Olive protested.

"You're wondering if I was in the field and didn't tell you."

The question hadn't even occurred to her. "Were you?"

She thought back to that time one and a half years ago when Cal confided to her about something he'd done. Because she'd been eight months pregnant with Augusta, he believed telling her would have caused more harm to her and their unborn daughter than good. But he'd kept the secret far too long, from Olive's perspective, and now in a deep corner of her mind—the corner that she preferred lay buried—questioned what he might be keeping from her now.

"I wasn't in the field."

"You might've driven by his body."

"Could've. It was pitch black outside." Cal rubbed his afternoon stubble, frowning. "Olive, leave the sleuthing to the cops. Look what happened last time. I don't want to go through that again."

"Last time" she'd injected herself into foul play, the time of the secret, they'd almost lost their farm to a horrid landlady who intended to develop the farm into condominiums and town houses. Cal was still recovering from "the last time." So was Olive. And the wounds from what each considered a betrayal were still fragile.

To Cal's point, he became untethered when she was distracted. As long as she was emotionally present, he could perform the grueling daily grind of farming. She knew this; she knew that even the worst drought in California's history couldn't undermine his faith that, if he put one foot in front of the other, things would work out.

But the color had drained from Cal's face. And his forehead

webbed up with new lines she'd failed to notice until now. He stood up abruptly, and she regretted the boot thing.

"The safe," he said.

She hadn't thought to check their safe. It held a cubic foot of prized tomato seeds. That single cubic foot was potentially worth tens of thousands of dollars. Cal had built a two-hundred pound safe into the cement floor of the office for that purpose—to store their most valuable seeds and cash from the markets until they could propagate or get to the bank. Olive realized, as Cal just had, that if their tomato starts were valuable enough to destroy—if a person had destroyed them—the stored seeds could also be a target.

Cal left to check the safe but stopped at the swinging door to the kitchen and shouted back. "Don't you hear that?" He paused in the doorway with a baffled expression that left Olive confused.

"What?" she asked.

"Gus. She's crying."

Olive tried to run up the stairs while Cal ran out to check the safe, but her legs felt like stumps, so heavy they didn't feel like hers. When she reached the second floor, she was light-headed and her heart literally pounded. Familiar creaks in the old flooring that normally voiced complaints were oddly quiet as she walked down the hall to Augusta's room.

Gus had one leg over the rail, reconfirming for the second time that day her crib days were numbered. Face streaked with tears, red and swollen. She reached out, groping Olive's chest with her sharp little fingernails, not for a breast, Olive realized, but for the charm necklace she regularly wore. The necklace was gone.

Her mind balked at remembering everything that had happened before this moment because, she was certain, of today's trauma. The necklace was beautiful, that she remembered, and held more sentimental value than any piece of jewelry she owned, beside her gold wedding band. Cal had ordered it from the *Sundance Catalog* for their third anniversary. He'd personalized it with charms and special birthstones, a light green peridot for Gus and yellow topaz for Byrd. She touched her chest and felt a loss.

"Something's burning," Cal shouted from kitchen.

Yes, she thought, she smelled it now, and rushed downstairs, finding him bent over and staring into the open oven door. She put on mitts. Heat rushed into her face, whipping her eyes, as she listened to him tell her, "the seeds are safe, no sign the office was broken into." She slid out the cobbler. The bumps of the sugary strudel crust were dark brown, the edges along the glass dish even darker. She hovered like a mare above her colt. When she lifted a small dark mound from the burnt top, revealing pale cooked apples beneath, she imagined brown irises dissolving into blue.

3

Gil Souza swore at the fifty-pound sack that lay at his feet. What worthless dumb shit was responsible for this? Juan, Pedro or one of his other nameless workers? He'd never find out, and what if he did? A month ago, Gil reassured himself, the pesticide he had used for a decade was legal. Today, this split sack spilling poison as white as Johnson's baby powder was banned. Government regs were a seesaw depending on who was governor, so he'd stockpiled the product because it was the only chemical strong enough to kill those bugger Lepidoptera that were hell bent on egg-burrowing into his test crops.

He pulled work gloves from his back pocket and hoisted the fifty-pound sack into a blue plastic wheelbarrow. His palms gripped the handles as he pushed a straight line to the barn. That barn in all its whitewashed glory stored more than a century of his family's history. Built by his grandfather, who'd created the business from nothing but the seeds he'd brought from Portugal, along with a lot of blood, sweat and tears. The barn had stood its ground against earthquakes, storms, and changing times. The tall sliding doors on iron rails added charm with each passing year. The dirt floor was tamped to a matte gloss by more than a century of hooved animals and worn boots. Hand-milled old-growth redwood beams held up the roof. They also held the weight of Gilman Souza, Sr., Gil's father.

As Gil pushed the wheelbarrow through the doors, pigeons flew from the main rafter where he'd found his father hanging by a rope four decades ago. A young college man home for the summer, Gil had fought his suffering like he fought everything. Alone.

He dumped the sack of pesticide onto the far corner of the barn, then pulled a thick canvas top over it and left. He slid the doors shut and strode to his office, head down, swallowing hard and punching his thigh to keep that emotional ball in his throat from rising any further. "Forty years is enough."

No surprise, really, that his father had chosen to die, Gil thought. His father was the weak link in three generations. But, luckily, the family's small fortune that ebbed under his father's ineptitude flowed again once Gil took control.

He sat in his captain's chair and pulled a yellow legal pad out of the top drawer of his desk where he kept his handgun. He plucked a Bic from the leather dice holder. Then made a list:

call attorney – status of lawsuit
check deliveries
Call greenhouse contractor.
Call County Recorder
USDA/APHIS
note to D

D stood for daughter. He scrawled a few lines to warm up. *If you don't get an education you'll never get anywhere in life. I want to help you continue your education and suggest you return to college. I'll pay for it. Maybe a business degree. Love, Dad.* Although he was convinced his intention to reach out to his daughter was honorable, when he read the note he imagined her reaction. More likely, she wouldn't even read it. He crushed the note into a wad, aimed at the wastebasket and tossed an outside bank across the room. The note overshot the rim and rolled a few feet along the floor as if the universe were saying, why bother?

4

Gil told the waitress, who hovered over his right shoulder holding a glass pot of hot coffee, to turn down the music. "A person can't hear themselves think in here."

The waitress, a young woman with long blond hair worn in a thick braid, stepped back, intimidated by his rudeness. Gil didn't care. She had tattoos. Her entire arm was a sleeve of tattoos, and Gil didn't like tattoos. They were cheap and dirty, even on a pretty young woman's perfect skin. Why did she have to announce to the world she was loose, or worse—a sheep following the latest trend. These days everyone was a poet, and everyone had tattoos. He waited for her to leave his table and turn down the goddamn music.

Gil felt a slight headache on the right side of his head. Just a pinch, but the first time he got one of these, he'd thought he was having a stroke until his doctor told him it was from gritting his teeth. He inhaled and loosened his grip on the coffee mug, meditated on the view outside the café's plate glass window. A row of cars had parked perpendicular to the front of the café, which sat alongside the two-lane Coast Highway. On the opposite side of the highway were the cliffs where, from Gil's perspective, only harebrains and surfers hiked down to the beach. It wasn't a friendly beach. Narrow and rocky. The waves were crunchers and the riptides killed at least one dumb tourist a year. It was hard to feel sorry.

The café was packed this morning with locals and travelers who wanted to enjoy breakfast and fresh baked pastries before getting on with their day. But the service was good because he was a regular and they knew he'd either never return or have the owner fire someone if they didn't treat him special. He drank his coffee, looking over the mug. On the opposite side of the highway an abandoned railroad track ran parallel to the road all the way through Santa Cruz proper to the south end of the county into the Salinas Valley. The track had carried lumber and sand, until regulations forced the cement plant to shut down. Now the track was a ghost rail and the town wanted to convert it into a goddamn bike trail. Gil believed if you were lucky enough to have a railroad track, you had an obligation to use it.

The waitress's long braid touched his arm as she hovered. "Refill, Mr. Souza?"

Gil leaned away and pushed his mug forward a couple of inches. "I'll have a bear claw. And can you watch your hair, please." Gil held up his hand. "Changed my mind. Make it two bear claws."

She smiled. "Yessir."

He wished his own daughter could be half as accommodating. She wasn't, even though Gil had raised her on his own, ever since his first and only marital bad lesson had run off with the driver of her Artichoke Queen float. That left him a single parent with a five-year-old daughter. He didn't mind that last part, raising a kid. Someone had to pass on his blood and inherit the wealth he'd worked to build. He just wished she treated him better. He wished she were less rebellious, loved him like a daughter is supposed to love her father. All she gave him was crap. She'd even changed her last name, that's how much she hated him.

"Mr. Souza," the waitress said with a cadence that made it sound like a question ahead.

"Yes?"

"Did you hear about that dead guy on that farm?"

Gil didn't answer, but, truthfully, he was still reeling from the news. Such bad timing.

"They say he cut his own throat. That seems so, what's the word, unsacred."

"Sacrilegious." Gil's ear itched and he didn't want to dig in a finger and scratch. Not in a restaurant in front of this young woman. "I know the farm. Farmer used to buy seed from me. A good enough kid. Shame about the dead man, though."

The waitress set the plate of bear claws in front of Gil as a small child raced across the room shrieking while his mother chatted with a girlfriend a few tables away. The woman had snuck in one of those small dogs and was feeding it a piece of bacon under the table.

"Ma'am," said Gil to the woman. "Could you teach your child some manners?"

The café went quiet as her expression changed from shocked to offended. Gil felt the heat as he cut his pastry, thinking of mother bear and how violently they'd react in defense of their child. Gil had grizzly in him and felt a sense of brotherhood with the four-legged beast, who, like him, was dangerous when hungry or riled. Kid aside.

The waitress sidled up to the table with her pot of coffee, again. Gil clamped a palm over his cup. Rule one: be the object of fear. Rule two: eat them before they eat you.

5

When Olive woke up, before she even put her feet on the floor, she visualized Cris Villalobos lying on his back staring at the chapped sky that matched his powder blue eyes. It had been twenty-four hours since she'd discovered his body.

She headed downstairs, feeling emotionally hungover. She heard Cal in the kitchen grinding coffee beans. She could smell the fresh beans. Cal had set the newspaper—top fold up—on the dining room table.

Local man found dead on farm. Cristobal Villalobos, 33, died from a fatal knife wound to his neck. Police have arrested a person of interest who was subsequently released. The Public Information Officer was quoted as saying, "Mr. Villalobos had a family history of mental illness."

Olive groaned. Thea's heart will rip another layer deep when she reads this insinuation.

She felt Cal's hand on her back. "I'm sorry, Liv. Really sorry you had to go through what did yesterday. Wish I had been there for you."

She, as well, but he sounded so remorseful that she kept it to herself.

"Cal, they're already implying it might be suicide."

"We didn't know Cris that well."

"He looked happy the last time I saw him walking on the road."

"We knew him for a year and he seemed like a good guy. That's the thing, we didn't know what was going on beneath the surface."

He poured her a cup of coffee and placed it in front of her along with a piece of buttered cinnamon toast. "Did you see the story about Best Seeds?"

She shook her head. She didn't care. He was trying to change the subject and her mood. She itched the spot on her chest where Gus had pinched her chest looking for her necklace.

"My necklace is missing," she said. "Have you seen it?"

"No." He asked when she'd last worn it and, then, she remembered. The farmers market. Last week. It seemed like a lifetime ago. She'd taken it off at the market to avoid a struggle with Gus. Whenever she picked up her daughter, the child immediately fixated on tugging the charms and stuffing them in her mouth. If Olive hadn't removed the necklace, her daughter would have broken it. Or choked. She'd placed it in the blue plastic cash envelope, the "bluey" they called it, which she'd stored behind the front seat of the box truck. That afternoon, when the market closed, Kat had driven the truck back to the farm.

Cal groaned. "How is that possible?" he said. Olive realized he wasn't talking about the necklace, and his words sounded so weary that Olive looked over to the headlines. Seed Company Heads to Court for Violating GMO Ban. She and Cal had been leaders in the local fight to ban GMOs from Santa Cruz County. And they'd won.

"I thought we'd killed that one," she said.

"Monsters sleep, babe," said Cal. "They don't die."

She didn't remember exactly when they'd stopped buying seeds from Gil Souza's company. Two years ago? Three? As soon as Cal got wind of Souza's intentions to take the fast route to what organic farmers and consumers considered agricultural hell. Souza was one of the reasons the community rose to the challenge of banning GMO agriculture in every form. Unbelievably though, Best

Seeds had ignored not only the will of the majority, but also the law. Bastard, thought Olive. Somehow, she believed, if the county supervisors voted unanimously to slap a moratorium on GMOs, that would stop research, test fields, and planting. Not.

This morning's story reported that Humpback Farm—highly respected members of her and Cal's organic farming community—had filed a lawsuit against Best Seeds, Inc. Olive, who knew the plaintiffs, thought to herself, good for them. Humpback had sold at markets every week until last year when a customer tested their produce for genetic markers, aware that Humpback was located near a nursery rumored to propagate GMO seeds. In otherwords, Olive realized, even after Santa Cruz County had banned GMOs, Gil Souza continued to secretly hold GMO seed trials. And here's the sad part, Olive recalled: When the test had come up positive, Humpback began its descent into bankruptcy. Their entire field was torn up and as much topsoil as possible had to be transported to a disposal site out of the county. They withdrew from the local farmers markets for tragically obvious reasons—Best Seeds, Inc. had ruined the bond of trust between Humpback and their seasoned customers. Their vacated vendor spots at the farmers markets had been transferred to Brody Hamilton. And now the family was going to court, and Olive took some comfort knowing that Souza would be brought to justice.

She couldn't bear to brush her hair. Her hair flew and crackled. The air was so dry it felt suffocating to breathe. The children's lips had chapped overnight. She couldn't remember a drier, colder morning. Even the finest hairs of Russian sage, which she'd planted by the front doorway, stood erect from static electricity.

Circles of fallen leaves lay on the ground, perfectly replicating the circumference of each fledgling apple tree that she'd planted last year, twenty trees in total. Each required pruning. Next year—not this year because the saplings were too young—Olive would harvest the apples and bake pies. If they could afford it, she would install an organic commercial kitchen and, if things went smoothly, she would teach community baking classes in the warmth of her own home. But first, the trees. And the trees had to be pruned.

She stood in the center of the orchard and stared through the bare limbs at the dawning sky, the various horizons of redwood groves, oak, and riparian thicket. The creek that bordered her orchard was dry. On the other side an empty field had remained surprisingly undeveloped. An ag outfit was set to lease the property. They'd let Cal know of their plans to grow commercial strawberries. If so, she and Cal would be legally responsible for creating their own five-acre buffer zone to protect their crops from the new neighbor's pesticide drift, which meant Olive would have to rip out half of the orchard or face the consequences of fumigant and pesticide contamination. The law was not on their side. In fact, the sheer irony that established organic farmers had to create their own buffer zones made her furious.

The eight o'clock whistle from the rock quarry tamped her rising anger. It was shrill and lasted so long that anyone who was still asleep was now awake. Just as well. With young kids, anger was her least preferred guiding force. She refused to let it shape her and, sequentially, shape her kids. Kids were as malleable as these young apple trees, saplings who needed thoughtful guidance and nurturing.

She unfastened her red-handled Felco pruners and ran a match book-sized flint along the small burrs on the blade. Byrd and Gus ran noisily in the dirt, scaring little brown birds from the bare apple branches. She stepped into the chore, sheers up, contemplating her first cut.

Pruning was all about light and, for the first few minutes, the moves felt awkward and counterintuitive. The tree's primary arms had sprouted lateral branches, and she had to choose which to let live and which to kill. Snip. Did the tree appreciate her for ridding it of excess weight? Did it feel the pain of an amputated limb, a discarded leaf? Olive contorted her wrist and angled a cut that would direct rain away from the wood and stave off rot, if it ever did rain. It might not. Slice. The bough fell. Without warning, the image of Cris in a bed of yellowed beet leaf rose. Those glacial eyes made Olive cringe as Byrd swooped in, plucked the cut branch and ran.

She forced cheer into her voice as she bribed him. "A nickel for each branch you gather and stack."

Gus quickly tired and fell down in the dirt, about to cry until Olive put her in the port-a-crib and pressed her favorite blanket to her cheek.

The leaves crunched underfoot, as pleasant to the ear as horse hooves or rain on a tin roof, a crackling fire in the hearth. She pulled a wooden spreader from her back pocket and inserted the forked ends between two branches to invite more light to feed their skins.

Olive had pruned six trees when the noon siren blared. At this rate, she could finish the entire orchard by the end of the month if nothing interfered. But, between weather and labor, pests and money, farming was all about interference. Gus, in sow-bug pose, whimpered from her port-a-crib. Byrd continued to play with his stick. She finger-pruned the main trunk of a tree with her thumb and first finger, catching the unwanted buds in her palm. She tossed them playfully at Byrd, and he shouted, indignant that she'd interrupted his sword fight with an imagined foe.

One more limb. The fleshy sound of the snippers on raw wood brought up Cris, again. She saw his killer take him from behind, left arm cinched around his midriff, right hand crossing the chest and jamming a blade into the carotid. A move like that took practice. But it was possible. She holstered her sheers. She searched the sky, but today the cloudless dome held no answers.

"Ha." Byrd extended his arm and pointed his stick, lunging. He fletched on cloddy, trippy ground between the apple trees, grunting as he advanced.

"Looking good." She swiped the tears with the sleeve of her sweatshirt before he noticed. "You almost got him."

He stopped and turned. "I'm not one of those quitters."

She reminded him that he was being paid to collect the branches. Byrd dragged his stick behind him as he walked to the small pile of sticks he'd accumulated.

"A nickel per branch." She listened as he counted to three. At five, Gus stood up in her crib, wide eyed, sucking on her pacifier. Byrd complained he was hungry. Olive broke open an energy bar, told him to take half and give the other half to Gus while she dug in her pack for sandwiches. As he walked to the crib, he held out the bigger half to his sister. As soon as she reached for the treat, he pulled back, eliciting shrieks of indignation from his sister.

"Byrd, give her half."

The wrath of Gus amplified the longer Byrd resisted.

"Byrd," she warned, picking up the pacifier that Gus had thrown to the ground. She brushed off the dirt and saliva and stored it in her apron. "Don't provoke your sister. Give it to her. Now."

Gus screamed and Byrd put his hands over his ears. "Okay. Here." He thrust the small half of the energy bar into the crib.

Olive looked up at the sky and took a deep, mindful breath. A cloud. From the west. One small cotton ball. From its edge, a stunted arc of rainbow.

"What does provoke mean?" Byrd asked.

"Provoke means, just when everything is going great, something happens to create chaos. Do you want to be the one who ruins your sister's fun?"

He scowled. "She always gets her way."

Olive pointed to the sky to distract him, more importantly, to coax his imagination.

"See the cloud?" she said. "What does it say about all of this?" She wanted him to look, listen to what this single puff of vapor evoked in his young mind, grab the thought and own it.

"Clouds don't talk," Byrd said.

The tourist train whistled. In a minute or two, it would pass their farm. She could hurry the kids out to the road. As the train crossed Shell Bean Way, Byrd would wave. Passengers would wave back, smiling.

"C'mon," she said. "Let's go wave to the conductor."

Byrd took off at a trot across the orchard, Olive went slowly to let Gus walk without rushing. They hit the road, Byrd yards ahead running toward the track until Cal whistled. "Hey, Buddy, get on over here and bring mama."

Cal's look as she approached made her smile. It also made her realize how the small muscles around her mouth had atrophied since finding Cris dead in this same field. But the smile assuaged Cal's self-doubt about this livelihood she'd wholeheartedly taken up with him, rerouting a promising newspaper career to marry and raise their children on a farm. He valued her talents—her intelligence, her verve and ways with the children—she knew that, and he enjoyed her stories about the crimes she'd covered as a crime reporter. His bad guys were devastating—light brown apple moths and bottom rot—but much less interesting.

Right now, he needed her to help lift and move a water pipe. Her end of the twenty-foot irrigation pipe felt light as they walked in unison over the rough ground to the next furrow. While they lowered it to the ground, Olive felt his admiration for her strength—the kind of strength that comes from physical labor, not the least of which was carrying their kids for the last four years. She pulled back her ruler straight shoulders and stepped over several beds to the next pipe. Before picking up her end, she arched her back for a stretch and twisted at the waist as she'd seen Cal do countless times.

When he put up a hand to signal a stop and rested his end of the pipe on his shoulder, she took the chance to glance over at the children, who were eating sandwiches on a blanket they kept permanently under the lilac tree.

Cal pulled out his phone. "Que pasa?" He stared at her while listening to his caller. When he looked down at his feet, the hunched shoulders told her it was probably Heriberto.

"Como estuvo la fronter? Fueron Los Gordos?" Cal was talking about the minutemen—los gordos—"Cuantos dias para pasar? Oh, tres."

Olive knew enough Spanish to understand that los gordos, the vigilantes who hung out on the border harassing poor people, were keeping Heriberto from crossing. He was Cal's foreman and could run the farm if need be. He'd grown up on a farm that his father owned in the country outside Oaxaca City. For generations, the family had grown primarily white corn, but after United States corporations were allowed to flood the Mexican market with cheap GMO corn, his family suffered so much financial loss that he had to find work here or, like so many already had, lose their ancestral land.

In the years he'd worked at Shell Bean Farm, Heriberto had created a second home in Santa Cruz. He'd married a woman who had grown up in a nearby farming community. They had a child, Lupe, who was three years old. It was Heriberto who had delivered Augusta a year and a half ago when Olive went into early labor on the railroad tracks that hot late summer afternoon. They named her Augusta, after the month that delivered her, Gus for short. Heriberto was as indispensable to Cal as he had been to Olive on that day when he used his lettuce knife to cut the infant's umbilical cord and cleared her throat with a finger until she wailed. It was Heriberto who had handed Olive the beautiful, bloody newborn wrapped in his long-sleeved work shirt. And as she put the infant to her breast, he cleaned up the afterbirth and saved it for her to bury. Like seventy percent of California's field workers, he was undocumented. Up until this year, Heriberto had managed to cross in one try. This year border security, in its infernal forms, had tightened.

"Disculpe un momento, Heri." Cal put his hand over the phone. "Heriberto's stuck at the border. He needs to borrow five thousand for the coyote. What do you think? Do we have it?"

Of course not. Cal and Olive's savings were drained. They were late on this month's mortgage payment. Their application for a new line of credit had stalled because of a federal government shutdown. The bills kept piling. Without Heriberto, Cal was screwed.

The crops, including their tomatoes, would not get planted on time, and they were already two weeks behind schedule because the recent vandalism had destroyed what would have been their first wave.

Olive balked for as long as it took her to mentally list their obligations and consider that she'd been putting money aside for a commercial kitchen. When she weighed the kitchen against Heriberto, the choice was obvious.

"We'll use the dream funds," she said.

Cal frowned. "You sure, babe?"

When she nodded, he pulled her to him and held her, but the feel of him didn't assuage her worry or dissolve her disappointment.

Cal told Heriberto they'd wire the money, and then he put the phone on speaker. "Olive encontro a un hombre muerto en el campo," he said.

"Muerto?" Heriberto repeated.

"Si, por el campo de remolacha. Cris Villalobos."

"Cuando regreses, avisame si eschuchas algo."

"Oh que malo es eso. Ella esta bien?"

"Si, ella es fuerte. Adios."

"Hasta pronto."

As they discussed Cris and how she'd found his body, it was the gravity in their voices that was comforting, as if they'd recognized, too, that the farm had unalterably changed and whatever hovered unspoken in his death was nonetheless real. Olive shielded her eyes. The cotton-ball cloud had dissolved to a wisp.

6

Gil was mildly surprised when a woman dressed in black pumps and a black skirt suit entered the meeting room. He looked around the place. A nice work environment. Tasteful, like the woman, who thrust her hand toward him and clamped his knuckles in a hard, bird-bone shake. He looked sideways at his attorney Kent Ferguson and scowled. He didn't appreciate not being informed that the lawyer for the plaintiffs was female. A woman was about to take his deposition and he didn't like women in authority, at least not over him. She stood cattycorner from him and clicked her pen, a black, fine point roller ball. The practiced way the soft black leather briefcase slid off her shoulder onto the carpet impressed him. Not a flinch to her face, not a twitch of her hand. She held the line of scrimmage with steady eye contact. It was all practice for the trial ahead.

"Let's get started," said Sternik, "by introducing ourselves into the record. My name is Clancie Sternik, and I am the lead attorney for the plaintiffs Humpback Farm against defendants Best Seeds, Inc. and CEO Gilbert Souza, Jr. I am taking the deposition of defendant Gil Souza, Jr."

The recorder rose from his keyboard to administer an oath. He was a serious looking young man with wire-rim bifocals, who had positioned himself in a corner of the room so he could record facial expressions and mannerisms, as well as words.

"Yes, I do"… swear to tell the truth, the whole truth, and nothing but the truth. Sternik sat down, her skirt hiking up above her knees, most likely, Gil reasoned, to draw attention to her legs. She put a yellow legal pad to the side and pulled a bundle of documents out of her briefcase, straightening the documents with short, manicured fingernails, polished to a high gloss, navy blue polish that seemed to be popular with bossy, liberal-minded women.

She said, "The defendants, Humpback Farm, claim that your company has contaminated said farm's commercial organic operations at great expense, including a loss of their organic certification and extreme financial duress. Is that clear?"

Gil nodded.

"We need a verbal," said Sternik.

"Yes."

"Are you aware of plaintiff's charge that your company's experimental field trials of GMO Brussel sprouts and glyphosate-resistant sugar beets not only contaminated but also irreversibly altered the genetic markers of another farmer's crops?"

"Brussels sprouts," Gil said. "With an s. People never get that right."

She leaned forward with lips that looked like hyphens and narrowed her eyes to nasty slits. Gil caught a whiff of her flowery perfume as she instructed him to "just answer the question. Yes or no."

"Maybe," Gil said. "For the record, GE as in Genetically Engineered is the proper acronym, not GMO. My company's focus in research and development is accurately named genetic engineering or transgenics or bioengineering."

"Thank you, Mr. Souza," she said. "We'll note your corrections. Furthermore, the charges against you include intentional violation of the county ordinance that bans researching, propagating and growing GMOs, including experimental test sites. You have been charged with conducting experimental GE seed propagation trials during this ban. Your illegal actions have contaminated Humpback Farm? Are you aware of these charges?"

"I am."

"Are you aware that the Supervisors of the County of Santa Cruz have banned propagating and growing GE crops in this county and that you are the first and only to violate this ban?"

"I am."

"You look so smug when answering that question. Why does an educated grower and community philanthropist like yourself, a man who sponsors a men's baseball team and sits on the Rotary Club, purposely violate a county ordinance?"

"The proper language is gene edited and outside the legal definition of GE."

"We'll see about that, Mr. Souza. Please answer the question, why did you purposely violate the county precautionary moratorium on GEs?"

"Objection," said Ferguson. "The language insinuates my client's intention to commit a crime."

"Mr. Souza, is that your position?" asked Sternik. "That you intentionally violated a county ordinance?"

Gil wasn't sure if now was the time to reveal his position. He glanced at Ferguson, who shook his head. What the hell. "Not a single state or federal law makes propagation and planting of GEs illegal. What I stand behind, if I'm forced to, is the fact that a county is not a sovereign body, and state law supersedes. I can plant what I damn well please as long as it doesn't violate state law. That is my position.?"

"This is California, Mr. Souza. Not Nebraska."

"Check out Maui and Oregon," he replied.

"Once more, are you aware that you knowingly violated the county law that bans GMOs?"

"I am," Gil said. "Someone has to feed the world."

"And that would be you."

When Ferguson objected, Gil almost wished he hadn't. Yes, someone has to feed the world and he was among those cutting-edge producers equipped to meet the challenge. What, he wondered, was so hard about that?

"The local court has recently awarded a local plaintiff for similar damages upwards of a million," said Sternik. "Are you aware of that case, Mr. Souza?"

Gil shook his head.

"Was that a 'no'?"

"Ambiguous. It was a jury trial. Lots of bias."

"Are you aware this will also be a jury trial, Mr. Souza?"

He shrugged. "Yes," he said before this self-appointed Wonder Woman could ask him to say it aloud. He had a plan. If the jury decided against him, he knew what his next move would be. Lemonade out of lemons.

"Federal law requires a grower to take containment precautions. What have you done to prevent exposing the plaintiff's property to genetically engineered material?"

"We cleaned up our test fields and disposed of plant matter according to federal APHIS regulations." He doubted she even knew what the acronym stood for. Animal and Plant Health Inspection Services, part of the USDA that oversaw all his GE permits. He watched Sternik for signs that she realized she was out of her league.

"Are you aware that GMO Brussels sprouts and your variety of GE sugar beet have not been approved for human or animal consumption?" asked Sternik.

"That's my business, seed test trials." He glanced at the stenographer, who was typing with a fury. Are you aware that this country's burgeoning poor are poorer and hungrier than they have ever been, and my goal is to feed them affordably?"

Gil perceived a shift in Sternik's demeanor as she sat back in her chair, surrendering to the plush leather, possibly dismayed she wasn't dealing with an idiot.

"Honestly, Mr. Souza, do you not realize your 'feeding the world' slogan is antediluvian?"

"Is that a question?"

"It is a question."

"That's debatable."

"What action, if any, do you plan to take if the court rules the plaintiff's crops were contaminated?"

As little as possible. It was time to stand up. He rose, fully aware of his stature, as he turned to the court recorder. "Are you recording the hostile expression on Ms. Sternik's face and the sarcasm in her voice?"

He retrieved his briefcase, which he'd placed at the opposite end of the table for just this purpose: unfolding his height and imposing his power by walking the full length of the long table. "The ban won't hold up, even in this county."

Ferguson spoke up for the first time. "My client was licensed by the federal government to manufacture GE seeds at a certified lab. Those seeds are his intellectual property to do with as he sees fit under the law."

Sternik leaned forward, her cheeks notably pinked up. "The county moratorium bans any and all manufacture of GE labs. Your unlawful experimental GE seed propagation sites in Santa Cruz County wound up contaminating Humpback Farm crops. The question is not whether or not what you'd done is illegal. The question is do you admit breaking the law?"

"Objection," said Ferguson.

"Where are those test sites, Mr. Souza?" asked Sternik.

Lucky for him, APHIS doesn't disclose the location of private parties' test sites. She had to know this, Gil thought. "If the USDA won't tell you, why would I?" Gil pushed back his chair. "I'm done here."

Sternik lay her arms across the table. "Mr. Souza, we are not done. We're in for the long haul."

"You have no idea of the long haul, Attorney Sternik." For Gil, the "long haul" was the story of his life that started when he was a kid, working summers and after school at his grandfather's seed company. "If surviving the long haul is key to victory, I'm going to win. And where's the question in that?"

He twisted his forearm and looked at his wristwatch. "I have a lunch meeting in seven minutes. Is there anything else I can clarify for you before I leave?"

"Do you care that you've violated the will of the community and, consequentially, brought to fruition what they most feared, contamination of their food system, in addition to ruining a long-time organic farm family's livelihood?"

"They are misguided." He walked out of the room, hearing his attorney snap shut his briefcase, and headed down the carpeted hallway, walls hung with black and white photographs of Santa Cruz surfers.

Goddamn surfers. "Figures," he mumbled. For some reason he didn't understand, he felt like crying.

7

Local man's death was suicide, Coroner determined. Cause of death was a fatal puncture to the carotid artery.

Olive reacted to every line of the story with outrage. "I'm calling Henry Rogers." Rogers was a detective with the police force, and he'd know what was going on behind the scenes. "It's only been four days. The police haven't even questioned me."

Cal set a cup of hot black coffee at her elbow. "We didn't know what was going on inside his mind."

"The police put it on a fast track to save money. They're ignoring the evidence."

"This is what denial sounds like," Cal said.

She didn't want to have a fight with Cal, but his quick retorts did absolutely nothing to calm her. "What about the greenhouse?"

"I'm leaving the evidence collection to the police, and you need to accept that we didn't really know Cris. He could have hidden his depression. It's really sad," he said, his voice turning soft. "That's how it is with suicide."

Wrong, she told herself. Discovering a dead man wasn't only sad. It was traumatic and measurably worse than being a reporter showing up at the scene of a murder. And she had, several times in her former career as a newspaper reporter. This was different. Cris and Thea lived in her and Cal's first home, the log cabin. Olive had passed him on daily walks up their shared road. She knew who belonged to the body she'd found, and the importance of that lodged in her brain wasn't budging anytime soon.

"This is your mu-ther," were the first words out of Ariela Murphy's mouth. "I saw you on U-Tube, Love."

As Olive walked to the laundry room with a basket of laundry, AirPods in her ears, she wondered how long it had taken the news to reach Kansas, where her mother lived.

"I swear I don't mean to be rude," Olive said, knowing rudeness was often the only way of making a point with her mother, "but I'm carrying a basket of laundry and I have to put it in the washer while the kids are napping. I'll call you back." She dropped the basket, pulled the phone from her back pocket and pressed "end." That she was busy was no exaggeration. After she finished the laundry and worked in the office, she had to make a couple of dishes for Cris's memorial, scheduled for tomorrow.

She had to keep moving. Her mother's last phone call, which was six months ago on Augusta's one-year birthday, had triggered a mild bout of depression. Her emotions were fragile enough after Cris's death and everything being delayed—Heriberto, planting tomatoes, their line of credit—without her mother cracking fissures out of thin ice.

The phone vibrated in her jeans' back pocket. Ariela, again. She let it go and folded Byrd's pants into a tidy stack next to Augusta's leggings. Olive could not remember her mother beginning a telephone conversation on a positive note. She and Cal had enough to deal with without Ariela casting her crazy-cloud over their lives. Olive's best guess was that she wanted to comment on how Olive looked in that U-tube interview. Stressed, she'd say, before twisting Cris's death until it was about her. Not that she didn't love her mother. She did, as long as she wasn't in the same room. Four states and two mountain ranges away worked fine. Even from that distance Ariela had claimed she could read Olive's aura. Green, she'd said the last time they talked, whatever green signified. Purple, if her mother were in a generous mood.

When her cell phone binged, signaling a text, Olive surrendered.

what's up? she texted back.

u didn't look well on U-tube, Ariela wrote.

Not according to Brody Harrington, she thought, which was exactly the defensive reaction her mother was fishing for.

found a dead body

u need me

no I don't

Thirty seconds later, another ding. Ariela had texted *rain dance*, as if she possessed the power to end the worst drought in the state's recorded history.

we're fine

coming to CA

NO!

can do reading on Cris Villalobos

no thk u!

listen to your mother or you'll be sorry

Olive felt like throwing her phone hard against the wall, but that would be childish, so she tucked it in her back pocket and flinched at the ping of her mother's next text. A visit was out of the question. She was raising two small children, managing a farm, and fending off the farm's rising debt until their line of credit came through. And there'd just been a death on their property. Ariela-in-the-flesh would be a wrecking ball. The metaphors were endless: A vacuum sucking up oxygen. A rat flea triggering allergies. A metaphysics monger devouring Cris's death. Listen to your mother or you'll be sorry! Jee-zus. Maybe she didn't love her mother from afar. Maybe she loved her mother when she wasn't thinking about her.

Olive and Cal walked silently into Thea's dirt yard, carrying their food offerings. Olive had decided to bake a cheese lasagna and toss a little gem salad with puntarella and shaved parmesan. That way the guests had a choice of warm comfort food and raw garden produce. The yard, hung with strands of twinkly lights across Cris's unfinished wood carvings, felt otherworldly. A nine-foot grizzly carved from redwood stood on its two hind legs as sentry. As their children ran past the sculpture, gleeful chatter filling the yard, Olive noticed all of the unfinished work: the trunk of a eucalyptus lain across sawhorses, rough cuts of bear, puma and coyote. Wood shavings in neat piles on top of the log, finer dust on the ground beneath. A chain saw on the ground beside a crowbar. He was not finished living is what Olive made of it.

She discerned voices inside, as they walked a woodchip path toward the cabin, passing a Virgin de Guadalupe candle burning softly in its glass cylinder. Bouquets of tulips and dahlias in glass jars lined the path. Trail mix had been sprinkled on the ground. Laughing Buddha. Bronze Shiva. Prayer stick with a blue jay feather dangling from white string beside a glass of water. They walked up the three steps to the front deck, steps they knew well because Cal had built them when he and Olive lived here before moving to the big house. Inside, people pressed against the glass-paned French doors. They held glasses of wine and small plates of hors d'oeuvres.

She side-stepped between people who'd come to pay their respects and placed the lasagna and salad on the crowded table between dishes of kale salad, lentil, hummus, fresh breads and crackers. Thea was speaking to a cluster of people by the refrigerator. As her kids reached for chips, Byrd especially seemed at home, as if remembering something in the depths of his first three years of life, when he'd lived in this fixed-up trailer. He and Gus gravitated to a corner of the carpet and played with wooden toys Thea had set out for them. In a small alcove, photos and small animal totems Cris had also carved were laid out on a small round table. Olive walked into the room, an addition Cris had built after the couple had moved here a year ago. She glanced out the window. The backyard had also been improved. Olive could actually see to the back fence. When she and Cal had lived here, a thick profusion of poison oak and wild berry bushes took up the entire space. Now, the area was definitely a yard, in fact, a charming yard. There was even a hot tub.

A wedding picture of Cris and Thea sat on the small table. They posed on a backdrop of Steamer Lane, a famous break for advanced surfers, like Cal. Thea's wedding veil merged with a breaking wave and Cris, in a white Mexican wedding shirt, beamed happily. A photograph of Cris the boy on a skateboard. Another more recent photo of him astride a life-sized sculpture of a bear, the contours smooth as a Henry Moore. He was smiling, and Olive was struck again that this was not a man who would kill himself.

Thea came up beside her, gripping a black pashmina around her shoulders as if it were Cris. Her soft curls framed a pretty, albeit weary, face. Fine auburn freckles seemed to have been flicked on her porcelain face with an artist's brush. Olive took her hand and was startled by its iciness. Byrd tugged on Olive's sleeve and Gus stretched her arms to be picked up.

"Would you say something about Cris?" Thea leaned into Olive. "Please. You found him."

When Thea put it that way, Olive had no choice, and no idea of what she would say. She and Cal stood shoulder to shoulder, eating from small paper plates. He talked and she was grateful for that because she wasn't sure how to begin her spontaneous eulogy or if she should even mention finding Cris in their beet field. The feeling of the humongous beets underfoot came back to her, round as river rocks, but softened in their early stage rot. Probably not. Surfers in Hawaiian shirts, familiar faces from the farmers markets, a Buddhist monk in a saffron robe. A man in a black tank top that showed off tattoos on every inch of exposed flesh.

Cal tapped his beer bottle with a metal spoon until the room quieted and the crowd's eyes turned to them. "Hey folks," he said, "time to say a few words. I give you Olive, a friend and neighbor of Thea and Cris."

Olive searched the room for friendly faces and was more than a little surprised to see Kat Granger, her employee who'd abandoned the box truck in the wee hours surrounding Cris's death. She was the reason Cal was roused from bed and gone when Olive needed him. A ruddy-faced surfer-looking dude stood next her, a boyfriend, Olive assumed. Not the reassuring faces she was seeking. But the man with brilliant tattoos who leaned against the wall with a bottle of beer, he caught her eye and nodded.

She took a deep breath, a sip of sparkling water. "Hi everyone," she began, feeling as if she were rounding a blind verbal curve with no idea of the words ahead. "Thank you for being here to honor Thea and Cris. I'll begin with his tattoo. I'd never really noticed it before that morning I found him, but it was a beautiful tattoo that's etched in my mind, a statement of his artist soul. It was his sculptor hands, though, that told me this was Cris. All that beauty and energy gone, leaving a hole I'm trying to make sense of. Lots of things I wish I'd noticed about Cris. His tattoo was a jellyfish, a sea creature from the natural world that inspired him. He was an artist and celebrated this source of inspiration in his work. Nature was the perspective from which his hands moved." She held up the wooden red fox that she had picked up from the table. "His death reminds me of what I take for granted every day. I'm so sorry he's gone."

Thea covered her face so only her red-rimmed eyes peaked from the pashmina.

"So, so sorry for Thea. The idea that Cris committed suicide leaves us stunned that a man with such a rich life in the deepest sense would choose death. I'm in disbelief, still." As murmurs rose and subsided, the only remaining sound in the room was Thea, sobbing.

"Every day my son Byrd and his little sister and I passed Cris on the road when he took breaks from his work. He always inquired about my family and our farm. He always asked about Cal's tomatoes. If I regret anything, it's that I didn't talk to him longer. But I know from our brief exchanges in the middle of our shared road that Cris loved people, and even more the person without the home, the alienated, and those who are so-called 'different.' Let's remember Cris by caring for the diverse body of the living and preserving the beauty we have." Olive glanced over at Thea, burrowed into in her pashmina, shoulders quaking.

Outside, Byrd and Gus played in the yard, scooping wood chips into piles, and the man with tattoos who'd nodded encouragement approached Olive. She tried not to stare at his lazy left eye.

"No way Cris did himself in," the man said, his voice reminding her of Tom Waits.

"I'm really interested in why you think that," she said.

"I know what made that dude tick, and he would never bail out on his life." He extended his hand. "My name is Cap. Owner of Captain Positively's Tattoo and Piercing Salon."

As Olive shook his hand, he glanced around the yard, as if he didn't want to be overheard.

"We should talk." He handed her a business card.

She thought to the week ahead, filled with bookkeeping and appointments. She'd have to check her calendar and brought out her phone. "Wednesday," she told him.

He winked with his good eye. "Until then."

They say this is a fragile time, and Olive feared that when the gathering was over and people left Thea alone in an empty home, she would sink into the bottomless pool of sadness. Olive was on watch in case she sank too deeply, too quickly. Cal had taken the children home and Olive remained. The fire had gone out in Thea's woodstove and without the heat of milling people the cabin had grown cold.

Bowls of vanishing quinoa and kale salads, deviled eggs and raw vegetables remained on the table, and the garbage bin was full of soiled paper plates. The counters overflowed with empty plastic wine glasses and beer bottles. Olive filled the kettle from the tap. She gathered firewood from the side of the house where Cris had stacked it and carried the split wood back to the cabin.

The kettle whistled as Thea stared into the woodstove's dark belly. Olive rolled out the wood onto the floor and gently asked Thea to turn off the kettle, thinking even minimal movement would keep her afloat. Olive balled up newspaper and placed each carefully on top of the ash, followed by two handfuls of wood chips and a bug-eaten pine. She struck a match and called Thea into the room. They stared at the orange flames and felt the heat emanate as they drank tea—black with milk and honey for Olive, chamomile for Thea, who had the presence of mind to place her cup on top of the woodstove between sips to keep it warm.

"He promised he wouldn't leave me." Thea lowered her head and took a deep breath, then straightened and pushed her soft curls hair back from her face. "I'm pregnant."

8

Cris had been dead for three weeks. The memorial yesterday had left them sad, the news from Thea offering hope weighted with even deeper sadness.

Olive stood back and studied their bed. The sheets resembled a paper airplane with folded back corners where each of them had risen from their side. No twisted blankets, which meant no love-making, not even cuddling. She didn't like what she saw, not one bit. She made the bed in two swift strokes, one on his side, one on hers. Then she put on her jogging shoes and left the kids with Cal.

Without the distractions of the kids and demands of the farm, running winnowed the trivial from the important until the an-swers to her most pressing problem remained. The endorphins kept the blues at bay.

At the Santa Cruz Harbor, she stretched and started her loop around the harbor, her head a popcorn maker of colliding ideas. Ten minutes later, she'd broken a sweat and what was the single most important issue became clear. She and Cal. If the two of them were strong, they could get through anything. Drought, financial stress, death, sickness, even her mother.

She noticed the bumper sticker on a bright black Dodge Ram truck: SAVE A TRACTOR. RIDE A FARMER. She put on the brakes and pulled her cell from the thigh pocket of her jogging pants and snapped a picture.

Back home, she found Cal and the kids in the strawberry field. The kids squatted, picking strawberries like pros while Cal pressed his cell phone to his ear, harried and talking loudly about electricity.

"It's taken a year already," he said, "because PG&E is biting it. We're going to drag the cooler over there with two tractors and a chair if we have to."

She wondered who was on the receiving end of his frustration.

"We need lights, and if I can bring in another cooler, that's good. I don't know … I've been talking about it for a year. Whatever you can do to speed things up. Thanks, man."

They needed electricity for the pump so they could water their crops. Although vast reservoirs of virgin water lived in the limestone beneath this ground, they didn't have the money to develop it. They could barely keep their present well running.

She scanned the fields. Their romaine had bolted and it was the end of February, the month Santa Cruz typically experienced the bulk of annual rainfall. Nothing was stationary about weather anymore. The farm in general was thirsty and the plants were ragged, even the clover and sour grass in last year's tomato field.

Heriberto had made it back. He arrived midday yesterday, while they attended Cris's memorial. She saw him in the field sitting on the tractor as if he'd finally mounted his favorite old horse. At the side of the farm nearest her, two farmhands stood in the back of a pickup and shoveled compost over the tilled beds of blown out beet and bell bean.

It was time to plan for the tomatoes. They'd go in the upper field where the soil drained, forcing the plants' roots to search for water. The stress developed the tomatoes' flavor and character. If that phenomenon transferred to humans, her family was developing more than its share of character.

Behind the farm's alluvial ground rose the Coastal Redwoods, endemic to the west coast. One of the trees was albino, a phenomenon of sacrifice for the greater good. The surrounding laurels had tried to poison the grove in their competition for moisture, but that lone redwood had sucked up the laurel's toxins so the rest could survive.

That evening when the kids were asleep and Cal was making their ritual fire for adult time, Olive walked down the stairs in her terrycloth robe, grinning to herself. She stood in front of the hearth and asked Cal to please bring her a cold beer. When he disappeared behind the swinging kitchen door, she undid the tie and let her robe slip to the floor. She kicked it aside and stood there naked, wearing nothing but a white piece of paper hung from her neck with the words SAVE A TRACTOR. RIDE A FARMER.

She'd say Cal's first expression when he pushed through the door with a bottle of beer in each hand was shock, followed by pure joy. As he walked toward her, they giggled. He put the beers on the dining room table and leapt over the back of the futon, reached up, grabbed her wrist and pulled her to him. Olive, straddling her husband's lap, felt his soft palms on her waist and the fire's warmth on her back, their skins alive and magnetic.

The next morning's residual pheromones in the aftermath of good sex were proof they loved each other. Cal was cheerful. She felt happy and sassy. The rest of the world was off kilter, but they were constant and bonded, and still in love. His eyes had a twinkle when she brought him coffee, and he couldn't have suppressed a grin if he'd tried. Olive realized she was smiling as she walked down the road to the mailbox, sidestepping potholes and loose asphalt.

Her office was a converted shed which doubled as the laundry room. She sat at her desk and gazed up at the clipping from the *San Francisco Tribune* that she'd thumbtacked to the wall above the desk. The story featured a half page, close up profile of Cal looking over his field. Iconic, she thought. And handsome enough to be one of those stud muffin farmers that magazines had begun to feature. Cal had accomplished what no one had. Over the span of five years of selecting out, saving and planting the seeds from a Best Seeds' original hybrid tomato (which could not replicate itself), he had propagated a tomato whose seeds could reproduce into the luscious likeness of their parent. Almost an heirloom, this open-pol-linating fruit—no longer a hybrid. Nurseries and seed producers had tried for decades to reproduce this popular Best Seeds hybrid. In the world of sustainable agriculture, Cal's accomplishment was a breakthrough. Like many creations, the Augusta Girl (named after their daughter) was an accident: At the end of one auspicious winter, five years ago—the same year she and Cal had met—while discing dying tomato vines into the ground, the tractor missed one plant because it was too close to the water pump for the plow to reach. That plant—a hybrid—went to seed and the following summer regrew a tomato that resembled the parent, while old surviving vines scattered here and there on the edges of the field devolved into ridiculous tomato renditions with no commercial value. One tomato looked like a donut on a stick. An awe-struck Cal began the generations-long (in tomato life) process of selecting out fruit and saving seed from this one fateful plant.

Olive sorted the mail—ads, seed catalogs, a farm bureau newsletter, and bills. She placed the three checks from restaurants in a separate pile. A letter from the County Recorder's Office gave her pause. She ran the letter opener's dull blade along the fold and pulled out a tri-folded white paper.

Notice of Default
California and Olive Post
111 Shell Bean Way
Santa Cruz, CA 95060

This had to be a mistake. The five-hundred-thousand-dollar mortgage on the farm and house was correct, but the lender was all wrong. She didn't even recognize the name, Inventiveness, demanding payment in full within thirty days or the farm would go up for auction on the steps of the county building without judicial recourse. She decided to call the bank to gather as much information as she could before telling Cal. A loan officer informed her that the bank had sold the loan and gave her the new lender's contact information which consisted of a phone number and a Post Office Box.

Cal didn't pick up his phone, so she texted him a note and brought up Quick Books on her laptop. As she'd thought, they had missed one mortgage payment and the second payment was still in the grace period. Missing one month and being late for another shouldn't be enough to trigger foreclosure, and that would be cleared up as soon as their line of credit came through. Olive pulled up the Santa Cruz County fictitious names website site to see who owned this company that claimed to be foreclosing on them. She typed Inventiveness in the "business name" line and clicked "search." Nothing came up. When she searched for the State of California's foreclosure process, she discovered that foreclosure in California was not a process but a quantum leap of injustice. A travesty, in fact, which was so badly tilted toward the mortgage companies that Senator Kamala Harris, when she was California's State Attorney General, had designed a website to advise the landslide of suffering homeowners who couldn't afford attorneys how to protect themselves. The best line of defense, according to Harris, was to write a hardship letter of response in "pro se" (without counsel) to the lender.

Olive began, *Dear Scumbags. I am flabbergasted with the Notice of Default your company sent me. You should be ashamed and you must be mistaken. Foreclosure based on missing one payment is extreme and unreasonable, and you have not given us fair notice.* She pounded out the words on the keyboard. *Furthermore, our last payment was sent less than two months ago to our original bank, not the institution you say you are. Who the hell are you, anyway? What kind of crap company name is that? Inventiveness. You're inventing a lawsuit. You can expect a letter from Shell Bean Farm's attorney.* Never mind they didn't have an attorney and couldn't afford one.

She deleted the foul language and continued: *A line of credit with our tomatoes as leverage will be disbursed shortly, at which time we will bring all mortgage payments up to date, including late fees. Respond to this letter immediately, please.*

"Foreclosure. Are you kidding me? Who the hell is Inventiveness?"

"I am not kidding and, yes, foreclosure." She watched the news sink in and waited until Cal's eyes focused on her before going on. "They claim we're behind in our payments and we have thirty days or they're auctioning the farm on the courthouse steps without even going to court."

"Son of a bitch." The anger in his voice she expected. "Can they do that?"

"Yes. I looked it up."

"Is this for real?"

"I called our bank. They sold our loan to another mortgage company that resold the loan to Inventiveness."

"I'll be right there." He hung up, and when he walked into the office five minutes later, Olive saw on his face tension that alarmed her. The corners of his mouth were commas drawing the fine muscles downward. The way his eyes darted around the room—anxious and bewildered—scared her. His cheeks seemed hollowed. His sun-kissed pallor ashen. She didn't know how much more he could take.

The county building was a monolith that felt like a morgue. Its interior cement walls and high ceilings amplified the oppression Olive felt as her footsteps echoed down the wide hallway. Even the schoolchildren's artwork displays couldn't warm this building. The elevator opened to the second floor. Directly across from the elevator was a counter, behind which a brunette woman wearing a headset was shielded from the public by bulletproof plexiglass. Behind the woman was a huge government seal that featured the handsome seven-point law enforcement star of the Santa Cruz County District Attorney, along with the California logo of a grizzly bear on a shoreline, redwoods in the background. Olive recalled Cris Villalobos's bear sculpture and realized a full twenty-four hours had passed and she hadn't once thought of him.

The clerk didn't glance up as Olive walked out of the elevator and turned right toward the County Recorder's Office. A young man promptly got up from his desk cubicle, came to the counter and asked how he could help her.

"Could you help me find out who owns the fictitious name of a company I'm doing business with? A mortgage company."

He walked the few steps to his desk and returned with scrap paper. He asked her to write down the name.

"Is the name search limited to Santa Cruz County?" she asked, passing the name Inventiveness to him.

"Affirmative."

"What if the business is located outside of the county?"

He glanced up as if the ceiling held the answer. "If the Doing Business As notice is out of the county, you go to that county. We don't interface fictitious DBAs with other counties."

"Do they have to file in the county they're doing business in?"

The ceiling again. "I believe so," he said.

"Shouldn't you know?" Olive mumbled, hearing the rudeness in her voice as the clerk returned with a piece of white note paper on which he'd written down the county's DBA website. "I can show you how it works, so you can try it out yourself."

"Thanks," she said, "but I've already tried that website with no success," and the chance this inexperienced clerk would do any better looked slim to none.

"I'm cranky and I apologize, really," she said. "But some mysterious entity is foreclosing on our farm."

He looked genuinely crushed. "Sorry to hear that."

She stood at the counter and typed the name of Thea's work into the desktop computer. Little Bee Bakery. The legal registrant came up quickly, a promising sign. Next, she entered her favorite downtown restaurant. She knew the owner, but the owner's name did not come up as the Registrant. Instead, a corporation's name. She turned her screen to show the clerk.

"How do I find the actual person's name? I'm getting corporations."

"Ah. When the registrant's name is a corporation, you go to the state. Corporations have to register at the state."

"Do you have the state contact?"

"Hmmm…" He wrote down two websites, both ca.gov sites.

Olive had one last question. "What if they're doing business but haven't licensed their fictitious name?"

He scratched his chin, having given up on the ceiling for answers. "That's a very good question. There's a law library in the basement and the reference librarian can help you. Good luck."

The law library was to the immediate right of the basement stairwell. She pressed the circular metal knob and the door opened, revealing a woman in a coral sweater and reading glasses behind a tall counter. She glanced up and asked warmly how she could help.

"I need to know the law pertaining to doing business without registering a fictitious name."

The librarian left and returned swiftly with a paperback edition of *Nolo's Guide to California Law* by Lisa Guerin, J.D. She turned to the back index, ran her finger down a column, flipped to the page, stuck a yellow post-it on the bottom paragraph, and turned the book around for Olive to see.

"If you don't register your fictitious name," the librarian read, "you can't use the courts to bring a lawsuit. California Business and Professions Code Section 17900."

Olive straightened her shoulders, feeling a sliver of hope. Maybe the foreclosure was invalid.

"Did you get that? Even if the business party could enter into a contract, they could never use the courts to enforce a contract if they do not register their name."

Olive thanked the librarian. It was a long shot, but she'd learned long shots could land in a small patch of truth.

9

Brody Harrington, who'd helped Cal set up his stall the morning
the box truck broke down, stood farm-boy straight, hands on hips,
watching her from the opposite side of the market before striding
across the converted parking lot, this time to help her. Byrd was
already putting up bird traps out of empty strawberry baskets and
string he'd finagled from the flower lady in the next stall. Gus was
asleep in her car seat inside the truck, and Olive decided not to
wake her.

"Let me give you a hand." Brody wrested the bundled E-Z UP
from Olive and propped it in the middle of her stall space. He
pulled out the legs in four directions, locked them and raised the
canopy top as Olive slid four tables from the back of the box truck.
He took the first table from her, kicked out the metal legs with the
toe of his worn Ariats and flipped the table upright. He did the
same with the remaining three tables as Olive unloaded a scale and
cash register. The flats of the season's first Albion strawberries were
next, which she strategically placed in their cardboard pint baskets
on the front table to lure customers into the stall's arrangement
of vibrant butter lettuces and beets—golden, red and the pepper-
mint-striped Chioggia.

"How are you holding up, Olive?"

She was pretty sure he was referring to Cris Villalobos.

"Sorry you had to see what you saw."

That again. She wasn't sorry. Not really. "I don't accept his death
was suicide."

Brody's gaze turned sideways, revealing an incredibly straight jaw and cleanly barbered hairline, a contrast to his grungier contemporaries, herself included. She attributed the difference to his place of origin, the hard ground of Anza Borrego ranchland, inland from San Diego.

"If you want my two cents," Brody said, "I'd say the cops probably know foul play was involved, but they don't want folks picking off the vagrants. They'd have even more problems on their hands."

Far-fetched, but she made a mental note to pass this by Detective Henry Rogers, whom she was hoping to meet tomorrow. Rogers hadn't returned her call.

Brody spotted a customer at his vendor stall. He patted Byrd, hard at work on his bird trap made of strawberry cartons, as he sauntered across the food court, turning his head side to side as if he were looking out for traffic. Olive noticed how his white T-shirt hit his belt, exposing the Wranglers label on his jeans. Jeans said a lot about a person, Olive thought. Levi's were old school. Gap jeans were young and affordable. Anthropologie's Pilcro shaggy chic. Wranglers signified cowboy.

"How much?" a young mother asked Olive. Her cinnamon-haired daughter was nose high to the strawberries, wanting to pluck one of the sweet ruby gems, but knowing better.

"Three-fifty a basket." Olive smiled at the girl and held out a carton of sample strawberries. The girl looked up at her mother for permission before taking a fruit and shoving it into her mouth as if it were candy. The bright red juice ran from the girl's chin and dripped on her flowered T-shirt.

Cal had just arrived. He got to work straightening the produce. It wasn't a full thirty seconds before one of their regular customers, a husband and wife who built boats, came up to him and asked when the tomatoes would be ready. The mother in front of Olive set her wooden food tokens onto the scale. Olive discreetly added a second basket to the bag.

"See you next week." Olive scooped up the silver-dollar size tokens, part of a government assistance program for single mothers to buy healthy food they otherwise couldn't afford. They made a pleasant clack as she poured them into the coin tray.

Cal had moved away from the counter into the greater aisle beyond the shade of the E-Z UP to talk to three of his buddies. He arched his back. When he twisted to the right, then the left, Olive wondered if it was habit or his lower back ached from disking the field yesterday for eight hours straight. The second, she quickly decided.

The words "contamination" and "GE markers" and "methyl bromide" and "Best Seeds" rose from the foursome.

Their conversation was therapeutic, Olive knew, generating endorphins and moving the isolation of farming into a communal endeavor. She overheard one of the men say, "Over my dead body."

Cal hugged himself and stared at the ground, his mannerism, Olive had learned, for trying to contain his frustration. Basically, he was a mellow, patient guy. Until he wasn't.

When Olive and Cal finished closing down the stall, they sat in the truck cab, kids in the back strapped in their car seats, and counted the money. Not a bad take, considering it was the end of winter.

Cal shook his head. "How much longer can we pay wages?"

"One month. Unless the credit line comes through exactly now."

"We have to tell Heriberto," Cal said, "so he can tell his crew and they can find other work if we don't come through."

"He'd be embarrassed if he heard it from me."

"Soon as I get back to the farm. He's working on the tractor. I'll catch him there."

"You could call him first and lighten the blow."

"There's no lightening the blow. I'll tell him in person."

Before dusk, as Olive bent in grating mild cheddar for macaroni and cheese, she heard Cal open the back door and listened as he dropped his boots at normal speed. He walked in and kissed her on the cheek. She was eager to know how Heriberto had reacted but waited for Cal to move through his routine. He opened the refrigerator. Instead of grabbing a Pacifico, he pulled out the half gallon container of milk and poured a glass, sat down at the breakfast niche and watched her drop handfuls of grated cheese into a pot of roux that had been heating on the stove top. She stirred the cheese into a thick sauce, relishing the fast melting, wishing more in life could transform so quickly into the form she wanted.

"He said he's going to finish out the season," Cal said. "Even if we can't pay him."

"That's nice." Olive turned off the burner.

"He's going to talk to the crew. Some will get work with a pot grow up the mountain. They pay more than we do, anyway. But Heri's staying on. Maybe some of his crew."

Cal downed his milk and took the edge of his T-shirt to dab the rogue tears.

Her cell phone vibrated in her back jeans pocket. She looked at the caller's name. Det. Rogers.

"Who is it?"

"Henry Rogers."

"What does he want?"

"He's calling me back."

Cal scowled. "Really? Didn't we agree to let the cops do their work?"

"And they're not. I want to see if he can run a search on Inventiveness. I didn't have much luck at the County."

"Right."

"What does that mean?"

"You're not going to bring up Cris Villalobos?"

Rhetorical. He didn't expect an answer, or at least not a truthful one.

When he headed upstairs to shower, she read the voice mail transcription from Rogers saying he agreed to meet with her at the Santa Cruz Diner the following day. She called the station and left a message confirming the appointment.

Rogers sat across from her in a booth at Santa Cruz Diner, pressing a mug of coffee between his palms. His confidence was palpable. In less than two years on the force, he'd been promoted from a rookie cop to detective, and Olive felt that part of his promotion had to do with his innate ability to listen.

"How are you, Olive?" he asked, meaning, Olive surmised, how was the person who had found Cris Villalobos' body surviving.

"I'm okay. But since you brought it up," and she was relieved he had, "I don't believe he killed himself."

He gazed over Olive's head as if reading his mind's reaction. "It's hard to be the first one at the scene of a death, especially a gruesome one like this. Sometimes we won't believe the truth until the denial wears off."

"I'm not in denial. I remain unconvinced. I saw enough circumstantial evidence to warrant an investigation. Our greenhouse was ransacked, and the plants they destroyed weren't only valuable, they were famous. I know there was a weapon at the scene. And I saw what looked like a boot print and a suspect tire track in the mud outside our wash area."

"A man's size eleven," said Rogers. "Or twelve. It didn't lead to anything."

"The knife?"

"The victim's carving tool. Flex point drop-point knife. We found it near his body. Sharp enough and long-bladed enough to severe the carotid."

"What about fingerprints on the knife?"

"Too much blood to lift." He scratched his face.

"How can you have too much blood to get a fingerprint? I know you can get fingerprints from blood. I've covered stories where they lifted fingerprints from blood and that cinched the case."

"We didn't need to," he said. "We had enough evidence to confirm suicide."

"You didn't have the wherewithal."

Rogers looked irritated, and a little mean, and Olive decided that this guy who she'd first met as a rookie had evolved into a real cop.

"Why couldn't Cris have run out of the house after hearing someone vandalized our greenhouse? He'd brought his knife with him and whoever was out there wrested the knife and stabbed him. Why is that so unbelievable?"

"No evidence."

"Henry, honestly. Who stabs themselves to death?"

"Rare, but not unheard of." Henry glanced sideways, checking out the booth across the aisle where a man slumped in his seat. Olive had noticed the man when she'd walked in—dirty, clothes with a sheen of grime. Down and out, leaning over his cup of coffee as if he were praying.

"Cristobal Villalobos," said Rogers, "chose an instrument that he had a relationship with. And had a family history predisposed to mental illness. A mother who killed herself with an overdose ruled intentional, siblings with records of addiction. His wife confirmed he was on a new cocktail of sleeping pills, including Ambien, and anti-depressants."

"He didn't look depressed or drugged to me, ever. And I saw him almost every day."

"Suicides keep their depression from the surface. You probably know that. Often, they elicit a state of calm once they've committed to the act."

"And why was he naked?"

"Good question. Went out of the world the same way he came in?"

Olive could tell Rogers wasn't sure of his own pat answers. "In the middle of winter? So far from his house?"

"Didn't want to leave a mess. His wife's a neat housekeeper. And it wasn't cold outside."

"Thea said he sleeps in the nude. Slept in the nude. He could have heard something suspicious and ran outside. He's the kind who would get involved."

"You're the kind who would get involved." He raised his eyebrows, touché. "Did you hear anything that night?"

"No."

"What about those two Aussies of yours?"

Pancho and Pixie, she told him, had died last year, after the first rain of the season was how she remembered. Pancho first, then Pixie. They never found out the cause. Cal suspected Pancho had been poisoned. Olive assumed Pixie died from a broken heart. They'd buried the dogs on a rise near the apple orchard so they could watch out for deer.

"Too bad." Rogers took a gulp of coffee. "Those were good dogs." Pause. "You know anyone who carried a grudge against Villalobos?"

She shook her head and glanced at Gus, asleep in her stroller. "But someone could have a grudge against Cal. Our entire first wave of tomato seedlings were ransacked that same night Cris died. It was only a week after the *San Francisco Tribune* wrote a big feature story on Cal and his success propagating a new tomato."

"I saw that story. Impressive." When Rogers leaned forward, Olive knew he was about to make a point. "The officer at the scene claims you spoiled the evidence trying to clean up the plants. And since the scene was spoiled there was no evidence to follow up on and no evidence to link it with Cris's death."

"There was an entire greenhouse full of evidence. I cleaned up one small seedling."

"The links aren't there."

"What about common sense."

"Common sense is great, but if it doesn't lead somewhere, it's useless."

"I found a tire track in the washing area. Our crew never parks there."

"The ubiquitous tire track. You have people going in and out of there all day."

"No, we don't. Not even the workers drive the trucks that close to the greenhouse."

"Listen." Henry tilted toward her on folded arms, his head of draining patience a mere six inches from hers. "I'm talking to you because I respect you and you're not going to let up. You're a smart lady, but who's going to murder someone because they got caught messing up a few plants?"

She scowled. "Those weren't just a few plants. They're our live-lihood. You just said you read the story of Cal and those plants. That kind of attention could create resentment."

"Know anyone jealous of your husband?"

She leaned back into the naugahyde booth and took a breath. "Gil Souza." It felt good to say his name to a cop. "We stopped buy-ing his tomato seeds when he went GMO. In fact, Cal originally grew out these famous ones from his family hybrid, a hand-polli-nated, secret process that Souza wouldn't share with anyone."

Rogers's expression remained as blank as a wall of gray cement. Still underwhelmed.

"No one's done that before," Olive stressed. "People have tried. This is a first. The story demonized Best Seeds."

"Best Seeds is a huge company. It can take a little bad press."

Olive's ideas were not resonating with Rogers. She could tell by his sideways looks at the poor man sitting in the booth across from them.

"You know, Henry, some people think the police have deter-mined suicide as cause of Cris's death to keep residents from at-tacking the homeless population. That's farfetched from my perspective, but I do know investigations and even determinations can be weighted by time and money. A suicide means no further investigation."

Rogers shook his head, dismayed. "You should be relieved. Suicide means there's not a killer on the loose." He pointed to Gus and took a deep breath, about to level something at her. "Look. We spend fifteen percent of our budget on investigations, second to patrol. I know that's not a lot, but we are constrained regardless of money to follow the evidence. There is no evidence to warrant further investigation."

Olive sensed that Rogers had reached his limit with the civilian across the table from him, so she tried a different approach. "What I'm about to tell you is confidential. Not only was our cash crop destroyed the night Cris died, this mortgage company I told you about is now foreclosing on our farm." She studied his face to determine if anything clicked. "Doesn't that sound even the least bit strange?" Olive asked.

He seemed to register her point with more focus. "The least bit," he said.

"I'm sorry to hear that." He looked earnest, the way his eyes crimped. "Didn't know you were having a rough time."

She shrugged. "We're farmers. Even so, we're not two months behind our mortgage payment and I can't get a real person to answer the phone, nor do they call back when I leave a message."

He pushed a notebook across the table. "Write down their number and I'll see what I can find out."

As she wrote down the phone number, which she'd memorized because she'd called it so many times, Gus stirred. Olive gently brushed back her daughter's hair, uttering motherly coos until Gus went back to sleep. Olive estimated three more minutes with Rogers before Gus was fully awake and needing her attention.

"It's not that I can't see what you see," Rogers said. "You'll remember, initially, we did arrest a man, but had to let him go."

"You mean Johnny Pogonip?" She remembered Johnny's face when the same cop who had confronted her in the greenhouse drove down the street with Johnny in the back seat. "What happened?"

"Nothing hard to go on. We issued a citation for illegal camping and released him."

"What does 'hard' mean, in this case?"

"No prints. No motive. Diminutive strength and stature to take down a man Cris's size. Yes, he camped in the woods illegally, but he took us there and the fact remains we had nothing to go on." Rogers handed her a card.

"I have your card."

"It's a new card. Detective Henry Rogers."

Being on such open speaking terms with a detective on the force felt good, like she mattered and like he was interested in her take. She read the card. "Suspicious. Only two years on the force and you're a detective."

"By your standards, everything's suspicious. Just so you know, I never said I was a hundred percent sure it was a suicide. I said there's no evidence of foul play to follow up on. Once the coroner determines manner of death—in this case, suicide—we officially stop investigating. You may see us cruising down your street now and again because of a residual pull to the scene. We're homicide. We're drawn to death. But in this town, we have enough cases to process without chasing air. If anything comes up ..." He pointed to the card.

Gus stretched her fists, her mouth scrunched in a lopsided yawn which she squeezed into a cry. Olive pulled her from the stroller and nestled her in the nook of her arm as the toddler pulled down the top of her shirt and reached for a breast. Olive gently pulled her daughter's hand away from her breast in a brief power struggle that Olive was determined to win and pulled a bottle of milk from her bag. Gus greedily drank.

"Someday I hope to have kids," Rogers said.

"I hope you do. Which reminds me to tell you that Thea Villalobos is pregnant."

Rogers sat back a few inches, perhaps startled. He spoke softly, as if he didn't want Gus to hear.

"I know what you're getting at. Why exit with a child on the way? Look at it this way: the prospect of supporting an infant and wife on an artist's salary could have been the last straw."

Olive looked down at Gus to hide her disappointment.

"Look, Olive, he was an artist. His wife said a gallery recently turned down his work and his application for artist-in-residency was also rejected. That's hard stuff if you're already depressed." He shrugged.

Rogers' belt radio went off. His parting words to her: "If you get a lead, do not go it alone."

"Okay," she said. "But if I find something and the police ignore me, I'm not going to wait around and do nothing."

He grimaced. "If you're about to do something reckless, think twice." He gestured to Gus, then walked down the aisle leaving Olive to brood, and when he was outside on the walkway and passed her window, headed toward the ubiquitous green sedan parked parallel to the curb, she looked away and slipped Rogers's card into the diaper bag. When she glanced out the window, Rogers was watching her from inside his car.

"Could I pay my bill, please?" she asked the waiter, taking a five-dollar bill from her backpack.

"The man who just left paid the bill."

She watched Rogers pull away from the curb. Paying for a cup of coffee was no big dent in the pocketbook—even a cop's—and the gesture confused her. She thought about what he'd said. Hadn't known Cris received a series of rejections. Did know, being a freelance journalist in the first year of her marriage, what rejection felt like.

She placed her five on the homeless man's table.

Maybe Cris did kill himself.

"God bless you," she heard the man say, as she strolled Gus down the aisle.

10

Victims of knife-inflicted neck wounds may be dead or coma-
tose, the article stated. Coma had been wishful thinking when Olive realized the body at her feet belonged to Cris. A wound to the
carotid artery does not result in as much external bleeding as inter-
nal. Exsanguination, in which hemorrhage occurs with little to no
appearance of blood. "Exactly," Olive said, aloud. For the wound
to be fatal the instrument must be thrust fully into the neck below
the jawline followed by a twist that severs the artery. Death is immediate.

She scrolled down to a photograph of an injured infant in war-
torn Syria and smelled graham crackers. Byrd stood behind her,
staring over her shoulder at the screen.

"What's wrong with the baby?"

"The baby's going to be okay, Byrd," Olive said.

"I'm worried about the baby," Byrd insisted.

"We can say a prayer for the baby," Olive said, although the
only prayer she knew was the morbid classic: Now I lay me down
to sleep ... If I should die before I wake, I pray the lord my soul to
take. Not an option.

She picked up Byrd, who wrapped his legs around her waist as
she carried him to his bedroom. As she sat on the edge of his bed,
holding his hands between hers, he said, "I'm still worried about
the baby."

Olive forced a gentle smile. "Let's go outside and ask the sky if
the baby is safe?"

Byrd threw back his covers, and they walked into the master bedroom out to the porch, sat on the wicker rocker and stared at the sky.

"I don't see anything."

Olive pointed out the Big Dipper, low in the sky. "Keep watching. You have to be patient."

A small cloud above the mountain ridge drifted upward. Another larger cloud followed. She was tempted to wake Byrd. The peaceful weight of his little boy body in her lap said let him sleep.

"Byrd," she whispered. "Byrd. Look at the clouds." She took his hand and pointed to the area in the sky where they traveled slowly across the sky. "Do you see? A baby and a mama."

He stirred and rubbed his eyes. "They're only clouds," he said, as the two merged and dissolved into the night.

Olive and Cal lay at opposite ends of the futon. The fireplace glowed and sent out cozy heat. She told Cal about the clouds. He massaged her foot, about to respond, when someone knocked on the front door. Olive unwound herself from Cal's legs.

"Who's there?" she called.

"I'll answer it." When Cal opened the door and she realized who was on the other side, her stomach dropped.

Ariela set down a square black suitcase with the finality of a missile launch. Then she shook off a large backpack. "Outlaw," she greeted Cal. She looked around him to Olive. "Daughter."

Olive rose from the futon and stood beside Cal. She looked outside, beyond her mother, who was smart enough not to expect a hug after Olive had expressly told her not to come. No signs of a car, taxi or Lyft. Whatever had delivered her mother to her doorstep had already departed.

Ariela's prairie skirt swished as she crossed the threshold and breezed by Olive and Cal. She was few pounds thicker around her midriff. Her ample cleavage, which was always a source of personal pride, cushioned a squash-blossom necklace. Olive stared at the black suitcase and recognized it as hers from her childhood, guessing it was probably packed with metaphysical trinkets and occult paraphernalia.

"This is not a good time for us," Olive said. "I told you that."

"Now is the perfect time," Ariela said.

"You should have called me."

"I did. But you said no. So, I contacted my spirit guides and they said go."

"No sense fighting spirit guides." Cal took the suitcase from Ariela and walked it to the futon.

"Thank you, Outlaw. At least one of you has manners."

Olive resented the nickname her mother so blithely assigned to her husband, Outlaw, and even more how nonplussed her mother appeared as she entered Olive's living room.

"I would've called you, Love, but you would've insisted you don't need me. Au contraire, you do."

Love—her mother used this pet name to mask her true intentions. Control.

"You found a dead man on your farm, knowing it signifies a grander scheme of some malicious intent, but no one believes you, not even your honey bunny. I didn't call because I'd made up my mind and didn't want to create any more anxiety."

"This is your version of being considerate?" She felt Cal drape his arm over her shoulder in an attempt to ease her.

"We'll work things out tomorrow. For tonight, Ariela, you take the futon," Cal said.

No. In less than five minutes. Ariela, who pointed her long, multi-ringed finger at her, had triangulated Olive's marriage.

"You're a skinny little witch," she said. "Don't tell me you're still nursing."

Olive hated comments about her body, and her mother knew this.

"I'll get some sheets and blankets," Cal said.

As he headed upstairs, the air soured as quickly as milk on a warm day. Ariela sat on the couch as if it were hers and flipped back her thick, wavy red hair. "So, what's new?"

"I'm looking at it." Olive turned and walked toward the staircase.

"Don't you want to know why I brought your old suitcase?"

"Can it wait until morning? I'm tired."

"Because you left it and me when you went away to college."

Olive turned at the landing as Ariela held up the open suitcase with its half dozen Hopi dolls, one for each Christmas from the time Olive was five years old. Even at this distance, Olive smelled the mold as it escaped the black velvet lining.

"You never liked these dolls," Ariela said, "so I'm giving them to my granddaughter, whom I haven't met because you haven't found time in your busy life to visit me."

Olive gazed at the dolls she had feared in her childhood. "You're the one who moved."

As a child she had yearned for normal dolls that came with outfits, moving appendages and blinking eyes. The kachinas had spooked her with their serious masks and hard-edged dance poses. They were meant to be powerful and they made her feel powerless, and all she could do was turn them to face the wall at bedtime.

"If you need anything, make yourself at home, but please do not come upstairs. You might wake the kids, and Cal needs his sleep. There's a half-bathroom in the hallway by the front door."

Cal was coming down the stairs with bedding.

"She is such a bitch," Olive muttered as they passed each other on the stairs. He patted her shoulder with a free arm, his other balancing sheets, blankets and a pillow, trying to tamp the coals her mother had stirred in her.

The living room smelled like patchouli when Olive went downstairs to start breakfast. Scent was one of Ariela's methods of staking territory. Their futon and hearth space, and now the entire downstairs. She hoped the smell hadn't slipped under the kitchen door where she was about to make breakfast.

Ariela sat up with a start. The sheets fell away, exposing her bare breasts. "So, Love, tell me. How did this Cris Villalobos lose his life?"

"Good morning to you, too."

"I'm interested in your perspective, Love."

There it was again. Her mother's term of endearment—love— was not at all about love. Like calling Cal "outlaw," which might have sounded cute to outsiders, but masked hostile feelings. Ariela's nicknames were, Olive knew, intentional manipulations to appropriate power and make Olive feel as if she had some intimate knowledge of their private lives.

"He's too young." Ariela, seated at the dining room table, objected to Byrd's preschool. "If you can't afford to come visit me, how can you afford preschool?"

"I never said we can afford it." Olive dunked a slice of sourdough into the egg and milk batter, remembering how her mother had routinely taken her out of school without a second thought. Educational road trips, Ariela had called them. Which would have been noble if the trips hadn't been one more expression of her mother's restlessness. Ariela couldn't bear the routine of raising a child and fled the small, rural town whenever she felt the least inclination. They'd only be gone a few days, Ariela would promise, but the days inevitably amounted to weeks, once an entire month. Most kids would relish the idea of a parent taking them out of school, but when Olive returned from one of these sojourns, her classmates had read their first book, learned fractions. Worse, they had forged new friendships that didn't include her. And there were consequences to truancy. Ariela would talk the Superintendent and school board out of pressing charges and threatening to notify Child Protective Services. Meanwhile, Olive quickly caught up to her schoolwork, but it took months to re-establish standing among peers.

She lay the egg-soaked bread onto a buttered grill. The sizzle of butter and egg assuaged a small part of the primitive brain Ariela had inflamed.

"Preschool is good for children." She spoke in her cheeriest voice for the sake of the kids. "It socializes them so that when they enter kindergarten they're not overwhelmed. More to the point, what kind of person barges in on their daughter and her family un-invited?" Wasted words, Olive thought, but at least she'd said them.

"A mother who cares for her daughter," Ariela answered.

Olive's hackles rose, but she kept quiet. Her mother sucked at parenting. Olive had vowed to be the opposite: a nurturing, affectionate mother on whom her children depended for consistency in a home where children were central. She strapped Augusta into her highchair and put a jar of maple syrup on the table. Cal entered and tousled Byrd's hair.

"I love you, buddy. Say it back or it's tickle interrogation." When Cal reached for Byrd's sides, he squealed, curled over, giggling in pain.

"Say it."

"I love you, Daddy." He shrieked.

Olive was grinning. The French toast was burning.

"How old are you, sonny?" Ariela asked.

"I'm five."

"He's eighteen," said Cal. "Old enough to drive."

"You're four Byrd," Olive said. "Barely."

"Oh, c'mon, Love," Ariela said. "Let him be five."

Now, her mother made her feel rigid. She stared out the window over the kitchen sink and saw the tin sign Cal had posted to the redwood tree in their backyard. SQUIRREL CROSSING. It felt auspicious. A black squirrel scampered up the trunk, stopped as if he sensed Olive watching him. His tail flicked as he clung to the trunk, sensing eminent danger. Olive sensed danger, too. As she watched Cal leave through the porch door, grab his boots from the mudroom and walk away from the house in his socks, the argument had just begun.

"Really, Love, letting your child leave home so early to spend the day with strangers, doesn't that give you the willies?"

The blunt criticism on how she chose to raise her children wasn't worth a response, but Byrd crossed his arms and proclaimed he liked his teacher and the pet tortoise.

"You think a turtle is worth more than spending time with me?"

Olive stood with a plate of mango slices and considered dumping them in her mother's lap.

"It's a tortoise," he said, indignant.

"You're smart, another reason to let me homeschool you. I have plenty to teach."

"That's the most frightening thing I've heard." Olive placed a piece of fruit in front of Byrd, as he ate a piece of French toast with his fingers, dripping syrup onto his pajamas.

"I don't want Ariela to homeschool me." He licked the syrup on his plate and Olive held off wiping the beads of syrup off his pajamas, remembering the day her mother had left California.

It was the same day Olive had left for UC Berkeley. Ariela insisted she'd chosen Kansas because it was the geographic center of the contiguous United States, where an energy vortex lay in wait. She'd rented an old farmhouse in the outskirts of Lawrence on a bend of a particular river with a reputation among the locals for its orographic deflection of the wind. In other words, no tornados.

"I'm serious," Ariela said.

"And I'm not?" Olive heard the high pitch of her voice. "What are you going to teach him? Spells and magic potions?"

Byrd piped up, "Magic?"

"There's my proof, Love. Modern technology turns them into zombies, changes their brain chemistry in a bad way. My god, it stunts their genitals."

Olive looked at Byrd. Fortunately, he didn't know the word. She glanced at the kitchen clock and waited for him to ask. It wasn't even eight in the morning, and chaos already bounced off the walls of her home.

She left the kitchen to straighten up the living room and heard Byrd and Ariela giggling. Their gaiety was so far from Olive's disgruntled mood that there was no way to be part of it. She couldn't even fake a laugh with the resentment filling her chest. She walked back into the kitchen, not because she wanted to destroy their fun, because in a way she did, but because she didn't want to be the kind of person who was so bitter she couldn't handle others' happiness, especially when it was her son's, inspired by someone else. And he had to get dressed for preschool.

She waited until she heard his feet on the stairs. Then:

"Ariela, you have to find an Airbnb or stay in a motel. I run my home a certain way that works for all of us. I plan things. We have schedules. I'm the farm's bookkeeper. I don't pick up and plant myself on others without a second thought."

The smug look on her mother's face seemed incongruous to the demand Olive had just expressed. Right now, forced to defend her territory, Olive was in more pain than her mother. "You're an imposition and I want you to leave. I can't be any clearer than that."

"I did have second thoughts, sweet, but you'd have told me not to come."

Olive didn't bite. "That is correct."

"You're in trouble, daughter, and you can't get out of this alone."

11

As she rounded the banked curve that paralleled Twin Lakes lagoon on her way to Pleasure Point, she thought of her mother as skidding into their lives like a car on black ice.

She parallel parked in front of Captain Positively's Tattoo Salon and wondered if the Harley Sportster on the sidewalk belonged to Cap, the man who was so convinced Cris had not killed himself. A paper clock hung on the inside of the glass front door. The slim red hour hand pointed to one. She checked her phone, twelve forty-five, and pulled open the heavy glass door. It opened with a jingle from the overhead bell. A woodcut of a buffalo hung on the wall behind the counter and beside that a ledger drawing of a Plains Indian galloping an Appaloosa.

"Lady," a man bellowed. "We're open in fifteen minutes." When she wheeled around, a thirtyish man with a two-day beard stood beside the water cooler. His angular face could have been handsome if he weren't so mean looking.

"Hold up, Surly." The Tom Waits voice. "She's mine," he said. "Send her back."

As she walked past Surly, who glared at her, one of the strands of beaded curtain got tangled in her hair. It took her an awkward few seconds to untangle. Cap, looking amused, sat in a cubicle in the salon room where the artists performed their work. She counted six stations, each with a brown leather chaise lounge that faced a triptych of mirrors. The exposed brick lathe and old redwood beams created an ambience of warmth and style that she hadn't expected. The fir floors had been sanded and lacquered. The sense that Cap had taste, by her standards, set her more at ease, which might not be a good thing. She was here to get information, not a tattoo.

"Glad I wasn't holding my breath." Cap sat on a round green stool and motioned to the chaise lounge. "Don't be shy."

"I'm not," Olive said, sitting down on the edge of the lounge.

"She's a virgin," Cap said to Surly.

He must've seen the doubt in her face that announced she'd made a mistake to come here.

"Meaning," Cap said, "you've never been tattooed. Am I right?"

"Never have been tattooed. And that's not why I'm here, but you know that. Thank you for seeing me."

The top half of Cap's hair was pulled back into a tight, slick bun, the lower half buzzed to his neck. A spider web covered his neck, replete with a spider in the center, same spot as the carotid. He put up his fist, in lieu of a handshake, and Olive gave it a bump.

"You know anything about jellyfish?"

"If you're referring to Cris's tattoo, not enough to make sense of his death."

"They're immortal," said Cap. "One species regenerates itself when sensing danger. It regresses to the polyp stage and grows again. Death becomes birth." See what I mean, his expression said.

Olive didn't. "Cris believed in reincarnation?"

His lowered eyes inferred wrong answer. "Jellyfish are going to be the earth's last surviving marine creatures. They'll outlive all of us. The next two-legged to walk out of the ocean will have evolved from jellies."

Olive sat ramrod straight and waited for him to go on, the way she used to wait when her sources brought her to unfamiliar places she didn't frequent unless they were about to divulge important information. "You have a story for me, Cap?"

"I record my stories on skin. This is about psychology. My clients go deep with me. Imagine you're sitting in a chair for an hour with someone pricking your flesh. It hurts. What do you do to pass the time? Breathe into the pain and talk, like praying. In a half-hour we're sharing our biggest fears and juiciest fantasies. One reason I love this job. Like you and your hairdresser, right?"

Olive hadn't been to a hairdresser in more than a year, but she got his point.

"Cris loved life too much to kill it." His good eye turned sad just as Surly entered the room and asked if Olive wanted a drink.

"We got bottled water, green tea and homemade kombucha."

Olive recalled a story she'd written about the risks of kombucha—kidney failure and anthrax—but said nothing as Surly retrieved the brew from the top shelf of their cupboard and showed her the thick pearly scum with its fine purple veins as if he were showing off a puppy.

He dipped his hands in the murky liquid and pulled out the slimy thing. "We call her Scooby for symbiotic culture of bacteria and yeast. I drink the liquid to heal the gut because health begins with the gut."

"Olive's inquiring about Cris," Cap interrupted.

Surly scowled. "You a cop?" He dropped Scooby back into her amniotic fluid.

"Does she look like a cop?" said Cap.

Surly shrugged. "She could. Why else would she ask about Cris?"

"She doesn't think he offed himself."

Olive inhaled another deep breath as Surly returned his jar of kombucha to the shelf. "I heard one guy used a box cutter to his neck," he said.

"Listen, Olive. My take? The cops just want to wrap up the case. I should know." Cap reached for the bamboo backscratcher on the wall hook behind him. "I was a cop before I lost my eye. LAPD. I know how it works."

Olive realized the orb she'd thought was merely lazy was, instead, a glass eye. She didn't want to digress too far by asking him how he'd lost it, but you never knew when a person's words could shed light.

"How did you lose your eye?"

"Surfing," he said. "In Huntington. A board ran right into it."

"My husband surfs. Is that why you moved here?"

"I came here because it's the next best place to Southern California with fewer people and cars." As Cap scratched his shoulder blade with the stick, a fleeting look of bliss crossed his face and he instructed her to "look real close at that redwood beam" in the center of the room.

"See the carving? It looks like bacon slices, but if you refocus and keep your eyes back you can see the bigger design. A pair of long-haired mermaids. Cris carved that. He loved the sea. He loved women, which has something to do with his death."

"He loved his wife."

Cap went silent. "Yes, he talked about her lots. Quite a woman from the sound of it."

"She's expecting their baby." Olive watched Cap's face, trying to discern if he knew this or not, or didn't care. She couldn't tell. "Did you know that?"

"I did not." He hung his head and clucked. "Damn."

Surly turned and headed to the lobby. "Time to open up."

That, or the sensitive nature of the conversation had driven him out of the room. Olive watched him leave, and as she turned her attention back to Cap, she took in as much of her surroundings as she could without being obvious.

"On the night Cris died, someone ransacked our greenhouse and destroyed a lot of our crop. Tomato seedlings. They were so special the newspaper published a front-page story on them shortly before Cris died. I don't believe in coincidence."

Cap crossed his arms and hugged his chest as if he were holding onto his truth. "I read that piece about the plants. Good photo. Epic. Your old man's a cool dude."

"Yep. Cris lived across the street from our farm and I think he heard someone breaking into the greenhouse. Could be he went out to stop them and the thief turned on him."

"With his rod and reel hanging free?"

The newspaper never reported Cris was naked.

Cap leaned back. "Sounds like we're both saying he died for tomatoes."

"That is not funny."

"Here's the thing, Miss Olive." He leaned forward.

"A guy goes down for offing himself and that's a serious bummer to his legacy and loved ones. A guy goes out for being in the wrong place at the wrong time, we can live with ourselves and the kid has a hero for a dad instead of a sick fuck whose genes he inherited."

A good point, but not evidence and not nice. She wanted more.

Olive said, "The police told me there's no substantial evidence of foul play for them to follow up on, and in the absence of leads, Cris's predisposition for depression and anxiety—which is medically documented—was paramount in the determination of manner of death."

"Anyone who isn't depressed in this fucked up world is who we got to worry about," shouted Surly. The front doorbell tinkled as someone walked in.

"Ignore him," said Cap.

"What about the jellyfish?" Olive asked. "What's that about?"

Cap tapped her knee. "Before I explain, you'd look good with ink. You have beautiful skin."

She shuddered, envisioning Cap creating art on her body.

"I saw that." He mimicked her shiver.

"I don't like needles. Thank you, anyway."

"Jellyfish, then. They excrete an iridescent fluid on their prey to protect themselves. Find the residue and you'll find the killer." He stared at Olive's arms.

"What does that even mean?"

"You have such smooth skin. Sure I can't convince you?"

"Positively. I need to know if you know something I don't, some piece of proof."

"Jellyfish are immortal. Cris wanted to live forever." He intended his answer to be meaningful, but … "You're the intellectual type,"

Cap said. "I could ink words from a nursery rhyme on the inside of your upper arm. In color. Keep your arm down if you don't want people to see."

"Actually, I'm the inquisitive type. And that's not the reason I don't have a tattoo."

"You have kids. Saw them at the memorial. Maybe a child's poem that would gauge your kids' progress as readers. Don't tell them what it says. They have to learn the words."

"That's tempting but I'm not in the market, Cap."

"How about a tat with experimental tomatoes on the buttock for your husband."

She shook her finger in his face. "Inappropriate."

He pressed his hands to his chest. "No. Rad. Less painful than a foot. You'd keep them to the outside toward the hip. The closer to the spine the bigger the ouch. You could make it seasonal. Ink the tomatoes in summer. What was in season when Cris died?"

Olive hesitated. "Beets. I found Cris in our beet field."

"I could ink beets. And by the way, sorry you had to see what you saw."

That, again. She hadn't admitted her truth to anyone, not even to Cal, but she was about to profess to this man who wanted to drill tomatoes on her buttocks that she was not at all sorry.

"I respect that you were the first person to see him," Cap said. "It is a sacred honor to be the closest one to a person's last stand. You have an obligation now. Finding his body makes you responsible for understanding his death."

That was exactly how Olive felt. She had been an ex-crime reporter for a reason—her intuition told her when there was more going on under the surface, and something in her DNA couldn't rest until she found out what it was.

"I nailed it, didn't I? You've been here thirty minutes and we're already talking deep. Just like the beauty shop."

Olive thought he might know about fictitious names. "May I ask you a business question?"

"Go for it."

"Did you file a DBA with the county for this salon?"

"Yeah, you have to. That's the law."

"With the county or state?"

"County."

"So, if I looked up Captain Positively's Tattoo Salon, your name would be there?"

"Hope so. Why?"

"Have you ever heard of Inventiveness, a mortgage company?"

"Nope. Does not ring a bell. Why, for the second time?"

"They're trying to foreclose on our land."

"Probably a scam. You should report them to the cops, and I don't say that lightly."

"I did." Olive pointed to the tattoo on the left side of Cap's neck. "The apex of your web is in the exact spot where Cris was mortally wounded."

Cap grabbed Olive's hand and pressed it to his neck. "Gotcha. Ha." He released her hand. "The arachnid's copulatory bulb reminds me every time I look into the mirror, I'm lucky to be on the living side."

He touched the spider. "Messengers from the spirit world, storytellers. I'm a storyteller in ink."

The gesture stunned Olive enough that she put her hand in her pocket and stood. "If that's all the story you're going to give me, I'm leaving." She started across the room but stopped and turned. "Did you murder Cris?"

Her bluntness didn't shock him, more like he'd been waiting for it. He let out a short laugh.

"What's so funny?"

"Hell, no, I didn't murder Cris," he said. "But someone who knew how to did."

"How did you know he was naked? The newspaper didn't report that."

"Small town."

"Obscure answer."

He shrugged. "Best I can do."

She walked through the beaded curtain. The bell jangled as she opened the door to exit.

Cap shouted, "Call for an appointment and we'll get something going. It's cash in advance, fifty percent down, but I'd take a trade in vegetables for the first session."

She walked past the Harley, imagining tomato vines inked across her butt and Cal nibbling the ripe red irresistible fruit. She liked the image but felt vaguely she'd missed something in that salon which refused to surface. Cap was holding back. She tried to formulate questions now that she hadn't asked in the salon. Instead, tomato vines tattooed on buttocks galloped across her mind. She turned back into the store.

"You changed your mind about ink?" Cap asked.

"If I did want a tattoo, would you require an advance deposit?"

"That's our policy. No different than any of my competitors. And a template, but I could make that up for you. I trade, but only if you have something to trade and only once. The rest is cash up front."

"Did Cris trade his carvings for ink?"

Cap's tone of voice changed, more serious.

"I liked Cris's work. But a man's got to make a living, so I had to charge for the color."

"His tattoo didn't have color when I found him. Did he pay up front before he died?"

"Affirmative."

"So, he paid you cash in advance for the color?"

"Ye-up. We had a lot of work ahead of us."

"How much cash did he pay up front?"

"Fifty percent cash, in advance."

"Did he make an appointment?"

"Affirmative."

Olive waited a few beats, determining if she should ask for the record of that appointment and decided not to, sensing she'd push him too far.

"How much is fifty percent?"

"Twenty-five."

"Hundred?"

He nodded. "Tattoos are a commitment."

"Why didn't you tell me he intended to keep working with you when I first came in?"

"You didn't ask until now."

"You knew why I was here. If Cris planned to color his jellyfish and paid cash up front, he'd invested in his future."

"You could be undercover." Cap leaned back, arms crossed against his burly chest. "Like Surly said. You're asking a lot of questions, not farm-girl type questions, if you know what I mean."

"I used to be a crime reporter. I asked questions for a living."

Cap looked satisfied with her answer. "If people don't put money up front, they'd flake on us. My creative mind-in-a-vise would go to waste."

"Cris Villalobos wasn't a rich man."

"Neither am I. If I'd told you he'd fronted me the cash, you'd tell his old lady—she's your friend, right? And I'd have to refund cash I've already reinvested."

Visiting Cap had been worthwhile. Olive learned that Cris had made a monetary commitment in his future. Not that a commitment guaranteed a person wouldn't kill themselves, but it certainly added weight to the homicidal side of the scale.

12

The conversation barbed her mind like a cactus needle as she hit her stride at the ridgeline and the undone chores of the day fell away. Cris had paid in advance for tattoo work. That was a lot of money to put up front if he was thinking of suicide. And if he'd been planning his death, he would have tried to get the money back for Thea. Not that there's logic when taking one's life.

She reached the fire road, formerly a logging road. To keep her blood pumping, she jogged in place, gazing down mountain to their farm that fanned out from the nape of the coastal redwoods into acres of rich alluvial soil that was cut in two by the San Lorenzo river. From here, she could see the river's path through the downtown to the river mouth lagoon and Monterey Bay.

The panorama was world class, offering a view of both lighthouses, the larger one at Steamer Lane overlooking the world class surf break. On the far side of the river mouth was the small craft harbor lighthouse that guided seafaring boats back to safety. The unmistakable Santa Cruz Boardwalk and its palms and arching roller coaster punctuated the town's fun-loving heart that attracted day visitors from around the state. Inland, the white mission steeple rose above the unmarked graves of the Awaswas, who were the land's first people.

The bay curved to leisurely Pleasure Point surf breaks and, in the far distance, the plume of billowing steam from Moss Landing Power Station. Five more miles south, the Salinas River dove into the Deep Sea Trench, cutting the bay in half. The seven-mile-deep trench, twice as deep as the Grand Canyon, sheltered troves of blind sea creatures who exist without names and light, relying on scent to survive. One species was especially grotesque: the male Anglerfish that sniffed out the female, bit her with his awl-sharp teeth and survived on her bodily fluids in trade for his sperm. Some trade.

Behind her, the rising Santa Cruz Mountains housed the University of California—the City on a Hill, as it was nicknamed—where the country's most progressive research and hands-on training in organic farming took place. Cal had graduated from that university and received a degree in Sustainable Food Systems and a certificate from the university's organic farming apprenticeship program, which trained people to farm organically. In other words, the university had Cal's back, figuratively and geographically.

Olive shook out her legs and started back down at an easy trot, testing her shins. She circumvented the sharp fingernails of manzanita brush, the West Coast version of a briar patch—impassible for the most seasoned hiker. She turned left on a narrower trail that led into the canopy of redwoods and a seep zone, where water unable to percolate into the mudsill pooled on the ground's surface, creating plant habitat that thrived in dampness and shade.

Johnny Pogonip stepped out of the trees into the path, his arms dangling at his sides. He tilted his head, indicating he wanted her to follow. "A widow, kneeling in the dirt."

Olive hesitated, remembering the way he'd suddenly appeared out of nowhere at the site of Cris's death, ordering her not to cover him up with her sweatshirt. He'd been correct. Among other things, covering Cris's body would have interfered with the medical examiner's determination of time of death, which had been estimated as between midnight and three in the morning. But she hadn't been thinking on those terms when she'd found him sprawled in the dirt and so vulnerable. She followed Johnny's lead off the trail onto a deer path.

Thea knelt on the ground by a small creek. She let out a startled shriek when she saw Johnny. From Olive's perspective, she looked like a beautiful, victimized woman out of a Keats poem. Olive lowered herself to the ground and knelt beside her on a soft carpet of sorrel. Johnny tipped his cap and stepped backward, turned and walked into the forest, softly disappearing into the shadows.

"Cris loved this place." Pink tendrils traveled up Thea's pale neck. Dried tears salted her face. "He'd drink from this very spring, even though I warned him people camped here and it probably wasn't a good idea." She cupped a wild azalea at its base, careful not to touch its petals. "We talked about naming our baby Azalea, if it's a girl. I don't know what I'm going to do if it's a boy. We were going to name him Cris, Jr." She leaned over and pressed her forehead into the dirt. Olive placed a gentle hand on her back, so Thea would know she wasn't alone. At least not now, in this place. When she rose, a circle of dirt remained on her forehead, as if the earth had blessed her.

"Walk back with me," Olive said. "We can hang out at my house and drink tea by the fireplace."

Thea gazed into the understory of redwoods. "I hear your mother is visiting," she said.

"I hope she's visiting. She has a way of sending out roots."

"I heard she's psychic." Thea's piqued look of interest resembled that same look of expectation and hope that used to come over Olive's girlhood friends when they realized her mother's metaphysical skills. Even her Christian girlfriends relished visiting her mother because she read their horoscopes in a way that helped them navigate their first love and salvage their shipwrecked hearts. Olive had often hoped that her mother's mystical bent would disappear from their gene pool, like the human tail and the whale's feet.

It was mid-morning when they walked in the front door. Ten o'clock by her watch. Byrd, who was drawing at the living room table beside Ariela, didn't look up. Olive noticed his fingertips. Blood red. She spotted the vial of dark liquid on the center of the table and picked it up. When she sniffed, the substance smelled earthy.

Ariela shrugged. "Don't worry so much. It's only Dragon's Blood. Tree resin. That's all it is. And do not look at me like that."

Byrd glanced up from his project. "I'm casting spells," he said with self-importance.

"Where's Gus?" Olive asked.

"I sang her to sleep and put her down in her crib. A lovely girl, who reminds me of you." She turned to Thea. "I've been waiting for you, dear," she said, her voice both soft and controlling. "Come over here so I can get a good look at you." Ariela regarded Thea's all black attire, buckled boots, and woolen cap with an approving smile. "I love your style," she gushed, turning to Olive with an accusatory is-it-so-hard-to-dress-creatively expression, making it clear that Olive, the thoughtful friend, was boring and the grieving widow was interesting.

It had taken less than five minutes. She'd timed it. Five minutes for her mother to spike a wedge between Olive and Thea and literally pull Thea to her side.

"Another record," said Olive.

Ariela waved her off. "My daughter. So sarcastic. She has my psychic gift, you know, but ignores it and channels it into" … she waved her arm toward the swinging kitchen door … "cooking."

Now there was something wrong with cooking? In middle school, Olive had begun to teach herself to bake by reading every cookbook she could get her hands on. She kneaded bread dough as if she were weaving the rug that her mother routinely pulled out from under her. Sometimes, it felt like she'd grown up on air. Cooking grounded her.

"Your outlaw is in the field, by the way," Ariela announced.

Byrd looked up, expecting his mother to react to the nickname.

Outlaw? Thea mouthed.

Olive rolled her eyes. Irritation was a progressive disease around her mother, boring more sorely with each exchange into tightly coiled barbed wire, set to spring.

Ariela had apparently placed a chair beside the fireplace before they'd even arrived, and a second chair facing it. She motioned for Thea to sit down as Olive led Byrd out of the room into the kitchen, hearing her mother shout, "Dismantle those walls, Love, and move forward."

Whatever. Olive pulled out the kitchen stool and scrubbed the resin from Byrd's fingers with a vegetable brush. When she turned off the faucet, Olive heard her mother talking to Thea: "When violence occurs. the spirit is unable to move to the next world until the energy is cleared. The sooner we start the better."

Byrd tilted his head to Olive as she worked up a pink lather on his hands. "What's she talking about?" Pink water ran down the white porcelain sink and spiraled into the drain.

Olive chose her words. "Spirits are like friendly ghosts."

"I want to see."

"Most people can't see them." She rinsed Byrd's hand and wiped them with a kitchen cloth. She guided him to the breakfast nook and put a glass of milk and a cookie in front of him. A faint smell of sage wafted under the kitchen door from the living room fireplace. Her mother screamed and a shadow moved across the kitchen as if a cloud had just passed over the sun. Olive looked out the bay window. No cloud. No wind in the trees.

13

Gil answered the cathedral door to find his daughter standing in the alcove, scowling. He loved his daughter. She was the heir to his fortune. On the other hand, she was a pain in the ass. For one, she took after her mother—Nordic features, petite, mouthy. Two, his daughter blamed him for her mother abandoning them when she was too young to remember anything except how it felt to receive a mother's hugs and kisses.

"Hello, Gil."

And he disapproved of his daughter addressing him by his first name as much as he objected to her changing her last name. She could do that when she married. He stepped aside. "Come in."

She balked, took a deep breath, then strode past him toward the kitchen.

"Why dreadlocks?"

"What did you say?"

He held out a cold can of Coke and offered it to his daughter.

"Why dreadlocks, for god sakes? You're such a pretty girl."

His daughter refused the soda, no surprise, uttering a string of profanities against Coca Cola, Republicans and high fructose corn syrup.

"Water, then?"

She slid into the breakfast nook with her back to the wall and a view to the driveway and woods. She put up her hand as if his offers were physical assaults. "Stop."

To what do I owe the pleasure, he almost said, but she always nailed him on clichés. He opened the flip top and gulped his Coke, then stared at her hair. She hadn't answered his question.

"I need money."

Why else show up on my doorstep? He waited quietly for an explanation, even a lie, that would at least acknowledge he was the one holding the cards here.

"I'm moving, and I need first and last months' plus a security deposit."

His heart sunk. "You're not leaving town?"

"Moving to the other side of town. I found a house with enough land for animals and a garden."

"What's wrong with your condo?"

She waved her arms. "You of all people should understand." She swept her arms around the kitchen bay windows. "You live on a mountain with a three-car garage."

"How much space does a single girl need?"

Her expression said, you bastard. "I want animals."

"The last thing you need are animals."

"I don't need you to tell me what I need."

"When did you start wearing your hair like that? You have such pretty hair."

"It's my hair, and if you're not going to give me the money, I'm leaving. I didn't come here to update you on my life or have my looks commented on by a man who alters the DNA of carrots."

The deep circles under her eyes made Gil wonder what was going wrong in her life. He had ways of knowing if she were sick or addicted or in crisis, but he'd heard nothing along those lines. "Do you need to see a doctor? I'll pay for a psychiatrist. Just say the word. I know some good ones."

Her raccoon stare made her look unpredictable. "I'm here for one thing. To ask you for money for a deposit and rent until I get a second job."

"I thought you had a job with that organic farm."

Her face puffed up, eyes glistened. "I never told you that." She slapped her hands on the table. "You're an impossible dick."

"You can't just leave everything and everyone to their own devices if you want to survive in this world. You need a skill."

"If we got rid of your devices for growing food, we could sequester so much carbon we'd reverse climate change."

Gil waited until her hand was on the front doorknob. She looked like a pixie deer, so small under the vaulted ceilings of his home.

"Check or cash?" he asked.

"That," she said, "is up to you. Unless your check's no good or your cash is blood money."

"How much?"

"Six thousand."

He hid his surprise—rents had gone up from the last time she'd asked—but he wrote the check for 6k, and as he wrote he anticipated her parting insult, since she held him responsible for everything from miscarriages to dead zones. After a decade of being the object of her loathing, you'd think he'd be used to it.

His daughter snatched the check and stuffed it into her jean pocket. He took a deep breath to buffer himself from the departing sting.

"You know that your death would go a long way to reverse climate change," she said. "At least two percent of carbon emissions are from conventional and GMO agriculture."

He almost laughed. "You're welcome."

"I know it's hard for people like you to accept, but it's true. It's impossible for me to accept it's okay to insert the DNA of Round Up into the DNA of a beet. Who do you think you are that you can do that shit?"

"People like me? You're acting like a brainwashed university brat. People like you store their money in their back pockets and lose it in the gas station bathroom."

"I do not want your advice." She turned and left, and Gil watched his daughter head toward her beat up Volvo, reminding him of her mother. "Jesus Christ."

She turned at least, looking so hostile the skin on his scalp tightened.

"Not like this," Gil said. "C'mon. What can I do to get you back?"

"It's too late," she said, clutching her skinny midriff. "The version of me that you want back was damaged too deeply and too long ago to ever come back."

Gil searched for a response. Nothing. "Please explain," he said. "You're kidding."

"Not kidding."

She retraced a few steps. "You ran off my mother because you're a bully. You didn't raise me. You hired a nanny. You were never there. And when you were, you scared me. You treated me like you treat the land. You contaminated and ruined me. I'm lucky I don't have cancer."

It's early, yet, a voice in his head said and he batted the thought away.

"You fed me the same poisons you put into the dirt and water, knowing."

"Exactly what?"

She wiped her eyes, smearing mascara down her cheek and looking horribly pathetic. "Maybe you don't know. Maybe you're too self-absorbed and stupid to know what's really going on."

"I know I gave you everything and you could have more."

"All those trips to the doctor when I had stomach blockages, missing so much school I didn't even pass sixth grade."

Her words felt like bullets and if he moved one iota, they'd pierce his heart.

"Your food."

"My food put a roof over your head."

"That I got out from under as soon as I figured out how."

His head felt like a pressure cooker full of his flesh and blood's insolence. "Grow up."

"I did."

Gil watched her turn again and walk away, and it was all he could do to keep himself from charging after her, spinning her around and giving her a shake. But he didn't. He wouldn't. He never had and never would lay a hand on his girl.

14

"**Who's lived here?**" Ariela sat in her chair by the fireplace looking especially wild. Thea sat across from her, bewildered.

"A lot of people have lived here," Olive said. "This house is old. Cal's great grandfather built it more than a century and a half ago."

"Anyone with negative vibes?"

"Why?"

"Why? Because Cris Villalobos was on the edge of this room." She pointed to the rafter above the fireplace. "He was about to enter when the darkest mass of energy came out of the fireplace. I thought it was soot. But do you see any soot? No. Thank Goddess it didn't enter me. Or Thea. Honestly, Love, it scared the bats out of me."

Olive was used to her mother's visions. She could never get used to the expression "Thank Goddess." It was so contrived. Even "Holy shit!" would sound better.

"A shadow flew through the kitchen while I was washing Byrd's hands. If that helps." Olive glanced around the room. The walls were bathed in sunlight. The wood floors glowed warmly. Ariela leaned forward and patted Thea's hands.

"We have to end now dear until I cleanse this room. Remember, all signs are a sign of the spirit world, and that's a good thing." Ariela rose and headed to the kitchen.

"What happened?" Thea asked.

Olive could only shrug.

Ariela returned with a bulb of garlic and sat back down in her chair. She peeled a clove, popped it in her mouth as if she were devouring milk to neutralize a habanero pepper, meanwhile peeling another clove. By morning, Olive forecast, the living room would wreak from the allicin sweat that would seep from her mother's pores.

Ariela pressed her palms against her eyes. "Oh my Goddess, child. I'm not sure how to make this go away. All your cooking and cleaning and folding laundry and occasional snooping isn't going to do the job."

"Don't encourage her, Ariela." It was Cal, standing in the doorway.

"When did you get home?" asked Olive.

"Just here to fill up on water. Then I'm going back to flame weed."

She stood there a moment measuring her mother's criticism and Cal's warning, the two on opposite sides of the spectrum.

Ariela's angst looped in Olive's head as she filled the wicker laundry basket with warm, fluffed clothes and carried it from the office to the house, the stairs squeaking with the extra weight. Any criticism of her spiritual life wasn't more or less hurtful than a mother's disapproval of her daughter's hair. She would never put down her own daughter, even if she didn't like her hairstyle.

As she folded Byrd's favorite T-shirt into a square, a dusky fear hunkered down, urging her to identify a nagging problem. She carried the basket to her room where Byrd had climbed onto the big bed with his books. She folded Cal's T-shirts and shorts and placed them on top of the dresser. Beside the pile was a framed photo of Cal, the boy, with his father. Grandpa Post had the same thick messy hair and smiling eyes as Cal. The two of them stood in front of his father's private Cessna that killed him the year Cal turned thirteen.

Cal's dad had encouraged him to become an engineer. Any ambitions he may have had to fulfill that wish vanished when his parents died—first his father and three years later his mother from breast cancer.

Olive ran her eyes over the spines of Cal's books, non-fiction, mostly. Aldo Leopold, Wes Jackson, Wendell Berry, Orin Martin and Jeremy Rifkin. *Collapse* on his bedside table. These were his mentors and intellectual shapers. When he forgot why he'd chosen the ceaseless hard work of farming, the indifferent weather and threadbare profit of farming, or when he panicked that he'd taken the wrong path, Olive would say, remember your role to farm so folks can eat healthy food. Focus on that and the money will come.

Insecurity was innate to a boy who had lost his father before he'd learned how to be a man. The trauma had probably altered his DNA. He wasn't an outlaw or an altruist. He was a trailblazer with a vision, and her job was to keep his fears below the surface and bolster his passions. It had been a hard road for Cal and, at some level, this was one element that attracted her to him. She'd experienced her own share of childhood trauma, and those experiences built an attraction into the psyche's radar. She was sure of this.

Olive stared at the photo of father and son and felt sad. He'd had a father. Olive had not. She had never known a father or anything about her biological father. She didn't know if she was a love child or begat from a sperm bank, and her mother, other than a few conflicting clues, had kept it secret. So, unlike Cal, she didn't miss her father because she didn't have one. Father was a mere concept until she had kids with Cal and watched him parent. Up to that point, living without one was her norm. When she met Cal, having her own children with a man she loved was so perfect it frightened her.

She pulled out Augusta's pink pajamas and held them to her nose. They smelled of bleach, and the smell reminded her of Cris Villalobos. She had detected chlorine that morning when she bent down over his corpse, searching vainly for a pulse.

Olive found Ariela in front of the open refrigerator, hanging on to the door handle and staring at its innards.

"What's wrong?"

"I'm blocked."

Olive reached around her mother and grabbed the parsley and cilantro she planned to mince for chimichurri. "How do you think Thea took the episode today?"

"She's fine. It shocked some adrenaline loose. And she has something to look forward to as soon as I figure out what in this house is freaking me out."

As Ariela continued to stare at the shelves of milk and egg cartons, Olive noticed the fading tattoo of a Celtic knot on her mother's shoulder. She'd never noticed the tattoo before. She touched it lightly.

"Is your tattoo without color on purpose?"

"I ran out of money."

"Really?"

"They wanted three hundred more up front for color, so I settled on black. C'est la vie." Ariela walked out of the kitchen, leaving the fridge door wide open. Olive watched her curl up in the corner of the futon, legs folded beneath her, eyes closed, arms hugged across her chest. Her mother was going into the "vanished" state, in the grip of what she called "the other side where clarity dwelled." Her eyes closed, she sighed and launched her liminal journey, "gone" for the entire time it would take Olive to prep dinner before the kids woke up from their afternoon naps.

After the spinner cranked and whirred, expressing excess water from parsley and cilantro, it clattered to a stop and Olive lifted the herbs from the basket into the blender. Putting the flat side of a kitchen knife to a clove of garlic, she smashed the clove and peeled away the papery white skin, grateful her mother hadn't ingested the entire bulb. She tossed the tender flesh into the blender with cumin and pepper, imagining the tip of Cris's wood carving knife piercing his neck deeply enough to sever the carotid. She rushed into the living room, holding the saltshaker.

"Ariela," she said. "Did you put bleach in the kids' wash? Their clothes smelled like Clorox. We don't use Clorox."

"Once in a while, Love" Ariela said, "you need a little extra kill factor. But the answer is no. I didn't touch your laundry."

If she told her mother about the phantom smell of chlorine that triggered the memory of Cris, she'd attribute the sensory mix-up to a metaphysical phenomenon. Olive was not going there. What mattered right now was the clarity of where Cris had been minutes before he rushed to his death on the farm.

15

The bay was dressed in silver tinsel. Only in winter was the sun low enough to cast such shimmers on the ocean's surface. The radiance was so glaring that ancients weaponized the phenomenon in battle. Olive was certain of this. Flotillas advancing east toward the motherland were intentionally cloaked in the swath of glinting southern light, blinding their enemy. She wondered how to use this phenomenon to protect herself from the forces working against Cal and her.

She backed into a parking space and began unloading the box truck and setting up the stall. A woman stood near the produce display. Her smile looked more like a grimace. "That is so expensive. How can anyone afford strawberries at three-fifty a basket?"

It wasn't the first time a customer had questioned the price of her organic produce, and Olive tried to regard the question as an opportunity to educate the public. She told her politely that growing organic strawberries and paying labor a fair wage for picking them was expensive. When the woman shrugged, Olive suggested she buy a flat for thirty dollars and freeze most of them for smoothies throughout the year.

"Then you're down to two dollars a basket," Olive said.

The woman held up her shopping bag, clinging to the handles as tightly as she clung to her anger. "I don't have thirty dollars for strawberries."

Olive suggested, "You could round up some friends to chip in for a box and split it up."

A man's voice interrupted, asking if she would trade "some of those onions for potatoes." It was Brody.

Olive smiled. "Of course, and we have five varieties—red, yellow, white, cipollini and leeks."

"Six." Brody held up a French shallot. "You forgot these."

Shallots were originally a separate species but are now considered an onion variety. "You're right, and we're the only farm in the county that grows them," she said. "If you take some, they're better eaten raw, since they lose their flavor pretty quickly when cooked."

Olive was sorry to see the disgruntled woman turn and leave. She almost called her back to give her a free basket of straws but restrained herself.

Brody was studying her with something between skepticism and humor. "Do you like being a farmer's wife?"

"I don't think of myself as a farmer's wife."

In her years with Cal, no one had even referred to her as a "farmer's wife." She was a woman whose husband farmed. She was a partner in farming, just like she was a partner raising their kids. She wouldn't mind being labeled an orchardist who was growing her own apples for a future commercial venture. A co-proprietor of a working organic farm and five years into a marriage with a man she passionately adored and with whom she shared the view that sustainable and organic agriculture was a solution to everything from carbon emissions, heart disease and cancer to world peace. A "farmer's wife" dropped short of describing the person she had become, and she might have laughed if she weren't slightly irritated.

"What kind of a question is that?"

"No worries," he said. "I'm testing my pickup line. 'Hello, how'd you like to be a farmer's wife?' Does it attract or repel?"

"That would depend on who you asked." She smiled at his silliness.

"You did marry a guy who farms and you are his wife. At least, I think you're married. Is that what you studied in college? Agroecology, or something along those lines? I assume you went to college. You look like you went to college."

"I went to college to train for a career in journalism, which I succeeded in doing until I married Cal and decided to raise a family and farm."

She glanced up at Brody as he scratched the back of his neatly buzzed hairline while a customer waited in front of the counter with a brown paper bag of produce. Olive peaked into the bag. Loose red beets. She placed them on the scale and said, "Six dollars at two a pound." He was a middle-aged man with long white hair pulled back into a neat ponytail. He visited her stall every week, rain or shine. As he found exact change, he said, "These are the sweetest beets I've ever eaten, hands down." He flashed a crooked smile. "What do you do to make them so good?"

She relived walking over that cobbled beet graveyard on her way to discovering Cris's corpse but pressed her lips into a smile.

"My husband grows healthy soil before anything else."

The man looked puzzled at the concept of "growing" soil.

"We compost organic matter and add the finished product to the dirt along with nitrogen from our legume crops, and we amend where needed with organic nutrients so that the plants receive everything they need to reach their maximum potential. You should try the golden beets, too. Accompanied with pecans, celery and goat cheese. A couple of threads of saffron. But don't overcook them or they lose their bright yellow color."

"Next time." He raised his paper bag and left. Meanwhile, Brody raised his eyebrows, as in "see, you're a farmer's wife," squelching more images of beet roots staining her fingers as red as Byrd's dragon-blood-stained fingertips and bleeding into everything they touched—from green salads to the kid's white T-shirts. Honestly, she shared Cal's love of the beet as a high energy, densely nutritious and storable traditional food. But after Cris had died among them, she loved them less. For hours, he'd lain in the field, blood dripping into the thirsty, rich dirt Cal had built up over the years.

Brody shoved his hands in his pockets, shoulders hunched up around his ears, not possibly knowing what Olive visualized at that moment—Cris, naked, one eye pecked out, the other leached of pigment and staring at the sky.

When the customer turned away, Brody held up a sack of what she assumed were potatoes. He sold corn, too, but only in the summer. Last fall, during Brody's first year as a vendor, she'd seen his infamous corn that he grew biodynamically, under the full moon and sprinkled with astragalus water. He left the golden tassels on when he brought them to market, adding to their beauty as the silken strands draped down the crisp green husks. But last fall Olive remembered watching customer after customer peel back the husk and discover with horror the fat green worm curled into the space once inhabited by kernels. The spaces were puttied with beige worm castings. Olive had advised Brody to peel back the husks and hack off the spoiled tops. He did, but she was certain he'd already grossed out customers who would not give him a second chance.

She handed Brody a large canvas sack and urged him to fill it. "Be sure to take a bunch of cipollini. They're sweet this year."

She watched him cross the food tables, looking left and right as if he were dodging cars, until he spotted Kat Granger, who'd just showed up. She walked down the aisle on the opposite side of the market, dressed in knee-high suede moccasins and a matching fringe purse, long flowing sweater over a short dress. She was late, and Olive could use a break, but instead of checking in she breezed up to Brody. He grinned. They hugged. Not a shoulder hug with pats on the back. A real hug so their hips touched when they threw back their heads in laughter. Olive felt not exactly old, but lackluster. And way too serious. She walked to the back of the box truck, hefted three fresh flats of strawberries to fill in the front table, musing over Brody trying out his farmer's wife line on Kat.

"How are those tomatoes coming along?" a customer asked.

"We'll put the starts in the ground after the first rain. Mid-March I'd say. Right on schedule." If we get a good rain.

Big if. Olive inhaled a purposeful breath and glanced across the market. Kat and Brody were still laughing, pheromones dancing, as Olive filled in empty spaces with vibrant pink blush lettuces worthy of a poem.

"So." Kat's voice startled Olive. "Brody tried his farmer's wife pickup line on me.

She was either oblivious that she was late or compensating for it by enthusiastically filling Olive in on the details of their flirtation.

"I can't do small talk, right now." Olive filled in the strawberry table with new baskets.

Kat pitched in, placing baskets in the holes and straightening them into neat lines. "Then I won't tell you what I said."

"I give up. What'd you say?"

"It depends on the farmer."

"I like that." Olive noticed the chartreuse leaves climbing up Kat's neck, glossy and new. Everyone but her seemed to have a tattoo.

"And then I flipped it and asked him how he'd like to be a farmer's husband?"

"What'd he say?"

"He said, 'if you're the farmer, I'm in.'"

"I didn't know you wanted to be a farmer, Kat."

"I've always wanted to be a farmer. Organic, like you and Cal. And, don't tell anyone, Brody's a stud muffin."

Ariela waltzed down the aisle, shouting, "Oyster mushrooms," waking up Gus from the port-a-crib Olive had set up behind the counter in the shade. She held up a vacuum-packed Ziploc of raw chicken feet. Her other hand held clusters of light gray fungi. "Burning sage can only do so much to clear a house of darkness. I told the young lady we'd trade for our strawberries and kale."

"Our?" Olive handed a customer change and forced herself to smile, then straightened the bundles of parsley on the ledge above the cash box until something caused her to glance up. Across the food court and its tables and chairs full of marketgoers, Brody and Kat were bantering again, and Olive wondered if they were seeing each other, or soon would be. They'd make a cute couple, a lot cuter than the rough-looking surfer dude who had accompanied Kat to Cris Villalobos' memorial, but for crap's sake, Olive was paying her fifteen an hour and the least she could do was show up on time.

Ariela, barefoot, carried a glass mixing bowl of oyster mushrooms across the living room and set it on the fireplace mantel. "We'll see what happens after three days." She wagged her finger at Byrd. "Now, sonny, stay away from the mushrooms. Don't even breathe on them or you'll ruin their magic."

Byrd brightened at the word magic. "Okay, Bubby."

"Bubby?" asked Olive.

"Yiddish," Ariela said. "For grandmother. I like the sound of it, and so does Byrd."

"We're not Jewish."

"Does it matter?"

"It might matter to someone who's Jewish." Olive headed to the kitchen to wash the dishes that had accumulated, thinking how brazenly and unapologetically her mother asserted herself into all things.

She heard Cal kick the dirt from his boots. The sound made her happy until she saw that hungry winter look that she worked so hard to fill out. He kissed her on the cheek and grabbed a Pacifico from the refrigerator. Winked over the neck of the beer. As he drank, his Adam's apple slid up and down his long neck with each gulp. Olive touched the deepening vertical line down his cheek, a line that embodied their life—the drought, the labor shortage, threat of foreclosure. More to come, she feared, before it got better. But he was home, and they were safe.

Cal left with his beer, through the swinging kitchen door to the living room, where he used to collapse on the futon until Ariela's arrival. Olive gave him ten seconds to notice the bowl of mushrooms on the mantel. One, two, three, four …

"Outlaw." Her mother cawed. "Do not even breathe on those mushrooms. And put down that beer bottle. Please. The glare is giving me an ocular migraine."

16

They needed one soaking rain. After the rain, they would wait for the mud to dry out. After the mud dried, Cal drove in the tractor to rip the soil deeply enough to break its capillaries and release moisture. Olive watched Cal rake his fingers through his sandy hair until it stood in thick peaks. Beneath all of this, she worried about the foreclosure. It loomed like a nightmare from the moment she woke up.

"Cannellini, cranberry," said Cal. "Aye, cuando?" He leaned back in frustration. "Que tiene a la lluvia antes de pone en los tomates?"

His pitch was higher than normal as he spoke to Heriberto over the phone, and a bit raspy. "Adios."

She waited until he looked at her, but from his glazed look, his mind was elsewhere. He straddled his legs and arched his back for a stretch that meant his lower back hurt. "So." He drew in a breath and focused on her for the first time. "What are you doing for the rest of the day?"

"I'm leaving the kids with Ariela for a couple of hours."

"Oh, yeah?"

"I'm taking Thea to lunch."

"That's good." Then, it clicked. He understood why she was standing there. "You want me to babysit Ariela."

"Please?"

Cal's cell rang and he was back on the phone, speaking seed jargon to his new supplier. He needed some heirlooms and chose the Brandywine Pink because it was the closest to Cal's Augusta

Girls. Although the 'Gusta Girls were gaining popularity, they were still in the early stage. If they failed or underproduced, Cal needed enough tomatoes in the ground to make ends meet.

Olive put an arm around his neck and kissed his cheek, then started to leave with Gus, headed to her mother, when Cal raised his arm and shouted, "You owe me, babe."

The restaurant was uncrowded when they walked in at noon sharp. They had their choice of tables and chose one in the center of the room.

The waiter brought them water and handed them menus. Thea ran a lemon wedge slowly around the rim of her iced tea.

"Do you believe in life after death?" Thea put down the lemon and leaned forward, her brow furrowed. The vase of lilies in the center of the table hid her face, so Olive slid the vase to the left.

"I don't have much time to think about that."

"When you do think of it, is it possible we go somewhere in any shape or form? A bird or a horse?"

"When I think of life after death, my first thought is my mother," said Olive. "She believes in thin places where spirits slip through, especially at certain times of year. The Ashwani, Day of the Dead, Samhain, Solstice, equinox. Like that. I mean, shoot, she makes a living communicating with dead people."

"You're being evasive," said Thea.

Olive looked down at her hands, sorry she couldn't give Thea hope that Cris had taken another form.

"I read the clouds," Olive said. "I look at them and pause until they tell me something. They always do. I don't know what happens when we die beyond knowing the living grieve."

The disappointment on Thea's face was profound, so Olive revised her answer. "That's just me. And there haven't been a lot of clouds these days, but next time I see one, I'll dwell on the question. It's an important question."

Thea rubbed the lemon wedge around the lip of her glass. "I want your mother to finish that reading. I really do."

Olive pressed her lips into a reassuring smile. "She will but she has to clear the house first."

Thea leaned forward, confiding in Olive, "I like your mom. I can see where you get your strength."

"My friends have always liked her." Olive's high school chums used to rave over her mother's fortune-telling at the kitchen table while Olive would prep dinner for the two of them— the price of having an interesting mother, Ariela would say. "Some considered her their second mother."

Thea rubbed her placemat, as if she were erasing a stain.

I talked to Detective Rogers. He said they've closed the case for lack of evidence. He also said Cris had been rejected by a couple of gatekeepers in the art world."

Thea's eyes blinked tears and fresh pain.

"Rogers did promise to investigate the mortgage company that's foreclosing on our farm to see if there's a possible link between his death and the greenhouse ransack."

"You can't lose the farm. You've worked so hard for that house." Thea crumpled her paper napkin, obliviously tearing off small pieces. "Cris wanted a house. He was ashamed that he was bringing a child into this world and didn't have a stable job or home of our own."

Olive reached across the table and squeezed Thea's hand. Her fingers were dainty and her gold wedding band nearly slipping over the knuckle from losing too much weight. Dark, wet splotches appeared on her white paper placemat.

"I didn't understand how much he was mentally suffering."

"If he was," Olive said.

The waiter, a young man, came to their table with an expression that showed concern and placed menus in front of them. Olive looked up at the intelligent face and didn't have to say it but did anyway. "Thea lost her husband a short while ago."

"Let me know how I can help you. Would you like some time?"

"Thank you," said Thea. "You're very kind."

He took a deep breath and announced the soup of the day—caramelized leak and potato in a thyme crème reduction—while Thea wiped her eyes with her shredded napkin.

"Our special is chicory salad from Shell Bean Way." He winked at Olive. "I recognize you from the market. I forage on weekends. If you want the salad, I recommend it with anchovies."

"I'll take the soup," said Thea. "And bread. You have good bread here. I know the baker." She almost smiled. Thea had trained at a leading culinary school in San Francisco and graduated to work for Chez Panisse, a famous restaurant in Berkeley. Since moving to Santa Cruz, she'd yet to find work that measured up to her skill.

Their server asked if he could bring them a glass of wine. Both shook their heads in unison.

"Water is fine," they chimed.

Thea smiled at the waiter with heartbreaking effort as he returned to place their order in the kitchen. Meanwhile, Olive noticed the restaurant had filled with downtown business clientele on lunch break and locals who sought quality food and were willing to pay a bit more—hungry patrons who appreciated a grass-fed beef burger and a creative organic salad. For those craving fat, the restaurant served pork confit and duck fries. Mixed media photographs by a local artist decorated the walls. The chandeliers of tiny asymmetrical lights added a whimsical appeal.

"I don't think Cris took his life, either." Thea poked the lemon slice in her water glass. "He wasn't unhappy. Stressed maybe." She sighed. "Life is so unpredictable. I can't imagine how I'm going to keep going."

Their server brought a plate of bread, butter and a small dish of salt. He placed a fresh napkin on Thea's lap as she reached for the bread. Her curly black hair, held back by a thin elastic ribbon, framed her face nicely. She wore mascara and lipstick and looked pretty in a simple black T-shirt and cream knit pencil skirt.

"You look good, Thea. How are you feeling?"

She rubbed her stomach. "Eleven weeks and I'm still suffering from morning sickness, which is the only thing in my life right now that I can count on. The doctor says the baby's healthy."

Olive remembered those early weeks of nausea when she'd been pregnant with Byrd and Augusta. The only things that diminished it were potato chips and cola.

"Even the thought of it makes me ill." Thea sprinkled salt on the butter and took a large bite of bread. Apparently, bread was Thea's remedy.

As the noise in the restaurant rose and the chairs filled with patrons, Olive spotted Kat Granger sitting in the window booth with three other young women. When Thea glanced sideways to see what Olive was looking at, she didn't seem to recognize Kat.

"That's my employee." Olive dropped her napkin on the table. "I'm going over to say a quick hi."

"Go for it. Me and the bread and butter are reasonably content."

The women were laughing when Olive walked up to their table. Kat, dressed up and wearing makeup, rose from her seat to greet Olive. She looked beautiful in her pointed, vintage cowboy boots and a knee-length print vintage dress, the same vibrant green as the sea kelp at the nape of her neck. "Taking a break from your small herd of adorable kids?"

Olive laughed, even though she didn't appreciate references to her children as a herd and pointed to the table where Thea sat staring at the wall. "I'm taking my neighbor to lunch. Thea Villalobos. Cris Villalobos's wife. You were at his memorial."

Kat blinked. "So sad." She chinned to her girlfriends. "This is my bachelorette lunch. I'm engaged to be married. Ladies, this is my boss, Olive Post."

One of her girlfriends held up a strip of photographs, the kind people take in a photo booth. "Kat and Lobster engagement photos."

They laughed among themselves as Olive checked out the series of four photos that showed Kat and her fiancé, the man she had sat with at Cris's memorial. The couple was smiling in one frame, kissing in two, and a closeup funny face in the fourth.

Olive was struck by the fourth frame and looked more closely. Her necklace. The photos were black and white, but the two small gems with two charms were unmistakable, one for each child. Olive turned over the photo strip and noticed the date. February 11, two days before Cris's death. Kat snatched the photos out of Olive's hand.

"That necklace," Olive said. "I had one just like it."

Kat's face went blank.

"Where did you get it?"

"A friend," she said.

"It's gold with my children's birthstones."

"Fuck you."

"I've been missing it ever since I took it off at the market and put it in the cash envelope. I'd left the envelope in the box truck, and you were responsible for closing up, driving the truck and delivering the envelope to the office that day."

"I did all of that."

"Except for the necklace. It wasn't where I put it, and we were short a hundred dollars cash." Olive restrained herself from accusing Kat of stealing in the middle of her celebration. "Do you know where your friend got it?"

"No. She always leaves me presents."

"Can I talk to her?"

"She went back to Mexico last week."

"Can you give me her phone number?"

"They're off the grid."

"I'm filing a police report and reporting these photos unless you give it back to me by the end of the day."

Kat sat down and reached for the sweet potato fries in the center of the table. Her girlfriends remained silent, except one.

"This is Kat's party," one friend said. "I don't care if you're her boss. You need to leave our table."

Olive walked back and sat across from Thea.

"What's wrong?" Thea asked.

"Don't look." Olive leaned forward. "My employee sitting over there by the window stole my necklace."

"Your gold necklace with the kids' birthstones?"

"She's wearing it in photos of herself and her fiancé."

"You're losing me."

"It's her bachelorette party and she brought her engagement photos. She's pictured in them wearing my necklace."

"Could it be a different necklace that looks like yours?"

"It's one of a kind."

"Is she wearing it now?"

"No."

"How can you be sure it's your necklace?"

"I know my necklace."

"She's leaving."

Olive turned and saw Kat walk briskly out of the restaurant alone, the girlfriends glowering at Olive.

As Olive drove up Shell Bean Way, her mother stood in the middle of the road beside a golf cart. A gawdy American flag was painted on the door of the passenger side with eagle wings spread across the small hood. A pair of trouser legs stuck out from under the cart's carriage. Olive pulled up, yanked the emergency brake and jumped out of the Jeep.

"Where are Gus and Byrd?"

Ariela scowled, hands on hips. "Settle down." She smelled like pot. "They're with your outlaw husband."

"You're supposed to be watching them." She put her hand up, shielding her eyes from the afternoon sun as she scanned the farm. "Where's Cal?"

"In the greenhouse with his tomato plants."

Olive pointed to the cart. "What's this about?"

"I love the flag. It's so irreverent. I bought it from Craigslist."

Any vehicle was bad news, as far as Olive was concerned. It signified permanency aka moving in, especially a golf cart which could never transport Ariela far enough away from Olive's home.

"I need transportation, Love." Ariela bent over and waved at Thea, sitting in the Jeep. "The house is almost clear, dear, so I can give you a reading. No charge. I never charge Olive's friends."

Thea smiled as the legs under the cart scooted out and Johnny Pogonip appeared. He smiled, his teeth surprisingly white, Olive noticed.

"A triumvirate of beauty," Johnny said. "Lay ladies, lay. Praise be to Bob Dylan."

Cal was walking out of the greenhouse with stacked trays of tomato starts, carrying Gus in a backpack, her arms around his neck. Byrd followed close behind with one of the trays.

Olive pulled Augusta from the pack and set her on the ground. Byrd looked up, his eyes bloodshot and glassy. She was furious. Even her mother's own grandchildren were second to her whims.

"She has not changed," Olive said. "Not one iota." She should have known better. But, no, she had let down her guard and her mother had swooped in like the fox from her youth. Back then, Ariela had helped Olive build a chicken coop. She had showed her how to center a nail and sink it with one blow of the hammer and how to feed the chicks by turning her T-shirt into a pouch and scattering seed. Olive had felt so happy to have her own chickens to care for. One afternoon while she was doing her homework, their mutt Pluto barked, and Olive looked up to watch her mother calmly open the front door and welcome a burly, bearded stranger with a sidearm into their sacred space. His name was Chuck. He was stupid and Olive couldn't figure out what her mother saw in him. It seemed like he'd be there forever until the night he left the coop door open and the fox did the rest. It was summer and sweltering in the California foothills. Their cottage had a ceiling fan that worked overtime. Everyone was cranky, especially Ariela, who didn't accept Chuck's lame apology for leaving the coop open—an accident, he claimed. She ordered him to leave, and as he opened his truck door and started to climb in, he shouted, "I want air conditioning more than I want you, bitch, anyway."

The living room smelled like pot, and the kids were starving and thirsty. She put down a plate of almond butter and strawberry jam sandwiches as Gus spoke baby talk to Byrd, then grabbed his hair and tugged. Byrd yowled and pinched her arm until she let go. When she started to cry, Byrd burst into tears.

The kitchen doors swung open and Ariela swept in. "It sounds like a litter of coyotes in here."

The kids stopped crying and stared at their grandmother.

"Your smoking got Byrd stoned." She told her mother for the third time she had to leave.

Olive heard the front door slam so hard the walls shook. When she went into the living room to make sure Ariela was gone, the pungent smell of weed hung like bat wings.

Byrd was beside himself over the sandwich. He wanted jam without almond butter. Tears and snot covered his face with a liquid sheen. He put his head on his arms and sobbed. Gus was a mess, too, her hair a rat's nest of tangles, her face smeared with jam and almond butter, a dirty shirt, and smelly diaper. Olive lifted her squirming from her highchair and walked her upstairs by the hand to change her diaper, leaving Byrd to his weeping.

After Olive changed Gus's dirty diaper and lowered her into the crib, she placed the favorite tattered cotton blanket against Gus's face and watched her greedily suck her pacifier, eyelids heavy. Olive pushed the hair from her little girl's face and bent down to her cheek. Gus reached up and touched the blank spot on Olive's bare chest where the necklace and its charms and gems used to be, then rolled to her side, which meant sleep. Byrd had stopped bawling. Olive breathed in the silence while it lasted.

Cal held her shoulders and told her she looked stressed. She watched his concern for her well-being shift to uh-oh as she told him that Kat had stolen her necklace.

"I saw photographs of her and her fiancé, Lobster. She was wearing my necklace in the photos."

"Are you sure it's yours?"

"Yes, I'm sure. I know that necklace—the charms and gems. She claimed someone gave it to her, but that person had conveniently returned to Mexico."

"Why would she steal your necklace and wear it in a photo that she showed you?"

"Her friends showed it to me. She was having a bachelorette party."

"Couldn't it be a similar necklace?"

"Cal. She stole my necklace. That was my necklace. One of a kind. And I busted her. She's lying."

Cal cocked his head and rubbed the stubble on his neck. "I haven't trusted Kat since she left my box truck on the freeway. The way I see it, if a person can abandon a box full of produce without even leaving a note, it wouldn't be hard to steal a necklace."

17

Ariela got as far as the tracks before convincing herself that she had a right not to be kicked out of her daughter's house when she had nowhere else to go. Olive had second thoughts, too. This was her mother.

"Did you see the way Johnny looked at me, Love, when he was fixing my cart?"

Olive turned the onion scapes she'd sautéed with Brody's fingerling potatoes.

Cal tilted his head sideways toward Byrd. "Do we have to talk about this when we're eating?"

"It's good for him to hear about the birds and bees."

"You're not an ingénue," said Olive.

"You wait, Love. Johnny and I are the same generation, both of us Pisces with Aries rising."

"Oh, in that case." Cal spoke with his mouth full of the rotisserie chicken that Olive bought once a week at the Wednesday market to give herself a break from cooking. "No wonder."

"Don't be sarcastic, Outlaw."

"My dad's not an outlaw," Byrd injected. "He's a farmer."

Ariela threw back her hair. "Johnny whistled at me, that's all I was saying."

Olive glanced at Byrd, who was picking his nose. "That's not the point."

Ariela said, "You're not going to get a girlfriend picking your nose."

Byrd dug deeper. Olive put her paper napkin to his nose and told him to blow.

Ariela wagged her finger. "You should know as soon as possible, sonny, that girls don't like nose pickers. Especially if you eat them. I broke up with my last boyfriend because of his bad habits." Ariela held her nose. "He farted."

Byrd laughed.

"In my face."

Cal whistled. "Over the line, Grandma."

"Bubby. Not Grandma. The word doesn't suit me." She wiped her fork with a napkin. "Johnny blows his snot into the road. That takes the lead out of the old pencil. And I'll bet you don't know why he keeps his hair short. The smell of unwashed long hair reminds him of sheep's wool. He used to herd sheep on the Navaho rez. How's that for service? Did you know sheep can't get up once they've fallen?"

"What are you talking about, Grandma?" Byrd asked.

"What did I say about calling me Grandma?"

Byrd looked like he was about to cry and Cal pushed his plate away with food uneaten, apparently having lost his appetite. "Tell us about your golf cart," he said. "Are you planning to take up the game?"

She looked offended. "I would never take up golf. How could you even ask? You of all people. Golf is a total waste of good water, and we're in the middle of a drought. I need transportation to get to the nude beach up the coast. It didn't start so Johnny fixed it. I'm calling her Beatrice."

Olive dished a portion of salad onto Byrd's plate. "You bought a golf cart that doesn't start?"

"Why are you always so negative?" Ariela mashed a fingerling and offered Augusta, who sat in her highchair, a spoonful. "And the Americana decor ensures other drivers will see me coming."

"Yep," said Cal. "That they will."

"When I outgrow it, I can sell it to help us pay the mortgage."

A brain blaze flared when Olive heard the word us. She regretted backtracking on ordering her mother to leave.

"Olive and I will get the mortgage straightened out without selling your vehicle." Cal speared a braised carrot from its serving dish and shoved it in his mouth.

"Stabbing vegetables?" said Ariela. "Do you two realize how shrouded in bad vibes your lives are?"

Olive cringed. Their lives were threatened with looming foreclosure, a vandalism and late planting.

"I know you don't want me to use the word with little sonny in the room, but d-e-a-d people are part of life, nothing to hide from, nothing to be afraid of."

"I know what that spells," Byrd said.

Olive did not want to bring up Cris Villalobos with the kids present. "I'm more afraid of your first-person plural pronoun. We, as in Cal and I, are taking care of the foreclosure. Not," she triangulated the three adults at the table with her free hand, "us."

Ariela pressed her folded hands to her chest. "I intended to find my own place, which I'm fully capable of, but as I was driving down your road, something hit me at my core. Something evil has leeched and continues to leech into your surroundings, Love, and I can help you get to the bottom of it."

Cal set his forkful of salad back on his plate. "Get to the bottom of things?" He rose from the table. "Your mother sounds just like you."

Olive heard him above, pacing on the upstairs hallway. The floorboards creaked as if to say even the house felt strained.

After she set Gus down in the port-a-crib with her blanket and pacifier, she pulled her sheers from their hip holster, walked up to the first tree, discerning the primary, fruit-bearing limbs from the rest, which she methodically pruned and clipped into twelve-inch lengths and left at the base of the tree to dry for kindling.

The empty space between the branches filled with shafts of light and air, the tree's two main sources of growth.

An explosion in the near distance was followed by a flurry of granules that fell from the sky and landed on Olive's head. Bird shot. Another explosion went off seconds later. Her neighbors on the cattycorner parcel behind Shell Bean Farm had rigged a propane tank to pop off every half hour to scare the robins and crows from their blueberry patch. The shots marked the unofficial start of blueberry season, and blueberries were great but the bird shot was not. The blast had clearly overshot its mark. Granules were in Olive's hair and they had landed in Gus's crib with a skitter. She bent over and picked up Gus, limp and heavy with sleep, complaining from being woken. When Olive ruffled the baby's hair, grains the diameter of pencil lead fell to the ground.

Add to her substantive to-do list calling her neighbors and letting them know their bird shot had wound up in her baby's hair. She talked to the husband, who at first denied the pellets could travel that far. He relented when she offered to bring a handful to his place and actually apologized by the end of the conversation, promising to "fix things." Next call was to the loan officer in charge of their line of credit. He very nicely claimed their loan was a mere week from being disbursed. At least he'd given her a time frame. Then, she called Inventiveness, the company foreclosing on them and waited out the same recording by a female whose voice sounded like chronic nasal drip: "IVT. Invest your funds inventively. Please leave a message and we will return the call as soon as possible." Which translated to never, but she had to try.

"This is Olive Post of Shell Bean Farm. If I don't hear from you by the end of business hours today, I'm calling my attorney."

She opened the metal desk drawer and flipped through the employee files looking for Kat Granger's file. At first glance, Kat's application looked in order. She had named several references, but Olive realized she had never followed up on those references because at the time of hiring the fields burst with produce and the urgency for more crew to pick and market trumped vetting new employees.

The phone number of Kat's first reference was out of service—a restaurant that had gone out of business. The second was a farmer, Paul Leverson. Olive knew him. He was an admired and seasoned farmer who ran a medium-sized farm that frequently hired university interns. Leverson answered the phone, his voice warm even before he knew it was Olive. She told him she was calling to check up on a reference her employee had given.

"Katherine Granger."

He repeated the name. "Doesn't ring a bell. Can you give me a time frame?"

Olive glanced at the form. "She said she worked for you roughly two years ago picking cherries and working at the vendor stalls."

"I'm looking in my records and I don't see a Granger. But I do want to say, I'm impressed with the strides Cal is making with that tomato, and I wish you the best. Drop by the farm with your kids and check out the ducks and chickens. You like duck eggs?"

Olive confessed she'd never tried duck eggs.

"You'll never go back to chicken."

She assured Paul she would, chalking up his answers as confirmation that Kat Granger was not only a thief, but also a liar. She pulled up Kat's number in her cell and punched it.

"Call me," Olive said, "as soon as you get this."

18

Olive wanted to finish up this one apple tree before she quit pruning for the day, but Kat Granger was driving up the road toward the office. She studied the tree for a few more seconds. It had been pruned open center style, like a palm-up hand holding a ball of light. From the five fingers grew secondary branches and upon those branches more branches that would bear the tree's fruit. On one branch, she strategically draped white kitchen string attached to a small cement weight—the size of an ice cube—over a lateral branch and fastened it with a clothespin to train the branch to grow horizontally. This limb would be her fruit bearer. She fastened the string with a clothespin. This little trick slowed upward growth and trained the branch to grow horizontally. In the orchardist's world, when you slow upward growth, the limb bears more fruit.

Olive pulled up a second chair and motioned for Kat to sit down, wondering how to coax the truth from this hard-shelled young woman.

"Looks like my fiancé's garage," Kat said, gazing skittishly around the office, grasping things to talk about besides the reason Olive had called her in. "How do you handle having a partner who surfs? Or maybe you surf. Not me. I'm a disgruntled bystander."

"Surfing is Cal's attitude adjuster. His church. I love watching him out in the water, and if it weren't so cold and the kids so young, I might join him on the little stuff."

Kat nodded. "Lobster's giving me surf lessons even though I prefer being a hard ass beach bunny." She rolled her eyes and took a deep ragged breath. "He bought me a wetsuit."

"He enjoys buying you gifts."

Kat shook her head and sighed. "Let's cut the crap. What am I doing here?"

"I'm updating my employee files."

"The tone of your voice mail sounded like you're going to fire me. If so, I want my severance check."

"I'm sorry I embarrassed you into front of your friends."

Kat's blond dreadlocks fell forward as she stared at her feet. "Putting it mildly."

"But I want my necklace returned and an explanation."

Kat bent down and retied her shoelace, which Olive read as guilt. "That necklace was a gift and I would never steal from you. Lots of jewelry looks the same."

"The charms were personalized with the kids' birthstones. A yellow topaz for Byrd and a light green peridot for Gus."

She saw the tic in Kat's left cheek and a missed blink of the eyes, and Olive knew she'd hit a nerve.

"You must have noticed the dates engraved on the back of the charms."

Kat shrugged. "It's a vintage piece."

"When did your friend give you the necklace?"

Kat rose to her feet. "I'd ask her, but like I said she went back to Mexico."

"Where in Mexico?"

"I'm done here."

"Can I call her?"

"I told you, she's off the grid. I don't know where your fucking necklace is. I've lost it, but I'll try to find it, and if I do, I'll show it to you."

"Do that. One more thing, I called Paul Leverson, your reference. He's never heard of you."

"No surprise there." Something in the bent of Kat's head reminded Olive of a sunflower, overburdened with mental weight. "Paul may not recognize my name, but he would know me if he saw me. I worked really hard."

"You lied about your references and you're lying about my necklace."

"I did not steal your necklace." Kat's palms were clenched, the knuckles white.

"And money was missing from the cash envelope where I put the necklace for safe keeping."

Kat stamped her foot. "What is wrong with you?"

"Nothing's wrong with me, but you are fired."

Kat moaned as if Olive's pronouncement were the story of her life. "Couldn't you have fired me when I first walked in? Did I really have to go through this shit?"

19

The last Olive heard before she fell asleep were the birds outside her bedroom window—noisy little brown sparrows that nested in the purple bougainvillea and ate from the feeder tray on their balcony railing. The first thing she heard when she woke up was her mother.

"Olive," Ariela called. "Olive." Each shout louder than the last.

The kitchen door wouldn't budge when Olive pushed it, so she shoved harder until she saw the port-a-crib her mother had shoved against the swinging door.

Gus stood in the crib and stretched her arms, yearning to be picked up. Byrd stood on the kitchen stool beside Ariela, who bent over the sink, mashing garlic, from the smell. Her mother glanced sideways.

"Do you smoke?" Ariela asked.

"Is that really why you woke me up? You want to know if I smoke?"

"Those oyster mushrooms," Ariela said, "have pulled in so much secondhand smoke it leads me to believe either you smoke or whoever lived here before you was a smoker."

"I don't smoke," Olive said, "and I credit you with that."

Her mother had smoked Camel straights because filters offended her. By Olive's tenth birthday, she'd tried all the stunts kids pull to get their parent to stop: hide the cancer sticks, flush them down the toilet, break them, reason, plead, rage and cry. Nothing worked. Ariela quit on her own when she had a breast cancer scare that turned out to be just that, a scare.

Olive didn't want to go into the history of tenants. "Lots of people lived here and lots of people smoked."

In fact, Olive and Cal's ex-landlady, who had lived here while hell bent on turning the farm into condominiums, was a chain smoker.

"I didn't smell cigarette smoke when I first moved in," Ariela said.

Moved in? "You are visiting."

Ariela placed a garlic clove inside the press and handed the press to Byrd. "Hold it firmly with both hands, sonny. Now, squeeze. Harder."

Once her mother placed her hands over Byrd's and applied her strength, small plugs of garlic meat squeezed through the holes of the press.

"Ariela. You are not moving into this house."

Ariela pressed her lips so her dimples showed. "Semantics."

Olive kept her arms to her sides to refrain from waving them wildly in front of the kids. Why did her mother so easily reduce her? Karma for firing Kat is all she could figure. She picked up Gus, feeling her little hand slip into Olive's shirt, searching for a breast.

"She's happy as a clam in there," Ariela said. "Why disturb her?"

Outside, where the forest shaded the yard, the afternoon grew dim, and the dull fear that came with changing light sunk into her psyche as deeply as the sun behind mountains. Times like this were why they invented Happy Hour. But Olive didn't drink. Not because she had a problem. She just didn't like alcohol, except for an occasional beer or glass or wine. She liked weed, until she decided to have children.

Thank god for a new day.

She sipped hot black coffee on the balcony that overlooked the farm and tried to read the morning newspaper, but the stress of finding someone to replace Kat weighed on her mind. The university was about to go on spring break and it was possible that one of the agroecology students needed a job. She could put the word out at the university farm. Word traveled quickly, like birds on a wire. The sparrows in the bougainvillea twittered, sounding anxious and three large crows cawed from the redwood tree. She heard a human noise, Ariela and Byrd running between the rows of kale. Her mother looked agile, cantering down the chunky dirt in a long skirt. While she ran, she managed to dip what looked like a branch of eucalyptus into a bucket of water she'd strapped to her chest and sprinkle it over the ground as if she were waving a magic wand. Byrd was trying with all his might to keep up to his grandmother. Halfway down the row, he tripped onto the rough clods. His crying quickly turned shrill.

When Olive got to him, his knee had a gash, white flesh showing and blood dripping down his leg. Olive knelt in the dirt and wiped his face with the tail of her shirt. The cut was deep.

"He's fine," Ariela insisted. "Dirt strengthens a child's immune system."

As Byrd wailed and his blood dripped onto the dirt, Olive worried that he needed a tetanus shot.

"This will bring the rain," Ariela said. "No doubt about that."

As Olive carried Byrd back to the kitchen and lifted him carefully onto the counter, she now understood why her mother reduced her. She rinsed the knee with warm water from the sink faucet while Augusta jounced on the port-a-crib rail. She dried it with a clean white cotton dish towel and applied Neosporin to the wound.

"A pinch of golden seal. Gotu Kola to keep the cut from scarring," Ariela injected over Olive's shoulder. She dangled an object in Byrd's face. A crystal the size of an acorn. "We'll crush this and mix it with water and refill our squirt guns. Now, smile for your Bubby."

Olive grabbed her dish cloth to control the urge to slap the rock out of her mother's hand. She didn't snatch the crystal though she very much wanted to. She wanted to so much that the mere thought jerked her body forward an inch.

Ariela, slots for eyes, spoke sternly. "You'll see, Love, the rain will come."

The rain came. Dust rose from the dry soil as the first drops fell. Olive opened the windows, inhaling the sweet ozone and tree resin, and walked outside to the middle of the road, craving the scent of wet asphalt after a long dry spell.

Cal smelled like rain when he walked in from the back porch. He kissed her softly on the mouth. The rain released weeks of unrelenting pressure. And when it stopped and the topsoil dried out, he would put the tomato starts in the ground.

Someone knocked. Olive answered the front door. It was Thea, who Olive had invited for dinner. Olive discerned the small mound of her belly.

They assembled around the dining room table. Olive asked how everyone's day had gone as she spooned chicory pudding onto Byrd's plate.

"I spent my afternoon at the nude beach," Ariela said.

"In the rain?" Cal asked.

"Rain-bathing. You should have seen the beautiful glistening people. Entire families. All ages, all sizes—big butts, little butts—"

Byrd's eyes widened while he shoved the savory pudding into his mouth. "Butts," he said with his mouthful.

"And pretty soon you didn't notice the rain or that people weren't wearing clothes."

"What did you notice?" Thea asked.

"Sand on my feet. Breeze flowing through my legs. All the little hairs tickling my skin as if I were a girl again. It felt like skinny dipping."

"That's beautiful," said Thea.

Byrd asked, "What's skinny dipping?"

"Going in the water without your clothes," Ariela said as Olive reached across the table and pulled the salad bowl toward her. "I did that, too. It's so amazing to be in the ocean when the rain's falling around you. The only downers were the two perverts on the cliff taking pictures."

"What's a pervert?" Byrd asked.

"Don't explain," Olive said.

"The kind of people," Ariela said, "who fart at the kitchen table."

Byrd threw back his head in glee. "She said fart!"

His other favorite word.

"Your turn's over, Ariela," Cal said. "What did you do today, Thea?"

Thea paused to swallow her food. "It's a boy."

At those three words, he let out a whoop.

"You should name him Cris," Ariela said. "After his father."

Thea looked at her plate, holding her fork, shaking her head. "I don't think so."

"Why not?"

"Oh my god." Olive pointed her fork at her mother. "Stop."

Thea lowered her eyes and dabbed her lips with a napkin. "I don't want to label my son with a name that represents abandonment. Especially if," she glanced at Byrd. "You know. So, here's another good event of the day. I received a check in the mail for two thousand dollars from Cris's tattoo artist. Cap. He said, because he couldn't fulfill their contract, he was returning money Cris had paid in advance."

Her visit to Cap had paid off, Olive thought.

"Which, by the way, I didn't know about. It's a windfall and I'm grateful. I need the money."

A knock. Cal stood quickly and crossed the living room to answer the front door. Olive recognized the voice. Kat Granger.

"Come in, child," Ariela said.

"Not so fast." Olive stood. "In the first place, she's a woman, not a child, and this is my house. You don't get to decide who enters and who does not."

Ariela leaned into Thea and whispered loud enough for Olive to hear. "Isn't this the girl who stole the necklace?"

Olive couldn't remember telling Ariela about her necklace.

Kat remained in the doorway, looking down at her feet in what Olive determined was some version of remorse. She walked to the door, intending to step outside before she sent her away. "We are not having this conversation in my living room in front of my family in the middle of dinner."

"Not a good time, Granger," said Cal. "There's more than dinner going on."

"Souza. My birth name is Katherine Souza."

It took a couple of seconds for the pronouncement to register. "As in Best Seeds Souza?" Cal asked.

"As in Gil Souza," Olive said.

"He's my paternal birth father. I hate him. That's why I changed my name."

"I'm confused," said Cal. "Gil Souza is your father?"

Kat flipped back her dreds. "Please don't use the f-word."

"Follow me," Olive said. "We'll talk in the kitchen."

Olive handed Kat tap water in a Mason jar as Cal tilted back in the corner chair. Kat sat across from him, speaking rapidly, and Olive knew she wasn't making it up.

"Why didn't you tell us when we hired you?" Cal asked.

"You wouldn't have hired me."

"Not necessarily," Olive said. "We value honesty and we're open-minded."

"Gil is your enemy. You'd think Gil hired me to spy on you."

"Did he?" Cal asked.

"No. He tries to kill me. Ever since my mother left."

"Kill you?"

"Not explicitly."

"Okay, everyone breathe," Cal said. "Start from the beginning."

Kat gazed at Olive, unblinking and not seeing as she explained how, at a young age, she knew she had to escape if she wanted to live. "He wasn't overtly violent. More like insidiously destructive." According to Kat, her pediatrician insisted she change her diet if she wanted to stop her chronic stomach aches that had landed her in the hospital three times before she was eleven.

"He's a fucking workaholic. That saved me." The color in Kat's face drained to a pale green. She rubbed her temples, as if they ached. "He got free boxes of cereal from his big wig GMO buddies in Omaha who turn soy and corn into processed junk food. Like, I was their experiment. Can you believe it? His own daughter. They hired a research firm to hold an experiment on fifty kids. Half of us were fed processed crap with genetically engineered corn and soy and the other non-GE. When my group, the GE group, started coming up with chronic gastrointestinal problems—one of us even got early onset Crohns—they suspended the trials. You can Google it. My doctor told me unless I wanted to die, I had to change my diet."

"Wow," said Cal. "Is this true?"

"You don't believe me?"

"What's not to believe," Olive said. "How old were you?"

"Nine."

Olive hurt, not for the adult but for Kat the child. "Did your pediatrician file a report with child protective services?"

"I don't think she did."

"If you were a minor, how did you carry out your doctor's advice?"

"I fed my breakfast to the dog. I threw away the paper bag lunch our housekeeper made for me. I stole Gil's pocket change from his dresser. He was never home at dinner, so the dog again—or the garbage disposal—when the housekeeper wasn't looking. I saved my allowance and I'd ask him for money based on some lie that he'd approve of—like joining the Girl Scouts. I also checked the laundry. He always had a couple of bills in his pockets. I'd take the money and stop at the health food store by the bus stop, and I'd talk the housekeeper into going to the farmers markets on weekends."

This was some story, and not a good one.

"I had to wait until I was sixteen to emancipate myself and when I turned eighteen, I changed my name. I was only seventeen when I worked for Paul Leverson after high school. I still went by Kat Souza back then. Ask him." She blinked away tears. "I've never told this to anyone before." She stared at the floor in a silence that sounded like truth.

Olive had questions about that morning she abandoned the box truck. "When you came to the farm to pick up the box truck on the morning of Cris's death, did you see anything out of the ordinary?"

"It was still dark."

"Why'd you leave the box truck on the freeway before Cal got there?"

She glared a few moments before answering, as if Olive should know her answer. "Because it was on the freeway. In Oakland. And it was dark."

"Cal was on his way."

"Not fast enough. I freaked." She looked genuinely afraid recalling that morning, alone on the shoulder of the freeway outside of a rough city.

"You had to come back to the farm to get your car."

"Yeah." She hugged herself. "Nothing. My friend dropped me off at my car and I left." She scratched a nervous itch on her cheek.

"And the necklace? Did you find it."

"Not yet." Kat looked up with pleading eyes.

"When did you lose it, if you lost it?"

"Not sure. After Lobster proposed. I had it in the photo. You saw that."

"The necklace means a lot to Olive," said Cal. "When you find it, we can talk about a rehire. Okay, then." He turned on the porch light, grabbed a flashlight and led Kat Granger out the back door to her car while Olive returned to the dining room. Byrd and Gus sat at the table looking content among the two women. Ariela doted on Gus, spooning chicory pudding onto her plate and Thea buttered Byrd's bread. Olive noticed color in her face. Almost a glow.

Maybe it was the pure whiteness of the clouds that scurried across the clean sky after the first rain that persuaded Olive to change her plans. Instead of pulling into New Leaf's parking lot to shop for groceries, she drove north out of town to the Coast Highway, feeling momentarily liberated from routine. And driving, especially up this serene and scenic route, clarified her thoughts.

Davenport lay ahead. The blink-of-a-town was an old shipping settlement, which had become a cement factory town in the early days before transforming to a charming tourist attraction of 408 people, according to the road sign. The stack of the abandoned cement plant speared the bright blue sky. Its stark geometric cone and massive length of gray buildings were an incongruous landmark among the chaparral of the coastal hillsides.

The plant had opened in 1905, just in time to supply materials to rebuild San Francisco after the Great Earthquake. But a century later, the SOx and NOx spewing monolith was forced to close down because it failed to reduce its carcinogenic chromium 6 emissions below EPA limits, becoming an iconic statement that powerful anti-environmental industries can be shut down.

Olive passed the stacks of logs at Big Creek's lumber yard north of town, abutting the cliff overhanging the Coast Highway. She glanced in the rearview mirror. Augusta had fallen asleep. Her neck hung at a crooked angle. Olive saw the street sign she was hoping for and turned right off the Coast Highway, continuing up a steep road that opened into a coastal terrace, then left onto Souza Lane where breathtaking industrial-sized greenhouses rose from the landscape like giant glass terrariums. They were cutting edge gorgeous and Olive wished she and Cal could afford one. What looked like a water truck was parked in front of a weathered barn. A double-wide trailer, which Olive assumed was the Best Seeds, Inc. office, sat on the edge of the terrace with a one-hundred-and-eighty-degree view of the ocean. Gus stirred as Olive idled the Jeep. When a middle-aged woman emerged from the trailer and pulled out her cell, giving Olive the snake eye, she turned the Jeep around and drove off.

20

Gil didn't appreciate the way Robert Johnson was checking out the woman who'd just walked into the café, a child on her hip. Ogling a woman carrying a small child was beneath Gil's sense of decency. And he didn't understand what Johnson saw in the woman. Maybe if she shed the flannel shirt and jeans, put on some makeup, and did something besides letting her long hair crawl down her back.

Gil's first finger stabbed the table. "We do the next thing because it's how we react that matters. It's the next action that flips the page. I'm not talking about a book, Johnson. Not a page you can go back to and reread. No do-overs in this life. Are you listening to me?"

"Yes, sir."

"You don't look like you're listening. I have a court date, and I need to make sure everything settles down before then. All ducks in a row."

The woman who'd walked in with the kid pointed her cell phone at them.

"Did she just take a picture of us?" Gil asked.

Johnson pulled down his ball cap. "I hope not."

What the hell? Maybe she was a tourist looking for local character, Gil thought. Or an environmentalist following his court case. A reporter wouldn't snap a picture like that with a kid on her hip. Whatever, she didn't look friendly.

"I know you," the woman said to Johnson. "You were sitting with Kat Granger at Cris's memorial."

It felt like a lightning bolt to Gil's brain when he heard his daughter's name.

"I'm Olive Post. Kat worked for me."

Johnson looked sucker-punched, too, and that disturbed Gil. This woman acted like she owned the place.

"I'd appreciate it if you could help Kat find that necklace she was wearing in your photographs. I had to fire her because of it."

Kat, fired? Gil put out his hand and stared down at the table as if that would stop this bird strike of bad news. "I'm Gil Souza, Best Seeds. Who are you?"

She didn't register surprise hearing his name. Instead, she shifted her kid from one hip to the other as an excuse to reject his handshake.

"Olive Post. Proprietor of Shell Bean Farm. We used to buy seed from you until you went GE, and your daughter worked for me until yesterday."

Gil, flummoxed with information, couldn't believe a former customer stood there measuring him up and talking about his own daughter, whom she'd fired for something Robert Johnson seemed to be involved in.

"It's curious," she said. "I've been trying to put the puzzle together. Every time I turn over a new piece, here you are. Mr. Souza."

"Maybe you'd better stop playing board games." She was a smart one, Gil thought. "If you would excuse us, we'd like to get back to our conversation."

The woman turned on Johnson, repeating her accusation. She didn't even go to the counter and order a coffee. Instead, she left the café and, as he watched her exit the restaurant's screen door, something told him she wasn't done. She opened the middle door of her vehicle, an outdated Jeep, and placed the child in a car seat. Gil stood so he could see her license plate. Yep. It matched the number Cloris had cited when she called fifteen minutes ago.

"What's with this so-called missing necklace, Robert?"

When Johnson shrugged off the question, Gil slammed his palm on the table. Coffee sloshed over the lips of their mugs. And here she came again, looking like a man on a mission. Only she was a woman, with a kid on her hip. Coming straight at them.

She addressed Johnson, ignoring Gil. "I forgot to congratulate you, Robert, on your engagement to Kat."

Gil coughed out his coffee and groped for a napkin.

"Considering Kat ..." She tilted her head toward Gil. "...how do you think she's going to react when she learns you're having a chummy conversation with her father?"

Gil raised his arms over his head to stop the coughing. He wiped coffee from the lapel of his windbreaker, and as she left for the second time, he almost called her back. Meanwhile, the sorry sonuvabitch across from him was apologizing.

"I was planning to tell you," Johnson said. "Kat made me promise I wouldn't tell anyone. You okay, man?"

Gil was salivating, still coughing. "Take out your phone," he said between breaths. "Now. Call it off. In front of me. And do not call me 'man.' I want to hear you say the words." This was what he got for hiring a screwup. "I paid you to watch out for my daughter and report back to me. Period. Not to fuck her. Especially not to marry her."

The tip of Johnson's sun-bleached hair dipped into his coffee mug as he hung his head like a dog.

"Raise that hole for a head and make the goddamn call."

"I don't know what to say."

"Call off the engagement and take care of that necklace thing or you're a dead sonuvabitch. And that is not a figure of speech."

21

Olive conceded, on first impression, that he was a somewhat attractive, barbered, late-middle-aged man. Neat wool plaid shirt and a high-end windbreaker. Someone to reckon with, and, Olive thought, Robert Johnson was probably on the reckoning end right now.

It had started innocently enough—a walk into the café for coffee-to-go and a treat for Gus. Cal would not approve of what she'd just done. He'd respond with a blank expression. A confused expression. Irritation. She doubted he'd consider these two men being in cahoots as anything worth confronting and risking her own safety. Hopefully, he wouldn't ask her what she was doing up north at the North Coast Café because she didn't want to lie. If she said nothing, it was still a lie. Every single lie was laying a brick between them. She'd tell him the truth. Which was her overpowering need to see, firsthand, what the Best Seeds, Inc. plant looked like because she felt deeply that company was linked to the series of misfortunate events on their farm.

She turned on the burner under the pot of chili and placed a bowl and a spoon in front of Cal.

"I ran into Gil Souza and Robert Johnson at the North Coast Café this morning while I was taking Gus on a car nap."

"Really. That's weird."

"I thought so, considering what Kat told us last night." She opened the refrigerator door and made room for the half gallon of milk. "They were at a table having what looked like a conversation, and now I'm trying to figure why. She'd never want her fiancé talking to her father."

"What were you doing up north at the café?"

"I stopped in for a cup of coffee and a treat for Gus, and there they were—the two of them together deep in conversation."

Cal stared out the window, his face tired, dirt in the lines under his throat from working on the tractor. He had to get the tractor ready for field work now that the soil was drying.

"There's something you're not telling me."

"I told Johnson I wanted my necklace back."

He grimaced. "I wish you hadn't. Alone. With Gus, up the coast. How wise is that?"

Since their conversation was on a bullet train to Baja, as predicted, she asked when he was taking the tractor into the field.

"Seriously? You're changing the subject?"

"There's something foul going on between those two men that Kat is unaware of. I don't know exactly what but add it up. Vandalized plants with a history going back to Best Seeds, dead neighbor, farm foreclosure, stolen necklace, Kat wears the necklace in an engagement photo with fiancé who has something going on with her father, whom she hates."

Cal rubbed his cheeks in frustration. "Where was Gus in all of this?"

"With me. I let it out that Kat and the Lobster were engaged. It felt deeply satisfying when their faces went blank." Cal's bottle of beer remained untouched on the kitchen table. So, yes, she'd upset him.

"You threatened the county's biggest ag man, Olive, who's also a big enough asshole to think he can violate a county GMO ordinance, and you don't think he's going to retaliate?"

"I'm saying he probably already has. Look, he's working with Kat's so-called fiancé."

"You think he's spying on us through this dude?"

"Indirectly, maybe, on top everything else."

"On top of what?"

"I don't know yet."

As he shoved his chair from the table, Olive wasn't sure if he was upset because she couldn't leave the investigating to the police or because she hadn't made her point.

"Ollie, we have so much going on right now and I can't lose you, not emotionally, not in the flesh. But if you can't leave it alone, take me with you next time."

She sighed, involuntarily—that's how profoundly those few words—six, to be exact—buoyed her.

22

Gil Souza tried to reach his daughter by phone. When she didn't pick up, he left a message, "Why didn't you tell me you got engaged?" and hung up. He shouted for Cloris and removed his reading glasses.

"I need your opinion." He breathed on his glasses and reached for a tissue to clean the smudges while Cloris shifted a cough drop to the opposite side of her cheek. Clack. That small noise unraveled him, but he needed her reassurance. Cloris had more children and grandkids than he could keep track of, and, although he wasn't in the mood to hear about them, he wanted her advice.

"Sir," she said, "Stanford Transbiogineers called you three times. They need a copy of your USDA license before they proceed."

"Fax it to them. And get a bid."

"Yessir," she said. "And County Planning returned your call. They didn't leave a message."

An emotional jam clogged Gil's throat. "She got engaged and didn't tell me. Neither did her fiancé, the scumbag who works for me. I heard it from a third party who enjoyed pushing my nose in it."

"Katy's being her rebellious self, but your worker certainly betrayed you. He should have asked your permission. He needs to apologize and you should consider firing him. But that's nice sir, isn't it, that Katy's getting married?"

"No, it's not nice." He couldn't think of worse news, not even the lawsuit. "What am I supposed to do?

"Sir, children go through stages that seem to last forever, but that's what a stage is. Not permanent but pronounced enough to be troubling. If you're having troubles with your daughter that are making you question yourself as her father, show her your love is unconditional and she'll come back to you. Parenting is a program of attraction."

"I'm not questioning myself, Cloris." As far as he could tell, Kat had been in a stage since her mother had abandoned them. He was sick of her stages. They were all bad. She was an ungrateful, spiteful daughter and an ill-prepared and uncooperative heir.

"Who, exactly, is she engaged to, sir, if you don't mind me asking?"

He did mind. Cloris had never met Robert Johnson and Gil kept his name out of the conversation. The less she knew the better. A little advice, that's all he was asking for. He held up his hand to say enough just as his cell phone buzzed on the desktop, showing Kat's number. His breath sounded labored when he answered the phone. "Hello."

"I told you not to call me."

Gil put the call on speaker phone as his daughter's rage filled the room. He watched Cloris.

"If I want to talk to you, I'll call you," Kat said. "If I wanted to tell you, I would've told you. Mind your own nasty business, Gil. In other words, fuck off." She hung up.

Gil slumped in his chair, shaking his head as Cloris uttered one loud rheumy cough. He heard her place another lozenge into her mouth, which she moved to the side with a clack before her next piece of advice.

"Okay, I see the problem," Cloris said. Clack. Clack. "If I were you, sir, I'd write her a letter. Tell her you love her."

Gil wanted to scream. Or maybe just walk out. "My daughter would spit on the envelope before she opened it."

"Excuse me, Gil. She'd know you haven't quit on her."

"You pick out a card." Gil reached in his wallet and pulled out a crisp twenty.

Cloris leaned forward to pluck the bill with her thumb and first finger. As she left the room, he heard one final crunch that punctuated her superiority in the matter of children before she closed the door.

Gil had broken a sweat. He ran past the raised open beds, the seedlings on drying racks, the hoops and greenhouses, his pace more a jog than a run, a slow jog. His knees ached as he passed the large glass enclosure, sun reflecting with such glare he looked away. It was the only way he knew to shake off the anger of double betrayal. He was used to his daughter, but that dickwad had thrown him off guard.

He'd almost achieved a rhythm, but the catch in his left shoulder stopped him. A pressure in his temples. They were killing him. He marched in place to keep the blood flowing and breathed deeply, filling his lungs to slow his heart rate, placing his palm on the exterior metal beam of the greenhouse to steady the head rush.

Once the pain ebbed, he started off slowly. His thoughts scattered and he focused the upset on Robert Johnson having sexual relations with his daughter behind his back. One thought rose from the scatter: if Johnson didn't leave his daughter alone, he'd kill him. He spit into the dirt. His vow was as clear as the new greenhouse glass. He checked the time. A drop of sweat hit the watch face. He wiped it clean with the edge of his T-shirt. Two p.m. He'd been running thirty minutes. Not bad for an old man.

23

Olive had ten minutes. Within that window of time, she had to park the box truck parallel to her spot, put up the canopies and set up the tables, spread out the flowered tablecloths, and arrange the heads of radicchios and cabbages in wicker baskets, along with bunches of chard and three varieties of kale, leaves facing out. Bins of vibrant beets—red, large goldens, chioggia. And, finally, the baskets of glossy strawberries—Albion, Monterey, Seascape. Damn. She needed help.

Wednesday downtown market was the busiest of the week, known for its carnival atmosphere and aisles jammed with all ages and lifestyles, some folks shopping for bi-weekly groceries and some showing up to hang out and grab a meal. The smell of rotisserie chicken, Indian food at the opposite end of the food court made everyone salivate. It was a vibrant market, bursting with commerce, conviviality and healthy food.

She set up the port-a-crib between the box truck and the counter, to the side of where she'd stand taking money. But before putting out the scales and cash box, Olive decided a New Orleans iced coffee could get her through the next five hours with a little more vigor. She bought the kids still-warm sourdough baguettes from the bakery and said "no" when Byrd asked for a brownie. She bought a ceviche for Gus and three oysters on the half shell, two for herself and one for Byrd, who had developed a surprising taste for the slimy salty creatures, without the dash of tabasco Olive craved. She placed the food and iced coffee inside a wooden crate she'd turned on its side and repurposed as a counter. She set the scales on top of the crate and cash box inside so the money was out of sight.

Mesa Grande farm, across the aisle from Olive, sold citrus—mandarins, tangerines, navels and Cara Cara for one dollar a pound. The farm was the only vendor that sold organic asparagus, which Olive planned to trade for strawberries. In another month, Mesa Grande would offer white corn for fifty cents an ear, driving down the price of their competitor Brody Harrington, who, today, sold fingerling potatoes the next aisle over. Maybe they knew someone who needed part-time market work.

Olive lifted Gus from her stroller and put her in the port-a-crib with her pacifier and favorite blanket. It was all about timing and routine. Gus fell asleep, lips puffed in peaceful slumber while Byrd sat cross-legged on the tarmac in front of a fiddler and banjo player. Two little girls danced in front of him as he tore at his baguette.

A man in an oversized army jacket hovered over the baskets of strawberries she'd set on the front table. She went up to him, knowing it was far too warm to be wearing a jacket. Before she could ask if she could help him, he turned from the strawberries and ferried across the aisle into the current of people, dipping his shoulder one way then the next until he stopped at Mesa Grande's. Olive watched him pick up a red pepper and stuff it inside his jacket. Then another, so obviously it was as if he were daring her to stop him. Olive glanced at Gus, asleep under her blanket, and Byrd, still sitting on a haystack watching the fiddler. Then she approached the man. Tap, tap on the shoulder, knowing he could explode on her, he turned slowly to face her.

"I saw you rip off the peppers," she said. "You know I saw you."

When the man sized her up what scared her was his demeanor, as if time were on his side. "You saw wrong. I'm talking to my friends."

Olive looked down both sides of the aisle and there was no sign he was with someone. She turned to him, "No friends." And when she looked into his rat-like face, her anger rose like a fever.

"You'd be surprised."

She pulled out her cell and punched 911.

"You're a real nosey bitch," he said.

"Maria," Olive shouted, "this dude is ripping you off."

"I can see why you pissed off my friend."

That was a strange thing to say, she thought, as he stared at her. Keeping eye contact while her phone rang, she tried to interpret his insinuation. He raised his left arm in a wave to someone or something behind her. That's when she knew he wasn't about stealing vegetables. She whirled around and sprinted to her stall. Gus wasn't in the port-a-crib. She had possibly woken up and climbed out, but Olive doubted it. She would've cried out first. She pulled up the tablecloth and searched the ground. No child. And when she looked up the man in the army jacket had vanished.

"Gus," she screamed, frantically scanning the market. She cupped her hands and ran into the aisle. At the top of her lungs, she shouted, "People."

Her voice froze everyone in their tracks. "Everyone! My little girl is missing. Her name is Gus. She's one and one half. Blond. Wearing OshKosh overalls. This is urgent. She's been taken from her crib. Look for her. Help me." She heard the last two words as a cry and instead of crumpling into a ball like one part of her wanted to do, she ran up the aisle, then stopped. The chances were that every direction she moved in would take her further from Gus. Her ears rang. People came up to her, asking questions she couldn't understand, clearly concerned. "My child's been kidnapped." She pushed past to the haystacks.

"Byrd." His face was startled by her voice as she pulled him up and held him. "Have you seen sister?"

He began to cry. Olive put him down and stopped a woman walking from the opposite direction. "Have you seen my little girl, or a person carrying a little blonde child?"

The woman pried Olive's hand from her arm. "Call the police," she said. "Now."

Every minute a child goes missing, the kidnapper has potentially traveled one mile farther away. Olive knew this. Which only spurred her panic that her baby had disappeared. She couldn't cry, she couldn't think clearly, and she couldn't fold. A man who identified himself as an off-duty police officer appeared at her side. She tried to stick to the facts.

"She was asleep in the port-a-crib behind the counter. A suspicious man—army jacket—came up to me and crossed the aisle to steal produce, right in front of me, so I left the stall and confronted him. He was unfazed and signaled someone behind me. I ran back here and Gus was gone. I checked under the tables and the truck."

The cop, on his cell phone, asked for the child's name, physical description and what she was wearing.

"Gus, short for Augusta. One-and one-half years old. Fair, light blonde hair, soft curls, blue eyes. Forty pounds. Wearing OshKosh jeans overalls and a long-sleeved pink-striped shirt. I'll be at the Shell Bean Farm vendor stall. I have long hair in a braid. Red plaid shirt." She listened to him repeat the information to Search and Rescue, hoping, hoping …

Her mind raced with what-if's. There were so many horror stories of what happens to children. An abducted five-year-old girl had recently been found dead in a Central California community. She'd been missing two days before they found her in a vacant lot. So many perverts preying on young children, so vulnerable and defenseless that Sheriff's departments throughout the nation treated a missing child as an immediate emergency. She knew this, too. But it only magnified her horror.

Her phone buzzed. An alert text from the Sheriff's department sent out to all citizens, notifying them that Gus was missing, likely abducted, along with her description. Every Search and Rescue volunteer in the county would drop what they were doing and head to the scene.

Please pick up. Please. Please. She was panicking, pacing in circles, gripping Byrd's hand.

Cal was in south county checking out a piece of ag land. Service was sketchy at best. A woman in an orange uniform shirt and red backpack walked quickly up to Olive. She introduced herself. Olive showed her the crib where Gus had last been, the area she'd been facing when Gus was taken. The woman put a firm hand on her back, the other on her shoulder and instructed her to breathe. Again. Three more Search and Rescue men arrived and two sheriff's deputies jogged toward her.

Spokes of a wheel, she thought, spread out quickly in pairs. No small talk. Maria stood beside her.

"Maria, stay with Byrd." She'd made up her mind and her body was already outside herself. "I can't stand here and wait."

The woman who was first on the scene told her just as firmly as she'd told Olive to breath that she needed to stay put. Olive took off running trying to catch up with herself. At the sidewalk, she turned right toward the busy part of town and the highway, shouting Gus's name, horror closing in from the edges of tunneling vision.

At a stop sign, the brakes of a Metro bus exhaled. Olive pounded on the glass until he opened the door.

"Have you seen anyone with a small blond child, one year old, wearing OshKosh overalls? My daughter. She's been kidnapped."

"I got the alert," he said. "We have our eye out. You need a ride anywhere?"

She kept running until she reached the library and pushed through the detector, interrupting a librarian as she checked out books. The librarian hadn't noticed a young child. Olive ran back to the foyer, shouted Gus's name. A siren screamed and somewhere upstairs a child wailed. She took the flight of steps to the children's section, ran along the aisles toward the far end of the room to the Storytime section. Her heart pounded and the wailing grew nearer, but she couldn't see the child because a woman blocked Olive's view.

"Gus," Olive said. "I'm here."

The woman turned, surprised, her sheltering hands on the child.

The jagged cry Olive emitted didn't sound like anything belonging to her. The stunned child stopped bawling as the woman pushed back her straight black hair from her eyes and wiped the girl's tears with her fingers. Not Gus.

Olive tore off back to the market. Search and Rescue would be knocking on doors, entering restaurants, stopping pedestrians. Maybe they had found something.

The incident commander looked relieved, not angry as Olive ran up.

"They just found her," she said. "You didn't answer your phone."

"Where is she?"

She pointed east. "Far outer edge of the premises. She's locked inside the porta-potty.

Olive pushed her way through the crowd that had assembled around the outhouse, shouting Gus's name. The outhouse door flew open and a SAR leaned in. On the grimy blue plastic floor that stunk of feces sat Gus. Olive swept up the baby. Her clothes were wet, and wads of soggy toilet paper stuck to her overalls. She smelled of urine.

"Ma'am," a deputy said. "The outhouse was locked on the inside. We used a crowbar to get inside or we would've gotten her out sooner. Any possibility that she could have walked into the john and turned the handle by herself?"

"No. Look at her. She's way too small." In fact, she wasn't. Gus was tall enough to reach the metal latch and curious enough play with it. "No."

"Hold on." The deputy pulled a piece of yellow paper that was stuffed down the back of her diaper.

Olive held Gus tight and craned to see as he unfolded it.

"This mean anything to you?" he asked.

On the paper were written in longhand the words: See how easy it is to lose the one you love.

"This is my fault." Hot crimson forks of stress crept up her neck as Cal stared straight ahead, gripping the steering wheel, clenching and unclenching his jaw. Byrd sat between them, Gus on Olive's lap.

"She was asleep in the port-a-crib," Olive said, shaking her head. "And this lowlife in an army coat was ripping off Mesa Grande. I went over to him and when I threatened to call the cops, he was looking as me as if I was doing exactly what he wanted. It was a setup and I fell for it."

"Not your fault, babe."

Cal shook as he removed his T-shirt and turned on the shower. Olive, seated on the toilet lid, held Gus, and imagined the thief's face etch deeper into her mind where it would remain until she found him.

Brown water ran off Gus and swirled around the drain as Cal held her up to the shower while Olive lathered the child, who didn't even put up a fuss. This worried Olive, as she dried and dressed Gus in fresh clothes then lay with her on their big bed.

Cal showered Byrd, whistled a tune to relax him. Into the bedroom they came, piggyback, Byrd in fresh pajamas, Cal in white T-shirt and sweatpants. Cal poured him onto the bed beside her, where the three nestled like baby birds under mom's wings. She read *Masha and the Bear*, waiting for Cal to bring them hot chocolate.

That night after the kids were in bed, Olive sat in the rocking chair wrapped in a blanket while Cal leaned against the porch rail, stiff with residual anxiety.

"This is what happens," he said.

She pulled up the blanket around her chin and braced herself for criticism. "Meaning?"

"Yesterday you confronted two men, pissed them off, and today someone takes our daughter and leaves her in the outhouse with a fucked-up note stuffed in her diaper."

"I know who wrote the note."

"No you don't."

"Cal. I do."

He turned. "How do you know?"

"I recognize the handwriting. It's Gil Souza's. He's up to something."

"Everyone's 'up to something' from your perspective."

"I drove up to Souza's plant before I confronted him in the café. A woman got my license plate. He knows I suspect him of something."

"Seriously? Our kids are paying the price for your suspicions."

"You outwitted him, Cal." She knew she had to impress upon him the truth of what she felt in her deepest self. This was no time for compliance, time for delivery. "You propagated an organic heirloom out of his conventional hybrid. You're getting the credit. And he's getting even."

"That is so far-fetched." The crease between his brow deepened.

"You used his product and made a hero of yourself, whether you wanted to or not, while demonizing his company and everything he stands for. Your success has turned public opinion further against him."

Like a vulture, Ariela appeared in the porch doorway, arms outstretched, poised to feed on their troubles.

Olive waved her away. "We're having a conversation. Go."

"No, don't go." Cal turned to Ariela. "Someone kidnapped Gus at the market. She was found in an outhouse, sitting in strangers' piss. Olive, tell her what the note said."

Olive recited the sentence, "See how easy it is to lose what you love? Stuffed in Gus's diaper."

"Your daughter thinks Gil Souza is the culprit," Cal said.

Ariela pointed a long finger at Cal, her bracelets tinkling. My daughter inherited instincts, son-in-law. "My money is on her."

"I don't need you sticking up for me right now."

"Where is this Gil Souza?" Ariela demanded.

It wasn't so much that her husband questioned her, as the way his doubt was a wall between them, a retractable, porous wall, but, still, a wall. When that wall appeared, she felt alone. And when she was alone, she went underground, slipping into the self-reliant survivor of her childhood, a precocious, wise girl who said to the adult Olive, "what took you so long?" At this point, she had choices. She could escalate the argument or she could stuff her resentment (not her style) or she could put it aside for a talk once the anger subsided, which the adult Olive knew was the correct choice. But here's the thing: his doubt, she told herself, was as damaging to their relationship as her lies.

When Detective Rogers arrived, and Olive insisted the handwriting on the note belonged to Gil Souza, unlike Cal, he didn't react, and this default detective face told her his brain was calculating the odds, noncommittal but open. She showed him the bill she'd pulled from their file that morning.

"I know his handwriting. He's handwritten notes to us on his bills back when we ordered seed from him."

The capital S. The l. A downward slant. He conceded to the similarities. "Does he have a motive for kidnapping your child?"

"I confronted him in a café and told him something he didn't want to hear. His daughter is engaged to the guy he was having coffee with, odd since his daughter hates Souza and would never tolerate her fiancé developing a relationship with him."

Rogers listened. "When was this?"

"Yesterday."

Small humpf and barely discernable nod.

"She hated him enough," Olive went on, "to emancipate herself as a youth and change her surname from Souza to Granger, and she'd go ballistic if she knew her fiancé was talking to him. They are up to something."

"Have you told her this?" Rogers asked.

"No. I'm saving that."

"For what?" He pressed his lips, a silent warning she'd better not go this alone.

"I don't know, yet. I think Souza hired her fiancé to spy on her, and I busted them." She felt a lump creeping up her chest, a sob or vomit, she couldn't tell, when she thought of Gus in the outhouse. "As I told you, he could be resentful that Cal's new tomato originated from his."

When Henry raised his chin and gazed to the right, Olive saw the hunch. Something added up. When he called the station and told dispatch he was heading up the coast to interview a person of interest in the Augusta Post abduction, she felt a small tragic victory.

They watched Rogers back out of the driveway, the sound of gravel crunching under the tires.

Cal's clamped her shoulder. He was shaking. "If that motherfucker Souza has anything to do with this, he's dead."

24

Gil didn't like surprise visits. He heard the knock on the door and asked the visitor to repeat his name. He didn't know how to react to a dark green sedan with a discreet siren parked in his yard. And he immediately disliked the man who introduced himself as Detective Henry Rogers. A city cop in sheriff's territory? What the hell? And he was on the short side for a cop, definitely not tough enough looking to call his attorney. Instead, he stepped onto the porch. It was chilly outside; the sun was low and offshore Westerlies drilled to the bone.

Gil squinted as the cop asked his full name, home address, name of business. He didn't feel compelled to answer questions from a stranger, even a cop. Until the cop informed him that he was following up on a kidnapping.

"Your name came up."

"Can I see your ID, again?" Gil immediately thought of his daughter, who habitually put herself in dangerous situations.

"Where did this kidnapping take place?"

"The farmers market."

Gil took a step forward. "I don't like games. Did something happen to my daughter?"

"No, sir, and the child has been found unhurt and returned to her parents. How old is your daughter?"

That's what happened when you got real with a cop, Gil thought. More invasive questions. "Twenty-two. No. Twenty-three." Sweat dripped slowly down Gil's spine even though it was cold. Drip, drip, drip.

"Someone took a small child from her crib and left her in the outhouse."

"Horrible. Why are you asking me?"

"The parents found a note on the child. The mother claims it's in your handwriting."

That made no sense. "Who are these parents?"

"See how easy it is to lose what you love? That ring a bell?"

Gil's scalp tightened. That was the exact threat he'd written in a note to Robert Johnson after finding out he planned to marry his daughter and forcing him to break up. He took a measured breath. He knew how the police worked—expressions were signs of guilt or innocence—knowing something or not. "Nope. Not a bit." His feet hurt from the shock. The note he'd written yesterday had ended up in the diaper of child. The low life deserved to choke on his own shit.

25

The hiss as he stubbed out the last cigarette before he quit created a sense of finality. Until the front door to his office flung open and a wild-eyed, windblown woman burst into his office accusing him of kidnap.

"Whoa." He held up a hand and tightened his grip on the edge of his desk. Reaching into his top drawer for the Smith and Wesson was not out of the question. He hadn't counted on this: a vintage hippy in a rage.

"Who the hell are you?"

"Ariela Murphy, and don't you forget it, Mr. Gil-the-man Souza."

More silver bracelets than he cared to count jangled on her arm as she shook her many-ringed first finger at him.

"I have something to say to you, Mister."

"I'm calling the sheriff, so make it quick." Gil wasn't about to call the sheriff, especially after he'd just been interviewed by a cop, but maybe the threat would scare this crazy off.

She raised an eyebrow. "Don't for one second think I'm crazy."

Gil leaned forward, placing his hands palm down on his desk. "Why would I think that?"

When the woman propped her arms on his desk and leaned over, daring him to look down her blouse, he smiled. Cleavage, lots of it.

She smiled back, and he wasn't sure if it was a showdown smile or a mutual attraction smile. "I'm a professional psychic," she said. "Want me to tell you what you're thinking now?"

The woman waved her arms in the air as if she were pulling strands of yarn. Gil cleared his throat, pushed back his chair and stood up, curious how she'd react to his height.

He could smell her perfume. Patchouli. He hated patchouli. It smelled like the dark days of the sixties. He hated the sixties.

"I'd like to know what your problem is." He thought she might be a devil worshipper and walked briskly around his desk to close the distance between them and show her who was in charge. He considered a swift kick to her apple butt to get her the hell out of there.

"Listen carefully," she said. "And do not attempt to intimidate me." She held up that first finger, again. "I know how men like you operate. Men like you are a plague to land, women and children. My children."

Yes, he'd taken his share of each, except the children, even though his own child hated him, but that was on her. Something about her eyes, their absorption, he'd seen those eyes before.

The woman slapped her hands on his desk. "My little grand-daughter, to be specific."

This was about the kidnapping. He picked up the desk phone. "Make it quick or 911."

"You kidnapped my Augusta Eugenia from under my daughter's nose."

Ah, that Post woman's mom. When she planted herself in the wooden armchair across from his desk, he assumed his threats didn't work. She wasn't leaving. His patience waned, and as she crossed her legs, revealing thick, frumpy sandals and shapely sun-tanned legs, he felt a mixture of disgust and desire. He couldn't help looking down her blouse, again. She had to be used to that, Gil thought, watching her scan his office walls and desk, zeroing in on the small wooden figurine of the standing grizzly bear that he kept by his desk lamp.

She kicked his desk lightly with the toe of her sandal. "I see you like wood, Gil. My daughter's neighbor was a woodworker." She gazed up at him. "He's dead."

What was this she-bear insinuating now? Gil pushed his face closer to hers. "You're not much of a psychic if you think I had something to do with a dead man and a kidnap."

"Don't change the subject. My daughter found Cris Villalobos dead on her farm."

Gil glanced at the wooden bear on his desk, wondering what else this woman thought, but now she was standing and her hands were on her hips, and there was that ringed finger and those jangling bracelets again.

"I've had visions of you, Gil-man Souza. It wasn't suicide and you know that. Cris was murdered. By someone who's done this sort of thing before. And that person will be brought to justice." She sidled over to his photograph wall and tapped an old one of him in uniform.

"You were a Marine." She tilted her head toward his framed certificate of honorable discharge, and Gil realized sweat was trickling down his spine for the second time that day. She'd have to leave and if she didn't leave soon, he'd drag her out.

"You sure don't hold back, lady, but you're done. Out."

She wasn't done. She wagged her finger.

"I want two things from you," she said. "The name of the person who kidnapped my granddaughter. And your promise that you'll leave my family alone."

"Or what?" Gil gave her a malicious smile.

She cocked her head and gave him a line smile. "Or else."

"Do you know who you're dealing with here? If I wanted to take the steam out of my competitors, and I don't include your small-time family in that bracket, I'd do a lot different than snatch a kid and leave her in an outhouse." Gil grabbed the woman's arm. It was soft and fat, and his thumb and forefinger sunk into her flesh before he felt bone. Something about the feel of her made him pause. What would it be like to screw a wild woman like her? Bad thought.

The woman yanked free. She began to speak in a language Gil didn't recognize. It was alarming and he tried to hide his bewilderment. He should've called the sheriff. He moved toward his desk and sat down, opening the top drawer slowly.

"Do not mess with me or my family." She held out her palms and moved them in crazy eights. Her fingers were long and expressive, reminding him of claws.

He sucked in his breath as she glared at him. He really didn't want to shoot the woman. He'd never seen anything quite like her face right now. It was fluid, like hot glass flowing from one expression to another.

"And you're an oxymoron," she said.

"Then you'd better watch out because whatever that means, I'm a powerful one."

She came around to him, and he swore she was about to kiss him with those full lips that probably had kissed a thousand men. But then, his head jerked back and he heard a snip. She held out a lock of his hair as if she were Judith decapitating the enemy.

"So am I." She placed his castrated lock in the voluptuous slit between her breasts as Gil met her gaze without blinking.

He shut the door quietly behind her and listened for footsteps, rubbing the stiff, uneven ends of his clipped scalp. The crunch of gravel meant it was safe to look out the window as this female who'd claimed to put a spell on him climbed into a golf cart.

He laughed. It was the loudest deepest laugh he'd ever laughed and he couldn't stop. He coughed and laughed and held his side until the spasm in his lung subsided, and when it did he stared at the photograph of his Best Seeds sponsored baseball team from the wall, ran his middle finger along the dust on the top of the frame and gazed at the assemblage of men. The short stop was Cris Villalobos, who seemed to be looking right at him with a mocking turn of the lips. Short stops. They thought they were such hot shit.

As Gil stashed the photo in the drawer beside his gun, he rummaged for a cigarette. The scent of patchouli hovered in the woman's wake. It smelled better than at first. He felt … elevated. This woman had made him laugh and he couldn't remember when he'd last laughed. He touched his scalp where she'd cut his hair. Maybe he'd get a crew cut. As he looked out the window at the dust rising from her putt-putt, he struck a match and lit the damn cigarette.

Gil woke up startled from a sex-dream that had left him hard and sore. In his dream, the broad who'd crashed his office was a gypsy. The swale of her dreamt-up hip lingered on his fingertips, and he could still hear her moan, Jesus, thick as maple syrup. Yes, he mused, he'd bet a new John Deere she was good in bed. As he rubbed the jagged patch on his scalp where she'd snipped him, the prickly stub shouted, ha, ha, ha. He swung his feet onto the carpet and stared down at himself. His erection throbbed, his head ached and he was thirsty.

That pleasant feeling just thinking of her left him in the quandary of wanting to see her again. The first time in decades he'd wanted to see a woman again. She was sexy, he had to admit. Looked like Susan Sarandon. An aging Sarandon with a few extra pounds. Sexy, but old. Then again, so was he.

"Now what?" Gil heard himself mutter.

The morning began with coffee and scrambled eggs, something he could do one-handed while he made calls to his foreman and got the day moving. And he had to clear up a few things before he went out to the ranch. Respond to the USDA. It was one thing for a county to ban GMOs, and another that federal law did not and the feds took precedence over local and state government. But, now, even the feds were threatening to shut down his GMO seed trials.

And that note: See how easy it is to lose what you love? Yes, he had written that. But he hadn't stuck it in a baby's diaper, for god sakes. His head ached and it wasn't seven o'clock.

Gil was about to pour himself another cup of coffee when his cell phone vibrated on the tile kitchen counter, showing an unfamiliar number with an out of state prefix.

"This is Gil Souza."

"I know it wasn't you." The caller's husky voice was unmistakable.

"Good morning, Ariela. You're already confusing me." As Gil poured coffee, put his cell on speaker, wondering if she was a psychic and how the hell she'd found his number. "Isn't it kind of early to be minding other people's business?"

"You are my business, Gil, and I believe now that you did not place that note in my granddaughter's diaper, but someone did and you know who."

If he asked how she'd come to this conclusion, she'd have the upper hand and interpret his interest as guilt. If he didn't ask, he'd never learn the extent of what she thought she knew. He cracked the second egg. "Am I supposed to be grateful?"

"Guess again."

"Ma'am." Women hated being addressed as ma'am. As far as Gil could tell, the word made them feel old. "I'm not following you."

Her burst of laughter didn't surprise him. She was a flagrant, brazen bitch.

"Why are you so afraid of me that you have to dodge the question?"

The tiniest breeze sifted through his kitchen bay window and cooled the mowed patch on his scalp. Goosebumps shot up on his arms. If this female from hell knew one iota of his plans, she'd show up on his doorstep as Medusa in the flesh, wild, dyed red hair snaking around her head in every direction but down. He said, "I don't recall you asking me a question."

"How do I know that it wasn't you? You want to know. So, ask me."

He tried to impress upon her that he didn't care what she thought. "You're psychic," he conceded. "Read my mind."

"That's not what I'm looking for, Gil. Dig deeper."

He restrained himself to sound indifferent. "I'm not following you," as he opened the silverware drawer and stared at the utensils stacked neatly in their organizer tray. He was looking for a whisk. He'd forgotten the whisk was in the adjacent drawer, with the kitchen knives, which made him think of those scissors she'd pulled out of thin air and applied to his hair.

"Everyone who knows me would agree that I'm not the kind of person who would accost a kid. They'd also agree that, bewitching as you are, I'm not the kind of man who enjoys people barging into his office accusing him of kidnap and thievery or calling him on a private number he never gave out."

"And murder." Ariela waited a second before adding, "Don't forget Cris."

"I never knew him." Gil heard his words, so far from the truth they didn't feel like his. He was used to that. "The cops said it was suicide." He changed the subject. "I dreamt about you last night."

Her silence signaled he'd managed to shut her up. Or maybe she was doing some hocus pocus dream-reading through the air waves. Protectively, he grabbed his crotch. "You casting some new age spell on me?"

"Did that yesterday, Gil. I'm wondering."

He sensed the hairpin turn ahead.

"You have something I want," she said, "and we both know what that is."

Wrong. He didn't have any idea what she wanted. "Miss Gypsy, someone always pays when I get irritated. And, by the way, you were young in the dream," he lied.

He chalked up the burst of laughter from her end as ridicule.

"You'd better eat your eggs and meet me this morning. I have something of yours, and I want to know who snatched my flesh and blood."

He looked down at the bowl of raw eggs awaiting scramble.

No big mystery. Everyone eats eggs at this time of day. Raising his wrist to check the time, Gil found himself staring at a band of white skin surrounded by brown. No watch. This woman, she was fucking with his mind. She'd be happy to know that. Not so happy if she knew his plans for the day.

"C'mon, Gil." She mocked him with contrived seduction. "You want to be a gentleman and choose the time and place," she said, "or do I have to take the bull by the horns, again?"

"North Coast Café. Eight o'clock.

"I drive a cart. Closer to town."

As soon as he recalled her piling into that silly cart and putt-putting away, he laughed. "Couldn't forget if I tried. We could meet at Starbucks downtown on Pacific."

"I don't like Starbucks," she said.

He didn't like Starbucks, either. The patio had become an office for homeless men who hung outside on the sidewalk as if they owned it. But that was the only coffee shop he could think of.

"St. Frank's café on Pacific Garden Mall. Eight-thirty."

Gil couldn't find his car keys or his wallet. He doubled his concentration. As he left the house, he activated the alarm system and drove down the long curving driveway from his secluded ranch house in the Santa Cruz Mountains and realized he'd forgotten his sunglasses. He kept driving through the gate and waited until it closed behind him before he proceeded two miles down mountain toward the Pacific Coast Highway. As he turned onto the open stretch of road and headed south toward town, he caught himself wondering what she'd be wearing, and he swore he smelled patchouli.

The woman was nowhere in sight. He glanced around St. Frank's looking for her, resenting all women who felt obliged to be late.

A scatter of young people sat on stools, working at their computers. Probably students from the University. Mothers in yoga getups
with babes in strollers waited to receive whatever coffee concoc-
tion they'd ordered. He couldn't figure how a business could make
a profit off customers who took up so much space and time, paid
so little, and didn't leave a tip.

The pretty barista asked to take his order.

"Coffee, black," Gil grumbled.

"What size?" she smiled.

"Large." He softened.

"To go?"

"I wish." He winked.

"I heard that." It was her. Standing in line behind him. Her hair
pulled back into a messy, complicated bun, wearing jeans and cowboy boots.

He looked her up and down. "You almost look normal."

"Trust me. I'm not."

He laughed.

The barista leaned toward Ariela. "Next."

"Small coffee, black. No room for milk. In a mug, please."

"Like a pro," Gil winked at the barista, who grinned back.

Ariela, elbow on the polished wooden counter edge, shook her
head. She was making a point, but he didn't get it.

"Old men who flirt with young women are disgusting. They
don't realize how disgusting they are. And you just insulted me by
flirting in my presence, not that I'm jealous, but the principle of the
matter irks me." Ariela pointed with her long first finger toward the
tables on the sidewalk. She'd polished her nails since yesterday, Gil
noticed. Navy blue.

"Let's sit outside," she said. "We can people-watch during our
awkward silences."

Gil didn't want to sit outside. People irritated him, especially the early-bird freeloaders who showed up from whatever hovel
they'd holed up in overnight, bumming a cup of coffee with the
rest of the freeloaders who'd survived another night without shel-
ter. And it was cold outside. Plus, he'd forgotten his sunglasses.

Ariela said, "Okay then. I see a table in the back corner of the room. You can have the wall."

She wound her way as gracefully as a horse between the room crowded with small round tables and empty chairs, and he followed. They sat across from each other and sipped their coffee, she staring at him over the rim of her cup. Her nails gleamed, making the skin on the back of her hands appear paler and smoother.

"I'm not a dirty old man, if that's what you're insinuating."

She rolled her eyes. "You wink at a pretty girl who could be your daughter? Do you realize how lecherous that is? You do have a daughter about that age, correct?"

"Hey, she smiled at me."

"That's old school 'roving eye' mentality. Women my age do not like that."

Do I care? Gil thought.

"And women her age are so caught off guard they can't help but smile. At you. They're being polite to the customer. That's all it is. That and a nice tip." As she started to remove her fleece jacket, he put up a hand "Please. Leave the jacket on."

But she proceeded as if she hadn't heard him and before he knew it, there they were, those lovely full breasts and the soft, fleshy cleavage.

He groaned involuntarily.

She winked.

"Please," Gil said, "if you have a hankering to go to bed with me, come out and admit it. We can get it done and move on."

There was her sleigh-bell laugh. "That would spoil the fun. And why is it that men can't see anything above the clavicle?" She reached over the table and placed her hands over his eyes. "What color are my eyes?"

"Hazel." Hazel was safe.

She pulled back her hands.

Brown. Gil sipped his coffee. "Close." He leaned on his forearms until he could smell her, not patchouli, but an old-fashioned rose scent. He was intent on taking control of the conversation, but the perfume softened him. "I'm here because you have something to say to me."

"Wrong. We're here because you have something to tell me."

"And what is that?"

"To whom did you write that note?"

He gave her a blank look. No. Not biting.

"Oh, c'mon. You know what I'm asking. If you didn't put that note there, the person you originally wrote it to did. They stashed her in a port-a-potty, for god sakes. You're connected. I want to know who and I want to know why."

"How do you know it's my handwriting?"

"From what I hear, you've done business with my son-in-law before that fork in the road."

"How so?"

"He took the high road and you the low. You'd written notes on the bottom of your invoices. You sent them a handwritten note congratulating Cal on his success with that tomato that originated from your hybrid. They told me."

He scratched the bald spot she'd created yesterday. "You owe me a haircut."

That's when her expression transformed and he knew he'd better give her what she wanted before she did something embarrassing, like kick him in the crotch with those pointed cowboy boots. "Whoa. First, tell me why you need to know?"

"My daughter, you met her, tenacious as a terrier," Ariela said. "She gets that from me. She will not let go of putting together the pieces until she's discovered the truth. It started with her discovery of the Villalobos man on her farm and now it's straining her marriage. I'm her mother. She doesn't like me, and she's pissed as an unneutered dog that I showed up on her doorstep, but whether she likes it or not, she's my daughter and it's my job to protect her."

Too much drama, but Gil tried to be polite. "Can't they work out this one without you? They're young, resourceful. People like them." He hesitated. "Anyway, why does your daughter care so much about this Cris person to let him disrupt her life? He's gone. Your daughter has a family to care for."

"You really think dead people are gone?" Her brow furrowed and her face looked entirely intelligent. "Someone tried to destroy their livelihood—those tomatoes. I think it could've been a trapped bobcat. Then again, you're the only one we can think of who would want to ruin your young competition's bright future."

"Think harder, then."

"What do you have to do with all of this, Gil?"

Gil put up his hands. "You tell me."

Ariela closed her eyes and put her arms on the table, fists balled up. He watched her eyes dart back and forth beneath their lids. "Hey." He tapped her wrist. "Are you in there? None of this séance crap. I work for a living, and I don't have time to play haunted house."

She turned her wrist and opened a fist. A small wooden bear sat on the palm of her hand. "Let's start with this."

Gil had an identical bear at the office. He kept it on his desk by the lamp. A sick feeling scraped his gut.

"I swiped it," she said. "Now, I'm giving it back. As soon as you admit something, anything."

Gil dropped his head. She was clever, he had to admit. The bear was a gift from Cris Villalobos, but he wasn't about to tell her that. It was none of her business. Cris had been glad to see him. It had been a few years since the baseball team. Gil wanted him to fashion custom beams for the guest studio he planned to build. He'd written an advance. They shook hands and Cris gave him the trinket. A small bear carving. No big deal. But the farm across the street from Cris had attracted him. It was full of charm. He wanted to own that charm. That was the problem with charm.

Ariela studied his face with power-tool eyes that bore so deeply he had to turn away.

She said, "You don't strike me as the kind of person who would lower himself to take children from their mother. You have far too much to lose doing stupid things like that. But I do believe you know someone who would."

"Maybe your people are just out to get me." Gil leaned in, measuring how his statement affected her. "You know, my kind of farming is not popular with that crowd, which is probably your crowd. I have nothing against a small fry trying to survive in a big pond. But I'm on the side of progress." He found himself leaning forward, not to be closer, but with an urge to confide in her the importance of research and development in the field of bioengineering.

"I'm trying to feed the world. That's what it boils down to."

"I'm thinking it boils down to poison."

"Nasty. If you were born and raised on a farm, you wouldn't be this way."

"Whatever that means. If I were born and raised on a farm, I'd run away."

"You know what I mean, then."

"The young resist their parents."

Didn't he know that to be true?

"Our young perceive the universe as a life source that our generation is destroying. But we can alter the innate disposition of our minds. That's a choice we have."

"I do my best to avoid altering the disposition of my mind. My mind works. It got me where I am today."

"How's that?"

Gil shrugged. "Your path is liking walking to the edge of a cliff on a moonless night with your fingers crossed."

She smiled. "That's lovely, Gil." He felt himself blush as she continued. "But something bigger is lighting the path on that moonless night. I don't have to cross my fingers. I give in to it."

Gil shook his head. "You have no common sense. Your path is fairy dust. I like solid ground."

"Really, Gil? Yours is one huge, frightening experiment."

Gil had work to do. Real work. He pushed back his chair and reached for his mug, planning on one last swallow of coffee, but the woman snatched the mug from his hand. "We're not finished here."

A few people looked up from their computers. He didn't recognize anyone in the room. She was behind him now, pressing his shoulders. He could smell the nail lacquer.

"I'm getting refills and while I'm gone, figure out what it is you want to say to me."

"There is nothing more I want to say to you." But he stayed, and she returned with the mugs and set them on the table, small drifts of steam rising from the hot liquid.

He heard his words tumble out with no forethought. "My daughter. She hates me."

26

Cal was gone when Olive woke up. He'd slipped out of bed without making a sound and made coffee. His boots were gone from the mudroom. She craned to see his Ford 150 and couldn't. She texted him good morning kisses and asked where he was.

He texted back that he was on the tractor, prepping soil.

Ariela was gone, as well. She grabbed the kids and dropped Byrd off at preschool then headed to the County Building.

Parcel maps, recorded after 1997, were on microfilm, and the public was free to search the records. In days of yore they were in the old bound black books. Those books still lined the bottom shelves under the counter. Gus sat on the floor trying to pull one from the shelf.

Olive remembered to breathe as she sat down at a public-use computer to search, using Gil Souza as the principle party. When nothing came up, she tried Best Seeds, Inc. Bingo. Best Seeds, she discovered, owned a dozen large parcels of agriculturally zoned land in Santa Cruz County. Olive picked up Gus and asked the clerk how much for copies of parcel maps. A dollar a page.

Once back home in the office, Olive took down the toys she had saved on the top shelf for special occasions. They weren't any more fragile nor carried more sentimental value than any of the kids' toys, but inaccessibility made them desirable. As Gus played, Olive laid the maps across the floor of the office in geographical order, starting south. The expectancy mounting in her core prepared her for the story these maps had to tell. Cross-hatches on every one. Meaning, each parcel abutted a railroad track.

"I got one over on Gil Souza." Ariela opened her palm, revealing a small wooden carving of a standing bear. "Yesterday, I confronted him at his office and took this."

Olive's face went hot as she watched Ariela set the bear on the kitchen table. "What did you do?"

"No one harms my family." Ariela reached down her blouse and pulled out a locket of hair. "Left him a bit worse for wear."

"What is that?"

"I took scalp as well."

"You assaulted him?"

"No. I put a spell on him. He didn't press charges, Love. In fact, this morning he met me at Frank's downtown café." Ariela tossed back her hair and pushed back her chair.

"Stay." Olive pointed at Ariela. "You are not leaving this room until you explain."

"I'm not your dog, Love. Although you could use a dog, at least for the children."

Olive leaned the broom and dustpan against the sink counter and picked up the smooth wooden carving from the table. It looked like one of Cris Villalobos's.

Ariela snatched it. "This is too full of juju and you have enough bad energy surrounding you without asking for more."

If it were one of Cris's, it meant Gil Souza could have known Cris.

"I scheduled a tarot reading at his house," Ariela said.

Cal opened the porch door and stuck his head in, calling Byrd. "Hey buddy," he shouted. "Let's go catch some ground squirrels." Cal's idea of catching ground squirrels was checking his traps and putting out more traps. If they'd trapped a ground squirrel, he'd transport it up into the park behind their property and let it go in a nice place as far from the farm as he could manage. He wasn't above killing the squirrels, but he never had as far as Olive knew, even though they ate as much of his crop as fast as they could.

The house reverberated with Byrd running down the stairs, through the living room, past Olive into Cal's arms with one leap. When they returned an hour later, sooner than Olive expected, Byrd wore a disgusted look and proceeded to describe the nearly-dead squirrel they'd found by the creek. Dead squirrels could be a problem on a farm. "We had to put it out of its misery."

Cal scratched his thick head of hair until it stood on end on his way to the fridge. Olive, never one to pass up the opportunity to impress her son to respect the animals they ate and eliminated, said, "Kind of sad, don't you think? Poor squirrel. Let's wash up."

The creek was dry and the opposite bank impassible with acacia, blackberry vines and poison oak. About ten yards up the creek, blackberry bushes had been tamped down into a narrow passage. Olive checked out the rumpled sleeping bag and garbage as she stepped up the opposite bank. The barren land on the other side was covered with bright yellow sour grass on what she estimated to be roughly a quarter-acre rectangle of land. The signs that this had been cultivated ground at one time was obvious to Olive, striding toward the residual humps of long-abandoned rows. She saw the commercial strawberry fields of its future, the fumigated ground, the required five-acre buffer zone to protect their organic crops from chemical pesticides. What she'd hadn't seen until this morning was the man behind the scenes, Gil Souza. According to the parcel maps, Best Seeds owned this property.

She kicked one of the stubs, uncovering the top of a large, stubborn bulb. White, like a turnip. Maybe parsnip. Could be rutabaga. She took out her camera and snapped photos.

27

The road to Kat Granger's house was seasoned and charming, an older rural neighborhood within the city limits without sidewalks. In this niche, university students, pot growers and the affluent dwelled side by side in everything from derelict homesteads and converted chicken coops to brand new ranchettes separated from each other by gulches of oak woodland.

Olive had driven before to the end of this road where a trailhead to the City Open Space Reserve began. Two years ago, when Byrd was still small enough to carry in a backpack. She'd hiked for hours down the hills to the coast, where Cal picked her up at a designated time.

The land was marine terrace, thin soil, which spanned fifty kilometers of the Santa Cruz coastline. It looked like short grass prairie and possessed a quality Olive remembered as dense silence. No crickets, no birds. The quiet so absolute it was freaky, as if the air deflected sound waves and a vacuous force held down the beauty.

"There." Ariela shoved an arm across Olive's face, pointing to the tin mailbox marked 1122. "Turn."

Olive cranked the Jeep into a dirt driveway that opened up to a weathered bungalow on its original mudsill. A few yards away an abandoned chicken coup sagged from neglect. More empty sheds leaned over a gully, supported by decades-old poison oak that looked more like red-leafed trees than vines. The property was unmaintained but charming, partly because the house was lop-sided from the early days and, largely, because the dun-colored dirt yard absorbed the warmth of the low winter sun and the Pacific Ocean sparkled on the horizon, even though it was miles away—across acres of terraced prairie. An atavistic nostalgia stirred inside Olive.

She backed in the Jeep against the sagging barbed wire fence, beside a vintage, faded, red and white Mercury sedan with grass growing out of its hood. A "For Sale" sign had been fastened to the barbed wire fence that separated the house from pastureland. The property owners were apparently waiting it out for the right offer after which the bungalow and deteriorating sheds would be put out of their misery, replaced by as many high-density townhouses as the city would allow. That was the tragic fate of Santa Cruz and much of California where natural beauty and pastoral artifacts were relentlessly preyed upon.

As soon as Olive set Augusta on the ground, she toddled across the flat yard, while Byrd headed straight to the rusty wagon wheel fastened to the barbed wire fence. Her mother was in charge of the kids. Olive climbed the three worn steps to the screened front door. No one answered her knock. She called Kat's name, heard footsteps. Kat came to the door looking hungover. "What are you doing here?"

Olive held out the white envelope. "Your severance check."

"You can't just drop in on me."

"I want to give you another chance to tell me where the necklace is."

Kat glanced across the yard. "Who is that?"

"That's Ariela, my mother. She was at the table when you barged in the other night." She hoped Kat would see that she wasn't the only one who didn't call first.

"Oh, yeah, her."

Ariela had made herself comfortable in Kat's front yard by collapsing in a vintage, faded red metal chair, her face tilted to the sun, eyes closed. Byrd poked a stick in the air and Gus squatted in the dirt to pet a cat.

"She makes a habit of acting like she owns the place?"

"Pretty much." Olive waited until Kat refocused on her. "Did you hear about what happened to Gus at the market?"

Kat scratched the tip of her green kelp tattoo. A tell, Olive thought.

"Which market?" Kat asked.

"The Wednesday downtown market. Someone kidnapped Gus from her playpen and left her in the port-a-potty."

The image of Gus stoked sharp pain in Olive's uterus, like it did when she thought of her children being hurt. "You have an ear to the ground. Do you think Gil could be involved?"

"I don't waste my energy on Gil. But if I did, I'd say he's a dangerous man, he doesn't like kids, but he wouldn't do that, at least not personally. He doesn't do anything on his own, except control people. He doesn't even farm anymore. Have you seen his hands? He gets manicures. Maybe his henchman did it."

"What henchman?"

"Don't know, don't care. Doesn't every rich man have a fixer?"

Since the question was rhetorical, Olive didn't answer. Instead, she glanced into the house. Several pairs of worn shoes at all angles were parked a couple of feet inside the door beneath a cinder block shelf, the kind poor college students put together.

"When Cal and I found Gus in that outhouse, she was soiled and wet from strangers' urine. There was a note in her diaper. It was written in Gil's handwriting."

Kat pushed open the screen to let out a second cat. "What did it say?"

"'See how easy it is to lose what you love?'"

"How do you know it's his?"

Olive expected a different response. More like, what is that supposed to mean?

"Your father used to write Cal an occasional note on his billings when we were his customers, the most recent one after we'd stopped buying seed from his company and the story about Cal's new tomato came out."

"Don't call him my father."

"I recognized the handwriting."

Kat put her hands on her hips. "That's what I don't get. Why you guys ever did business with him in the first place. You're supposed to be leaders."

"He used to produce untreated seeds before he got into Genmods. His hybrid was the original ancestor of Cal's Augusta Girl. Gil could be retaliating. The kidnapping could be a warning to stop nosing around."

"Who's nosing around? I'm not following."

Olive was still saving the fact that that she'd seen her father and her fiancé together. For now, holding back on Kat's check should get some answers.

"I think your father may be behind the greenhouse ransack, which means he might know something about the circumstances behind Cris Villalobos's death, and I know his company is trying to take our farm."

"I don't believe it. That bastard wouldn't wreck his competition's crops out of jealousy," Kat said. "He doesn't own emotions. He'd do it for financial reasons or if there's something for him to gain. I can't see him kidnapping a kid." Kat looked away, shook her head, eyes watering in a way that surprised Olive, until she remembered Kat at Cris's memorial when she wore the same sad expression.

"How did you know Cris?" The question came out of the blue. Kat reacted by shaking her head slowly.

"He was shortstop on the baseball team and I was the bat girl. Years ago."

Kat would have been in her formative years and shortstops were heroes. It wasn't that hard to imagine Kat as a girl dressed in a baseball uniform, rushing to the plate to pick up bats and into the field to pick up foul balls.

"Did Gil know Cris?"

"He sponsored the baseball team."

Kat retreated into the living room without inviting her in or sending her away, so she opened the screen and walked inside. Ariela followed with the kids, tossing her satchel on the overstuffed velveteen couch. Ariela pulled out a Ziploc with several perfect balls the size of walnuts inside. She opened the bag and the room quickly filled with unmistakable scent of herb. A Tibetan Tanka hung on the wall above the old stone fireplace. Buddha sat cross-legged facing the viewer. A diminutive woman wrapped her legs around his waist, her back arched in ecstasy.

"I'm not Buddhist, if that's what you're thinking. I take spiritual power wherever it speaks to me, and you don't have to be Buddhist to appreciate Tibetan art."

The Tanka's luster and stark white background on old yellowed walls indicated it was new.

"An expensive piece of art," Ariela said.

She shrugged.

Ariela gazed at the man and woman in sexual bliss. "I miss that feeling."

She had to stop her mother from digressing on one of her sexual tangents. "I remember you saying your boyfriend likes to buy you things."

"Robert. No. Eastern philosophy scares him. One more fracture in his dense skull." She pulled back her dreds, wound them into a bun, slipped the elastic tie and secured it in one practiced movement.

"I thought you loved him. Joined at the hip."

"We had a fight. He said he'd fix my bathroom sink. Which he didn't. Moron. Then he told me he couldn't see me for a while. Just like that. Cold turkey. Out of the blue. No explanation. He said it was none of my business why. Dick."

Right now, Olive knew more about Johnson and Gil Souza that Kat did, and guessed that Johnson had broken it off because Souza had threatened him. "Where is he now?"

"Right now, since it's noon on a Thursday, he's at the Beach Café playing pool, eating fish tacos and working on a beer belly." Kat's eyes narrowed. "Why are you asking about him?"

Byrd whined that he wanted to go home. As Olive scanned the room, looking for something to trigger an insight, Ariela took the kids outside. One wall was painted aubergine, the others were the color of yellowed teeth with black spots creeping up from the moldings. The random running shoes, boots and flip flops by the door made it clear the house was shared by several young, probably single, women who otherwise couldn't afford the rent. Paperbacks leaned against each other on the cinder block shelf.

"What are you thinking?" Kat scowled.

"I'm thinking cool digs." What Olive really thought was, a house with potential if you had money. If not, no matter how many times you painted, dusted, swept or wiped the place down, a palpable futility seeped from the walls. She handed Kat her severance check and went outside.

Ariela and Byrd sat cross-legged on the roof of the Jeep, staring out over the pasture. Gus was snugged into Ariela's lap. The last thing Olive needed right now was someone falling off the roof of the Jeep, so she whistled to warn the trio that she was on the approach. No surprise, no clumsy moves.

Her mother opened an eye and looked down from her questionable perch. "I'm teaching my grandson to meditate."

"No," Byrd said. "We're hiding from ticks."

Olive held out her arms for Gus and opened the middle door to place her in the car seat. Byrd balked. "I'm afraid."

Olive assured him he was safe, and when he shrunk from her, she grabbed his shirt and firmly pulled him off the Jeep.

"The ticks will get me." Byrd clamped his arms around her neck, choking her. He refused to put his feet on the ground until she placed him squarely in his car seat. He knew how to buckle up, thank you god, and as he did, she pulled out a square Tupperware container from her bag and handed each child a cube of cheddar.

"How does pizza for lunch sound?" she asked.

"Pepperoni," Byrd shouted, his mood a rapid shift from frightened to zealous.

Meanwhile, Ariela remained on the car's roof, still cross-legged, sweeping an arm across the meadow, her bracelets tinkling. "Look at this place. It's a petri dish for Lyme disease."

"That's what you told Byrd?" Lyme was no joke. Olive knew a farmer who had died from the disease last year, leaving a wife and two small children, but kids did not need to be instilled with the fear of deadly insects every time you took them on a hike.

"I have repellent," Ariela said, "but I left it at the house because I had no idea we'd be in wild lands. White vinegar. Ticks hate the smell of vinegar. If you'd told me, I would have brought it." She climbed down almost gracefully and slipped in the passenger seat. As they drove out, she rolled down the window and gazed outside, smiling slightly, the wind blowing her hair back. "We're a good team, Love, and I always knew we would be."

The sneaker wave comment hit Olive by surprise—she couldn't name the emotion that came over her, or more likely the cacophony of emotions, except that they didn't feel good. An undertow of acid reflux.

In ten minutes they pulled into the restaurant parking lot. The interior smelled like beer and yeast. Olive scanned the room and recognized the guy in the oversized army jacket that had distracted her the day Gus was taken. He rounded a corner of the pool table, rubbing blue chalk on his cue stick. Another pool stick leaned on the pool table, so Olive assumed he wasn't alone. She glanced around the parlor but no one else was here, except a couple at the beer bar. He bent over the pool table and aimed his cue stick to sink a ball. Smack. The balls scattered and before they stopped rolling, a man walked out of the restroom and grabbed his pool stick. Robert Johnson. Standing, and without Gil Souza, he looked more brutish than when she'd seen him at the café. His Billabong board shorts and his baggy T-shirt couldn't hide the soft beer belly, despite broad surfer shoulders. Flip flops, Polynesian tattoos around his ankle and wrist and buzzed red hair that framed a ruddy complexion and dumb features.

One look at Johnson and Gus screamed. Olive hugged the child more tightly and pressed her head to her neck.

"Let's go. We got what we were looking for."

But Ariela wasn't ready to leave. She pointed her first finger, jangling her bracelets. "Hey. You with the shorts." He looked up from aiming at the pool balls as Ariela spread her arms like a magpie ready for a fight. "Yes, you."

Johnson looked startled as Ariela walked toward him, thrusting her finger in his face. She chanted the language Olive had hated her entire life, until now. Then he saw Olive standing a couple of feet from the exit.

"What the fuck are you doing here?" he said.

Olive grabbed Byrd's hand and turned to exit, but Ariela wasn't finished. She walked up to Johnson and pinched his cheek. Then, she grabbed his cue stick and strode toward Olive. "How's that for gathering evidence?"

Both kids had fallen asleep and Ariela was atypically quiet after the confrontation with Johnson. They each took a child in their arms and carried them from the car into the house without a sound from anyone.

Cal sat at the dining room table, talking on the phone. He hadn't shaved. His lips were white and his face dehydrated. Olive sat down and waited until he was off the phone, then told him about tracking down Kat and Johnson.

He looked away, shaking his head softly. "Deep end."

"Yeah, I'm really sorry?" She had been so bent on finding a crack in this hard pan truth, that she hadn't planned what she would do if she found Johnson. The likelihood of seeing the man in the jacket was all she needed to be convinced. She told him this. But the words sounded weak, climbing over the boulders of shame.

She smelled the tinny scent of stress on Cal's breath as he called Detective Rogers's extension.

They both rose at the sound of a car pulling up on the gravel driveway. Cal opened the front door as Rogers parked his green sedan and walked to the front door that Olive had left open.

"This is not calling me first." Rogers remained on the front door mat, making it clear he had no desire to come inside their home.

"The question is, what would you have done if I did?" Olive looked at Cal as she responded to Rogers's criticism. He was still upset with her. She wouldn't have felt as bad if he'd been angry, but he was let down.

"We'd send a patrolman to question him."

"They wouldn't know what to ask, Henry."

"At least our daughter would not be traumatized."

"That wasn't my intention, Cal." That was lame, and there were no do-overs.

"What was your intention?" Rogers asked without sarcasm, so she answered as truthfully as she could find words for.

Ariela came in the room with the pool cue. "I have evidence. I took this from the jacket man."

"I'll take it," said Rogers.

Olive glanced at Cal, who looked as if he was about to track down Johnson himself, coiled so tight if she touched him with even a calming hand, he'd spring.

"Henry, you were going to look into Inventiveness, the mortgage company that is foreclosing on us?"

He tisked. "On my agenda."

"Meantime, Best Seeds owns at least a dozen agricultural parcels up and down the coast, including the parcel next door. I have the parcel maps."

Rogers appeared to be waiting for her to make a point.

"What stands out, all of the parcels border the railroad tracks."

Today, like every day since Cris had died, she was shot out of a canon and her information landed like a dud at Cal's feet.

"What does that tell you, Olive?" Rogers asked.

"I can't get my head around it." So many pieces of information didn't fit together in a clear picture.

Cal looked at Rogers, level-eye-to-eye connection of a man who suddenly understood. "Freight," he said, matter-of-factly. "He wants to use the rail to transport products."

Henry took out his notepad and clicked his pen. "What kind of products?"

"Don't know. But maybe you could find out before my wife does, for once."

Cal draped his arm around Olive as Rogers headed to his sedan with a promise he'd look into all of it. He waited until Rogers drove down the road before she felt him turn her shoulders firmly toward him. "I'm sorry for doubting you. Tell Ariela to watch the kids and get those parcel maps. I'll meet you in the truck in five."

Cal, behind the wheel of the pickup, his elbow out the window, gave her a shout. "C'mon. Time for a little field trip."

The first parcel was located on the outskirts of a quiet beach community in the southern part of the county at the end of a long dirt road in the cleft of gently sloping hillsides. Both sides of the hills were covered in strawberry plants.

The road ended at the railroad track. Fieldworkers bent over at painful angles and picked while others hustled to stack their flats at the edge of the field. They were paid by the flat, rather than the hour, spurring them up and down the rows, some running, not stopping for water or rest.

Agricultural fields filled both sides of the road as they entered the industrial zone of Watsonville and crossed the railroad tracks to the backside of town where colorful, repurposed buildings brightened the urban landscape. The funky charm buoyed Olive. Innovative people had transformed an entire block of old wooden warehouses into artistic storefronts. This cultural renaissance be-longed to the Mexicans and Latinos who worked and lived there—

skilled field workers and their families who grew and harvested the nation's food, who drove trucks, prepared food, cleaned houses, started small businesses, tended the sick and aged and taught in the schools. Many worked in the shadows.

She and Cal walked toward the small café. Inside, the walls had been painted in colorful murals and decorated with historic photographs of the town's old sugar beet factory. Cal handed her a coffee. They sipped from their mugs and studied the photographs.

They drove on a frontage road that paralleled the tracks, heading southeast out of the town toward the rural part of the county toward the large parcel that was zoned industrial. Passed the rusty remnants of a sugar beet plant to an old neighborhood that housed the families of sugar beet workers during the height of the industry. Today, the houses were low-income rentals. They kept driving on the outskirts of the neighborhood until they were forced to stop because a cyclone fence had been put up across the road with a large no trespassing sign posted on the chain-link gate. On the other side of the fence, the rails disappeared into the tarmac.

"Track's gone." Cal sounded disappointed, leaned back in his seat and raked his hair until it stood in thick tufts.

"Not gone," Olive said. "Underground."

They turned around and cruised down one of the streets lined on both sides with shoebox houses. Cal pulled the truck to the curb and parked.

They sat in silence for a few moments, thinking. The surrounding small houses had been built on postage stamp lots. All of them were painted beige. Bikes and tricycles had been left outside on dead lawns. Most of the lawns had plastic wading pools. Cal broke the quiet. "You know, I've researched sugar beets and they aren't a bad crop. Monotonous, but profitable if you do it right."

"Surprised to hear you say that."

"Let's just say I get why someone would grow them. The government loans on the beets because it's a commodity with a high demand. The loan pays for labor and expenses. Here's the clincher. If the crop doesn't make enough profit to pay back the loan, the feds take over the crop and use the revenues to pay down the loan. The balance owed is forgiven. It's pretty much win-win for the grower."

Olive found it auspicious her husband knew so much about sugar beets. She stared at the parcel map and looked up at their surroundings, waiting for clarity, but it just wouldn't come.

28

Gil Souza glanced down at his boots—round toed, worn but polished. His canvas windbreaker over the brown Polo shirt tucked into pressed Dockers and a wide-brimmed felt hat topped off his contrived appearance of a special kind of farmer, one with sophistication.

He rubbed his chin, which stung slightly from Aqua Velva and a close shave, and stared out the window of the county courthouse, annoyed by the vagrant who slept outside the building under an oleander hedge. Why was this bum, a filthy eyesore and a drain of county revenue, not the one on trial here? Answer: some small-time peckerwood organicos had a problem with progress.

Gil jumped when his attorney Kent Ferguson held out a cup of coffee in its brown cardboard sleeve. "You're formidable."

Gil took the coffee. French Roast, his least favorite, but he needed the caffeine for the fight ahead and took a bitter swig.

"Ready to set some precedence?" asked Ferguson.

"Lead the way."

For good luck, Gil patted the oak paneling as he entered Room 11 and walked up the center aisle to the front row. The plaintiffs were already seated on the opposite side of the courtroom and the jury hadn't entered. He imagined the hostile looks when they did come in and reassured himself that not everyone in this county was a liberal. In fact, some patches of the county were as conservative as it got in the rural Americana sense. Maybe the case would go his way. Probably not. But that didn't matter. He had a plan.

Gil waited until the jury entered before taking off his wind-breaker so this group could register from his attire that he was a well-groomed, working man whose livelihood, like all farmers, depended on the land and good weather.

The sound of nylons bristling down the aisle caught his attention. Clancie Sternik, in the same tailored black skirt and long fitted jacket she'd worn for the deposition, plus nylons. She strode toward the front of the room with her soft black leather briefcase dangling from a skinny wrist and settled in next to the plaintiff. The judge walked in. Another woman. If there were a god, he was playing a trick, or maybe god was a woman, too. Not that Gil believed in God. He didn't. Heaven and hell were right here on earth, comingling.

"All rise," said the bailiff.

Gil bowed his head, trying to appear humble.

"The case of Humpback Farm and Santa Cruz County v. Best Seeds, Inc. and Gilbert Souza will come to order." The judge snapped the gavel as if it were a locker room towel.

Sternik wasted no time calling Gil to the stand. He walked across the courtroom, feeling all eyes upon him as he put up an arm and pledged to tell the truth, the whole truth and nothing but the truth, "so help me God," his first lie of the day.

"Mr. Souza. How are you this morning?"

"As I said the first time we met, Ms. Sternik, I'd rather be working."

"And for the record, I would like to ask Mr. Ferguson to restrain his client from further snarky comments. Mr. Souza, the plaintiffs Frank Smith and Yvonne Searles claim you and Best Seeds, Inc. have violated their rights by contaminating their crops with a transgenic material originating from your experimental field of GE Brussels sprouts, which is in clear violation of the Santa Cruz County Precautionary Moratorium on GMO field tests and plants. Are you aware of this moratorium, Mr. Souza?"

Gil was aware, alright, of Sternik's thick black-framed glasses and her round brown eyes doing an endoscopy on his soul. "I am aware."

"Are you aware my clients are suing your company for negligence and for contaminating their crops, causing them to lose tens of thousands of dollars and, further, to sully their reputation among their customers?"

Gil glanced at the jury. They looked on the whole ordinary enough but looks were deceiving in a town where the Sierra Club was a conservative cause.

He would have to convey that demonizing GMOs was a misunderstanding based on left-wing propaganda.

"Your honor, please direct the witness to answer the question."

"Mr. Souza," said the judge. "Answer the question."

"My company applied for a permit from the USDA animal and plant health inspection service to conduct field tests before the moratorium. We procured a permit from the FDA since we're experimenting with a pesticide that will kill harmful Lepidoptera. You may not know the Brussels sprout is a tricky plant to grow, threatened continuously by fungi and the cabbage maggot from the time it's put in the ground to ..."

"Mr. Souza," said the judge. "Just answer the question."

"Yes, I am aware of the plaintiffs' claims."

"For the sake of the jury, Mr. Souza, can you explain the difference between genetically modifying a plant the old-fashioned way and GMOs today?"

"Innovation." Gil took a deep breath. "For millennia, cultivars like myself and my forefathers have been improving plants by selecting those with desirable traits, including wild species, and breeding them. Roses, peaches, string beans. Today, we use cutting edge engineering to breed plants to meet our current needs within specific landscapes."

"So," said Sternik, "the difference is traditional modification is between a plant and another plant. In the case of GMOs today, we're inserting into the plant kingdom the DNA of a, say, chemical.

Gil had it memorized. "A more accurate definition is that genetically engineered plants are made with techniques that alter the molecular or cell biology of an organism by means that are not

193

possible under natural conditions or processes, a miracle of technology."

"Very good, Mr. Souza. Now, I'm going to read into the record an excerpt from the United Nations paper on the biohazards of Genetically Modified Organisms, relative to containment."

"Objection," said Ferguson. "Irrelevant."

"Overruled."

"Quote, 'when a foreign gene, also referred to as DNA, is produced it is within the confines of a highly specialized laboratory with skilled scientists and people handling the product who are generally trained to deal with the positive output as well as the negative ones and the unperceived consequences which comprise the major amount of risk involved. However, when it gets out of the laboratory, the element of risk associated with it passes into the hands of those who may not be associated with the technology or who would not understand the technology at all. The commercial activities about the technology make the exposure still wider confounded with the risk involved in its release into an environment.' End quote."

"Your question, Ms. Clancy," said the judge.

"My question your honor is, are you, Mr. Souza, one of those who do not understand the risks of the toxicity of neonicotinoids in your experimental sites?"

"I do understand, but it's also my company's responsibility to weigh the potential risks against the proven benefits."

Sternik reached for something on her desk and Gil felt a foreboding. She was about to spring something on him.

Olive took a seat in the rear corner of the courtroom, where Souza could not see her. When Attorney Clancy Sternik called Souza to the stand, she moved behind someone large enough to block the line of vision between them. She watched Sternik introduce into evidence piece of paper that she waved in front of the jury.

"I have here a letter," Sternik said, "from APHIS, listing those entities permitted to propagate and grow GMOs in Santa Cruz County prior to the county-wide moratorium on GMOs. Are you on that list Mr. Souza?"

Ferguson rose to object. "Facetious, your honor."

"Restate," the judge said. "I want to hear what Mr. Souza has to say."

So did Olive

Sternik held up the paper. "Best Seeds, Inc. is at the top of this list. APHIS doesn't release the specific sites operated by private parties, as a rule. I submit this as evidence that Best Seeds, Inc. has, in fact, propagated and grown genetically engineered plant product."

"Mr. Souza, do you continue to propagate and grow GMO Brussels sprouts on these sites adjacent to the plaintiffs' farm, or elsewhere, after the county placed its moratorium on GMOs?"

"Objection," said Ferguson. "This case isn't about 'elsewhere.'"

"Sustained."

"The defendant has not answered the question."

"Answer the question Mr. Souza."

"Could you repeat the question?"

"Do you continue to propagate or grow genetically engineered plants on any of the sites that APHIS granted you a permit?"

Gil's chest itched. Scratching would indicate guilt. "No. I do not."

"Do you know what the penalty is for violating that ban?"

"Not offhand."

"One thousand dollars a day or six months in jail, for the record. That's for each day you violate the county ordinance. That adds up to three hundred and sixty-five thousand dollars a year. Do you realize this?"

Idiots. No one, not this smart-ass lawyer or the gawking jury realized that farming wasn't about growing things. It was about running a business. He stared down at his folded hands. The cuff of his Pendleton was frayed.

"Mr. Souza, answer the question," said the judge.

He nodded. "So I've heard."

"Are you aware that the USDA has not approved consumption of the strain of Brussels sprouts you're trying to grow?"

It didn't escape Gil's attention that she'd exaggerated the s.

"I'm in the process of perfecting that strain. That's the point of test sites."

"Are you attempting also to perfect your plants' unrestrained release of pollen?"

"You know as well as I do that it's impossible to control wind currents, the movement of fog and where a bird decides to defecate. In fact, I'd hate to try."

"Mr. Souza," she opened her notes. "In your deposition you are documented as saying you are aware of your responsibility for your products' behavior after planted. Is that true?"

"But not the bees. I have no control over the behavior of bees. Or wind."

"The plaintiffs beg to differ, Mr. Souza. What bees do is very much within your scope of responsibility. You must take bee behavior into account. But worse, pesticide, such as the ones you spray on your crops, kills bees. It also kills butterflies and other beneficial pollinators. Isn't it true that one of the worst consequences of pesticide resistant GMOs is that it allows growers to apply more pesticides in the field? Do you take responsibility for that?"

"Objection, your honor," said Ferguson. "Irrelevant."

"Not at all but withdrawn." Sternik seemed to study the jurors' reactions. Olive followed her gaze. Collectively, the jury looked, in one word, glum. "That'll be all for now, Mr. Souza. Witness dismissed."

The judge called a recess, and Gil walked from the witness box down the aisle and rows of spectators. Shock passed over his face when he recognized her. The Post woman. Not the Gypsy. The daughter. She looked straight at him with a disdain that people saved for criminals.

He wasn't a criminal, Gil told himself, as he strode down the courtroom's outer hallway, glancing out the floor-to-ceiling plate glass. The vagrant had vacated his spot in the oleander hedge. Across the street the Jury Room called.

29

If you asked Cal what the biggest issue facing farmers was, he'd say money. If you asked him what the biggest issue facing organic farmers was, he'd say money. His standing joke, if a farmer won the lottery, what would be their greatest need? Money. They never had enough. Some years were better than others, some longer, some years suffered worse weather, some years the work harder, but the pressure was unrelenting.

Olive and Cal had no savings left and the bank issuing their line of credit was slow as a herd of slugs. If they waited any longer, they wouldn't have a farm.

The bank was calling. Auspicious.

"We've decided to release a partial payment on your requested LOC," said the loan officer, a woman this time.

Olive didn't tell her the installment was insufficient to pay two months of mortgage arrears and the crew's bi-weekly wages. When she told Cal, they weighed their options—pay the crew (what was left of it) or pay the mortgage or pay the crew a partial payment and ask the mortgage company if they would accept only one month's payment, which was unlikely considered their chicken shit record so far.

Cal called a meeting of his crew in the packing tent. Some squatted on the tamped dirt floor, others sat on crates. Cal stood before them and Olive watched their faces. Disappointment. Glimmers of despair. As Cal went on, heads bowed. Deep sighs. Someone flicked a stone across the space. Two young men walked out. Lo siento, Cal said.

When the men and women disbursed, he repeated to Olive what he'd said: "'Those of you who wish to remain, I promise to pay you as soon as possible. Those who wish to go or must look for other work have my blessing. Ve con Dios.'"

The annual First Day of Spring Parade that Shell Bean Farm had participated in for the past four years was tomorrow. March twentieth, when the sun crosses the celestial equator and night and day are equal lengths everywhere on the planet. While the weather became more unpredictable with each revolution of the planet, earth and sun remained on course. Earth and sun were Olive's standard as she and Cal debated whether to drop out of the parade this year because of their pressures. They decided this wasn't the year to skip. This was the year to practice constancy wherever they could. Cal strapped hay bales onto the floor of the flatbed, the first stage of transforming the truck into a float. Brody showed up to help, tying down the shade canopy to the truck rails with hitch knots, the same knots he used at the market.

Cal turned the corner of Cathcart Street onto Pacific Avenue, the main street of town. Families lined both sides of the street for three long blocks. Ariela, who wore a low-cut peasant blouse and calf-length prairie skirt with cowboy boots, tossed walnuts from the flatbed into the street. The shells made a lovely clatter as they landed on the street. The teenage girls on the salt-water taffy float behind them threw handfuls of taffy. Byrd hung on the back of the truck and stared at the taffy that dotted the street mere yards from him. He watched enviously as the children scrambled from the sidewalk to snatch as much as they could, ignoring the walnuts.

Olive grinned until her jaw hurt and her arms were tired from holding Gus on one hip, waving with her free hand. Brody stood at the back of the truck bed, arms crossed over his chest, cowboy hat tilted down, chewing a piece of hay.

As they approached the announcer's stand, the Master of Ceremony introduced their float. "Shell Bean Farm owned by one of Santa Cruz's most beloved farm families, Cal and Olive Post." A blush rose to Olive's cheeks and she felt like hiding while Ariela took a step closer to the rails and blew kisses at the crowd.

Friends on the sidewalk hooted. Cal—his arm out the window—gave short waves. Another shower of candy arced from the float into the street. Little wrapped taffies bounced lightly as kids rushed from the sidewalks to snatch the treats.

The temptation was too much for a small boy. Byrd jumped off the tail of the flat bed onto the tarmac, intending to grab some candies. He tripped on impact and fell flat in the path of the approaching float. It happened so quickly the driver was unaware and Byrd was below his line of vision. Olive screamed. The driver—a young man wearing sunglasses—stared at her, confused. He raised his arms from the steering wheel, like, what are you asking of me?

"Halt." She put up her hands. Byrd had landed mere yards from the oncoming float. An out of body scream in a voice she didn't recognize issued from her mouth as Brody jumped from the flatbed and scooped Byrd up in one fluid motion. He tossed him back into the truck bed into Olive's arms and jumped back on board.

"You could've been smashed into a pancake, kid," said Brody, "and then we'd be eating you for dinner."

Byrd's mouth quivered and his lower eyelids dripped fat tears. "I want candy," he whispered, as the float rolled forward.

That afternoon Ariela and Byrd colored duck eggs in deep pastels. They stacked small rocks into cairns, which added a pagan quality to the dining room table. By six o'clock in the evening, everyone was assembled. Cal sat at one end of the table, cattycorner to Brody. A grandchild sat on either side of Ariela, who held up a wine glass of sparkling apple cider.

"Here's to the coming light. May it shine on us."

"And Brody," said Cal, "for rescuing Byrd."

They were laughing when Olive walked through the kitchen door carrying an Easter quiche with a hardboiled egg in its center. Brody rose from his chair as she entered the dining room.

Cal raised his glass. "To the cook, my wife who lines me out."

"I've never heard that expression," said Ariela. "What does it mean 'lines me out'?"

"She keeps his brain from knotting up." Brody, still standing, lifted his glass of cider.

Ariela tossed back her hair and pushed out her chest, leaning across the toward Brody. "Do you always stand when a woman walks into the room?"

"Only a woman I respect."

"Darling," she said. "I don't trust a man who stands when a woman walks into the room."

Brody took his seat as Olive set the quiche on the table and began to serve wedges. "Why's that?"

Cal shook his head. "Please don't elaborate. We have kids at the table."

Ariela scowled. "Careful, Outlaw. It was me who performed a rain dance. And did it rain?"

"It did."

"And now you can put those famous tomatoes of yours in the ground, correct?"

"Correct," Cal said. "We're prepping the soil tomorrow so we can put in the first wave on Thursday. Maybe you can perform a fertility dance."

"Careful, Outlaw."

"My mom doesn't like you to call my dad Outlaw," said Byrd.

Brody asked, "How many waves you planting this year, bro?"

"Two waves in two blocks. We'll stagger the planting with three to four weeks between. That way the harvest is spread out."

"You need an extra hand, I'm here for you, man."

Olive passed Gus a small serving of the quiche and a single string bean, thinking of the work ahead.

"Let's hold hands," said Ariela. "This will seal our good energy for Cal's tomatoes. Not only that, it's Olive's birthday."

Byrd pulled back his hand. "I don't want to hold hands."

"And it's not my birthday." Olive rose from the table and went to the kitchen to bring out the oval carrot Spring cake with cream cheese frosting she'd baked the night before. As she walked back to the table, cake in hand, Ariela was waiting for her. "It is your birthday."

Olive set down the cake. "No. It is not."

"Her birthday's in July," Cal said.

"She didn't tell you?" Ariela said.

"Tell me what?"

"Long story," Olive said.

"It's not a long story," Ariela said. "It's a good story. You tell it."

"When I was a child, she changed both of our birthdays to the Vernal Equinox so that, and I quote, 'no matter how disappointing the day, at the very least we can look forward to more light.'"

Ariela nodded. "See?"

"You never told me this," Cal said. "That's kind of cool."

"I try to forget it. As a kid, I believed March twentieth was my birthday up to applying for a social security card and being denied because the birthday I'd given didn't match my birth records."

Brody let out a long, low whistle.

"How'd you do that?" Byrd asked.

"The how isn't important, kiddo," said Brody. "The trick is when. That was a whistle moment."

Cal shook his head as Ariela pulled out a small silver flask with turquoise studs.

"Since it's my pagan birthday, too…" She untwisted the top and took a swig. Then another and, in case anyone were about to ask, which Olive, for one, was not, she informed the table that for fear of spreading germs she didn't share her flask with anyone.

An ubiquitous unmarked white van drove up Shell Bean Way as Olive walked along the edge of the farm toward the washing shed, carrying a red, gallon-sized jug of lemonade for the workers who'd stayed on. The driver made a three-point turn at the head of the road near the house.

The dwindled crew was taking their lunch break—four men and two women—after unloading one hundred flats of tomato starts from the back of the truck. They had stacked the flats at each end of the beds. Tomorrow they would walk through the rows and transfer the starts to the ground, grueling, backbreaking, repetitive work. They didn't complain.

As Olive filled their cups and thermoses with lemonade, the white van paused in the middle of the road beside the stacks of seedlings. Nothing especially out of the norm. She waited for the van's front door to open, someone to get out and join the crew. But that didn't happen. The driver wore a hoodie pulled up, a baseball cap and sunglasses. Ubiquitous. As the van moved forward, Olive noticed the mud-caked front license plate. The back license, too. She put down the lemonade and started toward the truck, leaving the shade of the canopy. Heri followed.

"Hey!" She waved her arms. But the van kept moving.

"Did you recognize him?" she asked Heriberto. "Quien?"

He shook his head, "No se."

That night Olive lay in bed while the full moon and its long shadows kept watch over the farm. Nature's sentry wasn't enough to keep her from visualizing the unfamiliar van with its dodgy driver in hoodie and shades that had cruised up the road that afternoon. She'd told Cal about the van, but he brushed it off as someone's wrong turn. As she lay on her side, cupping Cal's back, she couldn't stop worrying.

"I can hear you thinking," Cal said.

"Can't help it."

He turned flat and propped an arm behind his head.

"Is this your listening pose?" she asked, hopefully.

"Yep."

"Do you ever worry that our tomato flats will get stolen? They're out there in the open stacked at the edge of the rows right by the road and no one's watching them."

He shifted to face her, ran his hand down her back, his palm always surprisingly soft. "I worry about a lot of things, Petunia, but someone stealing the tomato flats isn't one of them."

Those were their last words before he fell back asleep, his breath collapsing into soft snoring. She concentrated on her own breathing, inhaling deeply to the count of five, exhaling, but after five rounds she remained alert and began listing the "things" they worried about: the mortgage, the foreclosure, their line of credit, when to pay the crew, and now the tomatoes. Maybe she would get a tattoo, after all. A deep green vine up her left leg with clusters of bright red Augusta Girls on her calf ... the feel of the needle staunching her worry.

Cal's face was blanched when he barged through the kitchen door the next morning while Olive sipped tea. He looked ill, and he smelled of cold air. His sentences broke, his voice was hoarse. She couldn't make sense of the urgency.

"Someone stole the tomatoes." He stood stalk still as their eyes met and his panic became their panic. "All of them. Gone."

The white van.

He shook his head. "We're gonna tank."

When the policewoman asked who would steal Cal's tomato starts, Olive couldn't think of one person except Gil Souza, her default scapegoat. But he would be too wrapped up in his court case to step over the line in this way.

She told the cop, a young woman, this wasn't the first time. Their greenhouse had been ransacked in February. The cop's voice sounded far off. "Ma'am. What make of van? Ma'am."

She recalled the plus emblem on the front grill. "Chevy. The license plate was caked in mud and the driver wore a hoodie and sunglasses so I couldn't make him out."

"A male?"

"Couldn't tell."

Cal shouted at Byrd to stop playing in the box truck, his voice so cross the cop stopped asking questions. When Byrd kept jumping with joy off the boxes, Cal leaned into the back of the truck and pulled Byrd out by his shirt.

Olive had never seen him be rough with Byrd, who was sobbing. She put her arms around her boy and held him while Cal harshly reprimanded him about playing in the box truck when they were trying to load it.

"This isn't about Byrd," Olive said. "Don't take it out on him."

Cal's shoulders shook. He choked and finally cried. He picked up Byrd and they sobbed into each other's neck. Losing it. The pervasive malevolence she'd sensed ever since Cris died had taken their plants and the farm. But, she vowed, it would not take her husband.

30

When the children fell asleep in their car seats, Olive pulled onto the shoulder of the Coast Highway and climbed into the Jeep's rear compartment as Ariela lowered the rear door, on Olive's instructions, but didn't latch it. As Ariela drove, Olive rode the rest of the way with a blanket over herself.

The Jeep slowed and Ariela chimed, "A gate across the road."

Byrd piped up, sleepily, "Where's my mom?"

"Go back to sleep, sonny," Ariela said.

"I want my mom."

Olive looked out from the blanket. The sky was dense with redwood branches, which meant they were close, but if Byrd didn't calm down in the next thirty seconds, she would call off their plan.

"She's back at the café, sonny," Ariela lied, "paying the bills so you can eat."

"I'm not sonny."

"For the love of Pete. We'll pick up mommy on the way back and I'll buy you a donut. Now, look out the window for bears and mountain lions. And do it quietly while I get this intercom thing to open the gate."

"Where are we going?"

"I'm going to read a man's tarot cards. He has cookies."

"What kind?"

Gil Souza's gruff voice came over the intercom. Too late to back out now, Olive thought, as Ariela answered with a sultry hello. The electric gate buzzed, and Olive imagined it swinging open as the Jeep inched forward.

"Nice big house straight ahead," Ariela said. "I'm backing into a grove of redwoods for parking."

"What are you talking about?" asked Byrd.

"You're my co-pilot. Make sure I don't hit anything." Ariela pulled the emergency brake lever. "Wake up your sister. Now, let's see what kind of cookies he has."

After Ariela unloaded the kids from their car seats, Olive checked her iPhone and set the timer for sixty minutes, the amount of time she had to find a way into the house and back to the car while Ariela distracted Souza by reading his cards.

From the back window of the Jeep, she waited until the trio walked up the driveway past a large circle of lawn toward the cathedral front door of a handsome ranch-style house with a detached three-car garage.

Ariela turned and gave Olive a nod as the front door opened.

Gil strode to the front door of his spacious foyer, catching his reflection in the hall mirror. He was surprised to see himself smiling. He adjusted the collar of his long-sleeved Pendleton shirt, a purposely conservative choice to balance the hard lefty at the front door.

Funny, he thought. The last time he'd worn this shirt was at the National Farm Bureau convention in Las Vegas. He didn't gamble because he didn't believe in using up his luck on cards but, he thought to himself, there might be more than luck in this gypsy woman's deck. This was a woman who knew how to talk to a man, even a man like him who was constantly on the defense when anyone tried to throw a wrench into his day. This was some wrench.

His boot heels thudded on the cold gray slate of his ranch style home, and when he opened the front door, she was standing there, her back to him, a small child on one hip and a boy clinging to her hand.

He almost shut the door. But she turned quickly and her eyes were so big, and her red lipstick had the effect of milkweed to a monarch.

"I wasn't expecting kids," he said.

"We never do." She laughed in a way that melted the barbs. "I'm babysitting. They're very well-behaved." The little girl squirmed from the woman's arms, trying to get down. "My daughter raises them with an iron hand."

Gil doubted that. Those lax liberal types let their kids get away with murder. "Is this the one that ended up in the john?"

She put a finger to her lip.

Okay, we won't go there.

She arched an eyebrow. "This is quite a place. I hope you don't have dogs."

If he had dogs, they'd be barking. "I used to have dogs. Ridgebacks. The last one died, and I don't have the time or energy to train another properly."

"What kind of cookies do you have?" the boy said.

A cute kid, but no manners, Gil thought. Maybe he did have a tin of shortbread somewhere, when the gypsy interrupted his thinking and asked for a tour of the premises before they got started.

"That'll give my grandkids a chance to get out their beans before the tarot reading." She smiled, flashing those big white bossy teeth that went so well with her full, red lips. "Where are your servants?"

Gil ignored her sarcasm. Never apologize for your wealth. That was his motto. He headed for the carriage house. His collection of cars would impress her.

A bright yellow convertible '65 Corvette gleamed next to the black Stingray. She uttered not a word. No exclamation, no gesture, He expected her to gush, like women normally do when men show them expensive cars.

He shrugged. "You're probably the Austin Healy type."

"Corvettes leave nothing to the imagination."

"Which is why you drive a golf cart." He smiled, couldn't help it.

She gave him a nasty look, and he was about to take it back when he realized he hadn't seen her cart out front because the kids had thrown him off. "Where'd you park?"

"In your redwood grove. I drove my daughter's Jeep because I have the kids. Car seats."

Gil remembered that Jeep. The Post woman had parked in front of the North Coast Café, minutes after he'd received a text message from Cloris that someone had been snooping around his plant. Maybe this was a ruse, Gil thought, and the woman was here to get information from him.

"My mom's at the café doing bookwork," the boy said.

"I parked in the grove so I wouldn't spoil your lovely view of that huge and very lush front lawn that's prospering in a time of drought."

"I have a well."

The kid piped up, "I like your cars."

Gil ruffled the kid's hair. "I like you." He'd always wanted a son. Girls were too much trouble and he didn't understand them. "You want to sit in one?"

"Yeah." The boy's face lit up, and the warm sensation in Gil's chest caught him off guard. His eyes stung.

"Say 'thank you,' Byrd," his grandmother chimed.

"No need." Gil hefted the boy over the driver's door and sat him behind the wheel of the convertible. "When you grow up, I'll let you drive it. Deal?" Gil glanced sideways to see how the woman liked the sound of a future.

She looked him up and down. "You're a tall man."

Gil felt jittery, probably because he'd drunk too much coffee and couldn't eat breakfast, anticipating her visit. Deep breath.

He couldn't help smiling when she said she liked his boots. But then she said, "I'd like to see the view. You must have breathtaking panoramic views."

He didn't feel like going on a hike. "You want a three-sixty or will a one-eighty suffice?" He guessed a woman like her had caught the innuendo.

"I've seen the one-eighty." She jounced the girl on her hip.

"You're carrying her?"

"No. She has feet. Sturdy shoes. Soon as we get outside, I'll put her down."

Gil took the lead on the foot trail up the mountain. He couldn't remember the last time he'd hiked this path. Ahead was a view of the meadow where he grazed his Herefords, farther a creek and waterfall that collected into a pool where steelhead lay eggs and swam to the sea. Unlike salmon, they repeated the cycle for years. Gil liked that about steelhead. A fish that survived all that hard work of swimming up and down the mountain, out to sea, and back, instead of dying like salmon. It made the struggle worthwhile.

The boy darted off the trail toward a stand of tan oaks.

"Hey, son, careful of the poison oak." As Gil walked after the boy, he saw a cluster of Amanita phalloides. "And stay away from those." Gil could tell that his voice shocked the boy, who cringed as if he might start crying. "Step away." Gil put his arm in front of the boy and pointed to the poisonous mushrooms. As the boy slunk back to his grandmother, Gil slipped his buckskin gloves from his back pocket.

"You just hunted the first death caps of the season, son." He gave him a wink. "But these mushrooms can kill a grown man. Even me." His knees ached as he got down to examine the telltale filament beneath the cap. "Yep." He might not be able to get up without a grunt or two. "These little things can poison you just breathing their spores."

"I don't want to die," the boy said.

"Don't worry," said Ariela. "Your Bubby has an antidote."

"There is no antidote," Gil said, gruffly, "and you shouldn't give him false information."

Once the woman turned her back to console the kid, he quickly picked two deadly fungi and stuffed them in his breast pocket. He looked around and marked the spot.

"I almost lost my little girl after she sucked the nectar of a trumpet vine. Worst week of my life. She hallucinated for two days." Maybe that's why she turned out to be such a wreck. Great eye, boy. You found some good ones."

The kid looked puzzled. "Why do you want to keep it if it's poison?"

Yes, smart beyond his years. "I like keeping a few around for my enemies." Gil laughed. "See all these woods? They're full of monsters."

Olive ran along the thicket parallel to the driveway. She slipped through the unlocked front door and ran through the foyer, past the high ceiling living room on her left, taking the stairs two at a time, noting how the fourth step squeaked. She walked into the master bedroom, a spacious, masculine room with dark wood paneling. A king-sized bed with a navy-blue comforter and expensive-looking silk pillows dominated the room. Meticulous. The cream-colored popcorn rug denied a livelihood that depended on dirt. A leather chaise lounge—also navy—with indigo patterned pillows offered a panoramic view of the forest.

The room exuded *Architectural Digest* style but revealed zilch of the person, except money. No dust, no articles of clothing. No telltale books on the bedside table. Not a pillow at the wrong angle. The room was all veneer and said nothing of Gil Souza's interior.

The woman—he resisted thinking of her by her given name—
raised her arms, revealing a fleshy, surprisingly tanned midriff.
Her eyes were closed and she was breathing deeply, everything
so demonstrative. When she asked where "the last light" was, he
didn't understand. Did she mean the sun? Was she asking for a
cigarette? He could use one right about now. When she pointed to
the ridge and asked him where the last shaft of light shone when
the sun finally set, he thought it was a weird question. He'd have to
guess. And, of course, it depended on the season.

"Where you find the last light of the day," she said, catching his
gaze, "at the point where earth meets sky, the first people believe
we are closest to the spirit world. I'd like to see that place."

Hippy shit. He regretted ever inviting her to his home, yet he
pointed up mountain. Pico Verde, a unique coastal mélange, was
the highest point on his property but too steep to climb, especially
with young children. And she was wearing Western boots.

"I want to see the top," said Byrd.

The girl started to cry.

Already these kids were whining, and it would get worse if they
went farther, but this gypsy picked up the girl and spurring the boy
on with a promise of candy seemed to do the trick. She stopped
abruptly and pointed to the ground.

"A sign," she said.

"I'd bet just about everything is sign for you."

"Coyote scat. Coyote is a messenger from the spirit world."

"Wrong. Come over here, son. You'll like this."

Gil appreciated the way the boy bent over the ground to the
spot in the dirt he pointed out.

"Do you see that animal track, son?"

"I'm not your son."

"Okay, apologies. Byrd's your name. Byrd. See the paw? That's
a mountain lion. Not coyote. They have retractable claws. See how
he's kept those claws inside his paw when he's walking so you don't
see the nails in the track?" The boy nodded. "Look at the shape of
the paw." He traced the letter. "M. Like Mom. Now that's a sign."

The boy's eyes were satisfactorily round with awe, Gil decided, but he didn't want to scare the child. "Don't worry, the sound of your grandmother's bracelets has scared him away."

She straightened her shoulders, sexy without trying, and he felt a pleasant feeling, until she opened her mouth, chiming, "This is such a magical place. I'd love to be here when the light lifts from the mountain and enters the sky. I can tell you a story about the time I was on an ancient Miwuk crying spot."

"I have no patience for a story about Indians." Those stories went one of two ways, tragedy or new age ga-ga, and he didn't like either. But she went on because, as he had quickly learned, she didn't care what he thought.

He waited for her to lose her breath as they climbed the grade. She didn't. When the top of the ridge was in sight, she turned to him, flushed and—he had to admit—ravishing for a woman her age.

"Kids," she said. "Stay with Gil while I scale the peak for a quick glimpse."

"I wouldn't recommend it." She was making him nervous. He pointed to her cowgirl boots. "Those boots don't have a grip."

But she took off, scrambling like a mountain goat on all fours until she reached the peak. It had to be twenty feet straight down from there. She stood up, spread her arms over her head and looked to the sky, eyes closed as far as he could tell.

"My god, woman, sit down." He held his breath until she sat down and slid back toward him on her cushioned rear end. She came at him, exhilarated and brushing the seat of her jeans.

"Please don't do that again," he said. "You're gonna give me a heart attack. I don't want someone falling off a cliff on my property. My insurance rates would skyrocket."

She laughed. That infectious earthy gut laugh—the way women do when they've bested a man or watched him make a fool of himself—and then she held out her arms for the little girl.

Gil's legs felt weak as he headed back down the trail in the wake of her dusty rose scent.

Her mother was laughing, that robust laughter that always made Olive smile. She wasn't smiling. They were in the hallway, Souza's booming voice talking about letting the kids take a nap on his bed. She checked her watch. She had fifteen minutes before she had to get back to the Jeep.

She didn't know what she was looking for, and she wouldn't until she found it. At the end of the upstairs hallway was another door. Souza's study. The desk was tidy except for a few pieces of mail strewn beside his PC. Built in white filing cabinets took up one wall of the office. The other was covered with architectural blueprints. He was up to something. She knew it. And the blueprints were key.

She took photos, then tried the filing cabinet. The top cabinet was locked. The middle cabinet slid open. Files were arranged in alphabetical order. APHIS. Agricultural and Plant Health Inspection Service of the USDA. Inside were official permits with numbers and a lot of bureaucratic jargon she couldn't make sense of. A piece of paper was stapled to the back of the file. She lifted the file, flipped to the back cover. Stapled to the file was a two-column chart, what she guessed were APHIS permit numbers in one column and APN parcel numbers in the other. She took a picture and turned to leave but tripped on the small area rug and fell on her knees. Damn. She regained her balance and gripped the back of Souza's desk chair. The noise had probably traveled to the kitchen below. She looked more closely at the three envelopes on Souza's desk. Each had a County Recorder's office return address.

He guided her inside by the elbow, feeling a jolt to his groin from that one small touch. He repeated, "Big bed's upstairs if you want to put your grandchildren down for a nap," hoping he had the same effect on her. But she'd already staked out her territory in the kitchen and made a bee-line to the cushioned bench seat against the wall—his place.

"Gil, could you get water for the children, please?" She rummaged through that bottomless satchel and asked for green tea, placing her chin on her palm as coyly as a twenty-year-old. Gil didn't have green tea, and she grimaced at the offer of Earl Grey. She tapped the table for him to sit down across from her as the boy fidgeted with the salt and pepper shakers and the baby girl sucked one of those ugly rubber nipple substitutes.

"I don't approve of pacifiers, either," she said, "but in these situations, they're helpful at times like this."

"You're reading my mind?"

"Your facial expression. Don't worry. The children will settle in a minute or two, and when they do you can ask them, meaning the cards, a question."

The boy sat on one side of his grandmother and stared so glumly out the bay window that Gil felt like offering him something, but he didn't have kid food. No cookies. No juice. He dug into his back pocket and held out his pocketknife. The boy reached for the knife, and once more Gil wished he'd had a son.

"Now, Gilman, what is it that you want to learn from this reading?"

"Just call me Gil. What do I call you?"

She pressed against the table, her bosom swelling as he put two glasses of water on the table. "Well, you could start with my name. Ariela."

The boy guzzled his water and, panting, held out his glass. Gil refilled it.

"Is that your real name? Ariela?"

"No more questioning me. Time to ask the cards."

"I feel silly."

"That's your tough guy persona softening. If you don't want to feel silly, think of those last words you spoke to me at the café." She paused and looked into his eyes, but he couldn't meet her gaze. "Ask something general, but not vague."

The idea of voicing a question on demand felt to Gil like standing at the edge of a cold lake. He could not jump in.

"Gil?"

"I'm worried about my next land deal." His voice had caught, but she either hadn't noticed or pretended not to. He cleared his throat.

"Beautiful but reframe your statement into a question."

"You're pushy. Anyone ever tell you that?"

"It's not about me. Metaphysical protocol."

Whatever. "You're telling me what to do. I don't like that." He took a deep breath. What the hell. And spoke on the exhale. "Will my current land acquisition pan out?"

A noise from the ceiling surprised him. He pushed back his chair.

She leaned forward and whispered loudly, "Spirit ruckus." He stared at the hand she placed on his forearm.

"Damn woodrats." The thud had been a little loud, though, even for rats.

"Pay attention now, Gil. What I'm going to instruct you to do next is very important. Do not close your eyes and keep your feet on the floor. Can you do those two things?"

"I'm not about to close my eyes." He slid out from the table to fetch a broom.

Olive opened the metal brad on the reverse of an unsealed manila envelope addressed to the County of Santa Cruz Recorders Office. Now she was guilty of mail tampering. A federal offense. But she was too close to stop now. She pulled a thick white packet of papers from the envelope, knowing the contents had everything to do with her:

FORECLOSURE FOR LACK OF PAYMENT

111 Shell Bean Way. Her address. Her and Cal's names. Inventiveness had been typed on the debtor line.

Gil Souza was the instigator of the foreclosure. This proved it. He was probably responsible for last night's theft. She opened the second envelope and found a quit claim deed that hadn't been filled out. Except for the address: 111 Shell Bean Way. The third envelope was sealed and addressed to the Universal Rail Restoration Bureau. Apparently, Souza had big plans.

She checked the blueprints on the wall. On both sides of the railroad tracks, oblong buildings had been drawn—too large to be houses. Possibly industrial warehouses. The parcel numbers matched those in the neighborhood she and Cal had driven through outside of Watsonville. She stared at the blueprints, waiting for them to speak. A redevelopment project. Souza planned to raze blocks of homes to build a plant. But Shell Bean Farm did not fit. The railroad track that ran along her farm was an isolated spur off the main rail, clear on the other end of the county and too insignificant to contribute to this high roller scheme.

The woman's effect on him had worn off for now, replaced by a nagging mistrust that she was after something more. The ceiling noise bothered him.

"Ariela." The first time he'd addressed her by name produced a horrible feeling in his chest. "I'm checking the upstairs."

"I'll go with you. If your offer's still good, the kids need to stretch out."

As she followed him up the stairs, the rug rats trailing, a question hit him and he stopped. Felt her on the step below him. He turned around, his groin level with her face. A thrill shot through like lightning.

"Why did you bring your grandchildren? I've met your daughter and she clearly does not like me. She would never approve of allowing her kids in my home."

She laughed, probably at him, Gil thought.

"Which is why I didn't tell her where I was going. Just that I'd return after the kids finished their car naps. C'mon. Move it. The cards will wait, but not for long. Waiting too long is metaphysical coitus interruptus."

He let out a short, irrepressible laugh and turned, shaking his head. "You're a damn bawdy woman, Gypsy." The nickname felt better on his body. He looked back and saw her lift a flirtatious shoulder.

The two children filed into his bedroom as he held the door open. Her smell as she passed electrified him to the degree his skin ached. He'd never felt such a sensation. When the kids climbed onto his bed and jumped and squealed, the sensation went dead.

She pulled them off by their arms and dragged them into the hallway. "That is not going to work."

"Fuck it, then."

"Not in front of the kids, please."

Fuck the kids, he thought, as he herded the trio back down the stairs. The little girl looked like she might fall, and when her grandmother did nothing to help her, not even take her hand, he picked up the girl and carried her. What was her name? Gus. Bad name for a girl.

She took his hand and placed it on top of the deck. "For this to work, the cards need to get a feel for you." She closed her eyes.

"I'd rather get a feel for you."

The corners of her mouth turned up. She was feeling it, too. Or playing him for a fool.

"I'm a conduit between you and what the cosmos has to say to you through these cards," she said. "You are matter, the cards are matter, and between the two is energy."

The boy knocked over the saltshaker. He'd taken off the top. Salt spilled like the Milky Way across the table. "I want to go home." The girl had fallen asleep on the bench cushion next to her grandmother.

"Byrd, I said I'll buy you a donut if you're good. You're not being good."

"You said candy."

"I'm not in the mood for tantrums."

The boy threw the saltshaker onto the floor and buried his head in the crook of his arm.

So much for conduits, thought Gil, until the woman pressed her hand with those silver bracelets and ringed fingers on top of his and her big heat passed through him. Her intelligent forehead, eyes, eyebrows filled in with pencil. Even the fine lines above her upper lip appealed to him now, and the small crescent scar on her right cheekbone sparked concern. He hadn't noticed the scar before. He would ask her, sometime, not now.

"Mix them up." Her voice softened.

He picked up the cards and started to shuffle.

"No." She moved her hand above the cards to demonstrate the stirring motion she wanted of him. He slid the cards over his kitchen table in figure eights, as she'd demonstrated.

"Good." She picked up the cards and squared them, instructing him to spread the deck in an arc. When she flashed an unabashed smile that startled him, he visualized her naked. Couldn't imagine her in bed. Yet.

"Pick three cards. We're doing the short version. Present, future and outcome."

Gil pushed his first card toward her. An old man.

"Present card," she said, seriously, as her two lovely gifts of abundance billowed in a wind of temptation.

"Next, the future card."

He turned another card over. A maiden walking across a log.

"And a third. Your outcome card."

A water wheel. The carefulness with which he chose the card mildly surprised him. He felt a need to remind her this was strictly for entertainment.

"You weren't having fun, Gil, when you told me your daughter hated you." The jingle of her silver bracelets relaxed him.

She tapped the old man in the forest which, she explained, was The Hermit.

Gil said, "I live alone but I don't consider myself a hermit."

"Loner, hermit, recluse," she said. "Same archetype. A man who lives alone by choice or chance."

He shrugged, thinking he didn't really live alone by choice. He'd never met a woman he wanted to live with. Not on purpose. Anyway, he didn't mind living alone. Especially if sharing a space meant he had to endure someone else's bad habits. "Something wrong with a single man living alone?"

"Absolutely not. I live alone." The Gypsy pointed with too much enthusiasm to the young woman balancing on a log high above a creek. Two men dueled in the background.

"Your future," she announced. "The woman is in a precarious situation." She pointed to the men in the ravine who appeared to be dueling. "She's above the danger but be forewarned."

"Always a 'but'?" He tugged the flesh beneath his neck and wondered, finally, if she knew as they played, he was foreclosing on her daughter's land. He shook his head, shaking off sudden guilt. God only knew how she'd react if she found out. Cutting his dick off was not beneath her.

Gil forced a smile. "Did you stack this deck?" He pulled a toothpick from his breast pocket and stuck it between his teeth.

"Of course not. That would be bad karma for me." She pointed to the card. "You may win whatever it is you're fighting for but winning without a good heart will upset the balance."

He folded his arms over his chest to ease the sting. She was closer to the truth than he could let on. Or she was baiting him.

A stricken look came over her. She tilted her chin to the ceiling, eyes darted back and forth as if following flies. She trembled, and a chill rose on Gil's arms and chest. He was afraid to touch her.

She took a deep breath and touched the third card. "The wheel. Luck and fate are turning in your favor."

Let's finish this. He waited impatiently for the "but."

She rubbed her temples, for drama's sake, he hoped.

"The outcome of your land acquisition is ambivalent." She reached into her satchel and produced a bottle of Advil. Asked for water.

Gil realized how pale and clammy she'd become. He got up and poured her a glass of tap water, worried she was too impaired to drive home. The last thing he wanted was a fainting woman and two squirmy kids extending their visit.

Olive heard their footsteps return back down the stairs. She took one last look around the room and decided she'd found enough.

Her exit options were limited. If she took the stairs, she'd be spotted crossing the kitchen. Gus or Byrd might catch a glimpse as she passed.

She unlocked the sliding glass door of the master bedroom and walked onto the spacious deck, which overhung a bank that dropped into a gully. She climbed over the railing and eased down to the support beam. A splinter of wood stabbed her groin, she winced and dropped, landing on a cushion of redwood duff. Nothing seemed broken or cut. She ran crouching, hoping the trees and brush provided sufficient cover.

As Olive neared the Jeep, Byrd saw her coming out of the woods and ran down the driveway full speed. Ariela must have let him run ahead. She ducked behind the car and when he reached her, she pulled him down to the ground beside her. "Shh, Byrd, get in your car seat, quickly. I have to hide. A bad man is after me."

After Byrd was in his seat, she climbed into the floor of the middle seat. Souza and Ariela were halfway down the driveway.

"We can't let Gus see me, okay, buddy, or she'll give us away."

"Is it one of the monsters?"

"The man with Grandma is a monster." She squeezed onto the floor on top of discarded bread crusts and food wrappers and pulled the car blanket over herself as Byrd thought to cover her foot.

Something fell on her back. "What was that?"

"Buzz Lightyear. He'll protect you."

"Grandma knows I'm here. But the man doesn't, so don't look at me or talk to me. Pretend I'm not here." She squeezed his calf. "You're so brave."

"I see them."

"Okay, here we go."

"There you are!" Ariela's voice sent shock waves through Olive, and Byrd's entire body flinched. "Why are you crying, Sonny?"

"My mom's not here," Byrd said.

"Don't do that, please," Olive heard her mother say. "The boy doesn't like people ruffling his hair." Olive heard the door open and Gus climbed in, resisting Ariela's attempts to fasten her car seat. Another heavy object, this time dumped on her head, probably her mother's satchel.

"Call me if anything comes up for you surrounding the cards," Ariela said.

Souza grumbled something that Olive couldn't make out as Ariela turned the ignition key, shoved the gear into drive and lurched forward. "Sorry. I'm not used to four-wheel drive. Back away, Sir Gil." She ground the gear into reverse and the Jeep lurched backward.

"Next time, no kids." Souza's voice diminished as the Jeep jerked forward.

"See you later, cowboy."

They waited for the gate to open. Three sharp curves down the road, the brakes squealed and the Jeep came to an abrupt stop. Gus bawled at the top of her lungs.

"Time to switch drivers." Ariela got out of the car and Olive threw off the blanket and tried to sit up, flicking the remains of a jam sandwich from her shirt.

Gus squealed, "Mama."

"Gussy." She climbed out of the back seat and over the console, slipping behind the wheel while Ariela went around and got into the passenger side.

Olive told her about the foreclosure on Souza's desk, the quit claim that hadn't been filled out, and a check made out to the federal railroad agency. "The wall in his study is lined with blueprints for developing an industrial plant and, somehow, we're part of that. And I took a photo of his list of GE test sites."

"Then, it was worth the risk." Ariela breathed in slowly, exhaled loudly. "What are you going to tell your husband?"

31

Olive found Cal upstairs in bed, facing the wall. He was supposed to be overseeing the crew transplant the seedlings. He'd slept all night in the same T-shirt he'd worked in the day before.

"Are you alright?"

He didn't move or respond. "I can't do this anymore. What's the point?"

She was prepared for Cal's criticism, but intolerant of his despondency. "I broke into Souza's house," she said, "and found the foreclosure papers and a list of test sites."

"You what?" He turned over, at once snapped out of his morose state of mind. "What kind of a stunt is that?"

"We need to confront him, and if you don't come with me, I'll go alone. He's planning to raze that neighborhood we drove by and replace it with an industrial plant of some kind."

"Sugar beets." He was alert, now. "The bastard plans to bring back sugar beets."

The office wreaked of stale cigarette smoke. But that was all Olive registered because Cal reached over Gil Souza's desk and grabbed his collar. In the other arm, he raised the golf club his father had given him.

"My wife says you're foreclosing on our land and you stole our plants."

Souza didn't say a word, but Olive noticed his body tilt as if he were pulling out a drawer.

Cal's face had turned crimson. "A child. How could you do that?"

"Watch out."

Souza had reached in the drawer and pulled out a gun. Cal released Gil's shirt and swung his club, sending the gun skittering across the room as a woman appeared in the doorway of the adjoining office.

She held up a phone. "Sir, do I need to call the Sheriff?"

Olive recognized the woman's voice, that gravelly smoker's voice on the Inventiveness recording, the voice that had never returned her calls.

"You crossed the last line, man, and we're the ones going to the cops."

Souza shook his head, bent over his thwacked arm, clearly in pain. "There's nothing to tell. It's all above board."

"Stealing crops to drive us into debt is fraud, which invalidates your foreclosure scheme and sends you to prison."

"You have no proof of any this."

"I do. I have photographs of you and Robert Johnson in the café. I have more photographs and parcel numbers of your development plan. And copies of your blueprints." That got him. "And I discovered a boot print in our beet field next to Cris's body. We're doing a forensic palynology test to see if the soil around the body matches Johnson's boot, which I took from your daughter's house when I delivered her severance check."

Cal shot her the processing new information look.

"Drop the foreclosure," Olive said.

"Get out before Cloris shoots you." Gil cradled his injured arm with his good one and nodded at the woman standing in the doorway.

She held the gun and pointed it straight at Cal. A deafening shot filled the trailer.

When they'd driven out of Souza's range, Olive opened the truck's passenger door, leaned out and threw up. Cal's hand gripped her shirt while she puked and he kept driving.

"That man is dangerous."

"You figured that out?" She sat back in a sweat. "I can't believe she shot at us."

"I can't believe she missed. What's with the boot?"

"The boot was a lie."

She sat in the office chair, staring at the newspaper clipping of Cal celebrating his propagation success. Envy-inspired retaliation was not far-fetched. Tacked on the wall beside the clipping was the handwritten note from Souza congratulating Cal on his success. Above that, a copy of the note that had been found on Gus. She reassured herself, again, the two handwriting samples had similarities—the slant, the lack of dotted i's. The ou. Yet, the S in Souza's signature was different from the S in See how easy..... The former a snake-like S; the latter a lazy cursive. But people practiced flourish and uniqueness with signatures. And Souza was clearly a flourish guy.

Olive sifted through their files of business receipts, looking for something. She didn't know what. She found a payment to his compost supplier for shaping the strawberry rows. A receipt from Best Seeds, Inc. for tomato seed, dated two years ago January. Behind that, an earlier bill from Best Seeds, which was accompanied by a typed letter dated February eleventh. Augusta would not have been born and they would have been renting Thea's cabin. The idea of buying this house, the Post homestead, and the land wasn't even a dream at that point.

She read the words of gratitude from Souza for Cal's steady business over the years, followed by a statement of the company's

vision for the future, which included diversified innovation, a eu-
phemism for GMOs. The third paragraph took her by surprise: an
offer to buy Shell Bean Farm, the business and its lease on the land.
Olive didn't remember Souza offering to buy their business or Cal
mentioning anything even close.

Olive stood at the edge of the beet field while Cal worked with
the crew flame burning. She held out a water bottle while he kissed
her on the cheek before taking a long drink then asking, "How
much should we tell Rogers? You did break into his house and I
attacked him in his office."

"That was self-defense and Souza doesn't know I was in his
house." She glanced at her watch. "We should tell him everything.
You never know what detail will be the catalyst for a cop's mind.
Cal, do you remember Souza offering to buy our business a year
ago?"

"Can't recall him making an offer."

She held up the note for Cal to read. "He's been scheming on us
for awhile, maybe trying to capture the organic market because it's
a thriving economic niche."

"Why don't I feel like we're thriving?" Cal went pale.

It was April and customers already asked when the tomatoes
would be ready. Olive had hired a new person, Mateo Esperanza, a
young man who'd grown up in a farm labor family in Santa Cruz.
He had just finished a farming program that trains teenagers from

poor backgrounds to find a place in the just and sustainable food movement. Olive liked him immediately. His teachers wrote glowing recommendations. Cal made plans to train him.

"Mid-August," Mateo answered, without taking his eyes off the customer. When they groaned, he smiled kindly and told them with a small mellifluous tint of Spanish accent, "yearning is good for the soul." Olive hadn't told him this season's tomato supply would not meet her customers' demand. She hadn't told him about any of the travails she and Cal had endured this year. Heriberto had told him a few bits and pieces, enough to make him realize how important he was to them.

"How does dry-farming work?" a customer asked. "I mean how is it possible to grow tomatoes without water?"

Olive folded her arms across her chest, held her tongue and listened to Mateo. It was such a relief to reserve her energy and take in his soft deep voice explaining that "holding back water made the plants dig deeper to find the moisture they needed and effort developed their unique character." He spoke knowing these tomatoes were more than a metaphor of their lives. They shared this life—the tomatoes, the redwoods, the squirrels, the people.

So when her phone rang, she wasn't ready for the harshness of a bank. When the loan officer on the other line relayed her condolences about the crop theft, the yet unspoken words that Olive sensed hit doubly hard.

"We were hoping they'd caught the thief and retrieved your product," she said.

"We never reported to you the crop stolen," Olive said.

"It was in the newspaper. We made a call downtown and the police confirmed."

"We were lucky, actually. We put a new wave of seedlings in the ground, and the next wave is thriving in the greenhouse."

"I'm glad to hear that, really I am. It's numbers. Half the crop leverage we loaned on is gone. I'm sorry to have to tell you, I really am, but we're rescinding the line of credit."

"All of it?"

"We're not extending credit until we reconfigure the LOC because your leverage has changed dramatically, and we have no assurance that you can re-pay the loan."

"We'll be staking our second wave in a couple of days." Olive heard the despair in her voice. The farm wouldn't make it to summer without the LOC to pay for labor and overhead. Their crew were already overextended. Olive didn't know how they'd managed to survive this last month.

"We'll get back to you, Ms. Post, as soon as we reconfigure the loan to asset risk and projected profits. Can you send us the new numbers?"

Did she have to recite to this loan officer the suicide rate of farmers in this country? Twice that of the general population. Globally, the highest suicide rate of all occupations. She squelched the hysteria in her throat and with a measured voice—careful not to torch her side of the bridge—and told the loan officer she'd send the figures and hoped to hear from her as soon as they reconfigured the loan.

32

There was no good time to deliver bad news. She left Mateo to the stall and went to tell Cal in person. He was in the tomato field sinking stakes. He took off his cap and scratched his head, waiting. She stared at his face, and though she saw he was expecting something, he wasn't expecting this. It was a miracle anyone remained in this occupation and understandable why the average age of farmers in this country is increasing—young people, repelled by the idea of working to the bone for a threadbare livelihood, chose lucrative jobs in the tech industry with at least the potential of affluence. Or a startup in medical marijuana. You know what sustained farmers? Customers. Their gratitude. And the media. Their talent for putting farmers on a wobbly word pedestal. Even if the pedestal fell, the words stayed, they floated above the dirt and sweat in cultural mythology that was warm sun on the sore bone.

"They pulled it?"

"Until they reconfigure the crop loss and what our leverage is now worth."

Cal's mouth drew down and lips quivered. His eyes turned red. He turned and walked to the end of the row, picked up one of the green metal stakes the crew had laid out every three yards, and shoved it a half-foot into the broken soil. He pulled back his sledgehammer in a wide arc and came down hard. His muscled back was lean and his loose brown cotton T-shirt dark covered with sweat. He wiped his forehead with his arm, moved three feet down the row and slammed in another stake.

33

The Big Dipper hung on the northern horizon, and the Milky Way streaked the middle sky like a wedding veil. Between the occasional downshifting of distant trucks and the hum of the hot tub motor, it was quiet. Olive slid cautiously into the one hundred and four-degree water, enveloped in steam that rose into the cold evening. Cal, she thought, could use a good hot soak but he'd gone to bed before the kids.

Thea perched on the tub's top seat, soaking her calves. At six months her stomach had blossomed into a tidy dome. The animation in her voice was contagious. She'd been offered a job as head baker at the new downtown restaurant where they'd eaten lunch. She tilted her head and stared at the stars. "I miss him so much." As quickly as her smile faded, the hot tub's motor stopped whirring, and silence filled the yard.

Cris was everywhere. He had transformed the matted blackberry and poison oak from Cal and Olive's tenancy into a real backyard. In the span of a year, he had turned the thorny jungle into an oasis of lavender and Russian sage with small solar lamps that lit the crushed rock path toward a Tibetan Buddha. Strings of small overhead lights, strung from one side of the fence to the other, created a sense of enchantment. He had lain sandstone slabs around the base of the hot tub, with chamomile planted between, so when Olive had walked to the tub, her feet crushed the herb, releasing a fragrance that almost erased the smell of chlorine.

The hot tub, Olive realized, was where Cris had been before he met his death on her farm.

She leaned on the hot tub ledge and floated her legs behind, feeling the heat on her stomach and the cool air on her back. It was a dark night. Which was why the glint in the chamomile caught her eye. She raised herself over the hard edge of the hot tub, feeling the clutch of anticipation, and reached for the shiny object. It resisted her gentle tug, so she pulled harder, bringing a twig of yellow blossoms and root and bits of dirt with the object.

"What is it?" Thea asked.

Olive held it out and poured tub water to rinse the dirt. She knew what it was. Two small gems sparkled. A light green peridot for Augusta and yellow topaz for Byrd.

"My necklace."

Thea stood and held up her arms. "Cris. He's here. A messenger bird plucked it from wherever and let go of it here."

Olive doubted the bird theory. A sign, though. Good for Olive, not for Thea. In the distance, the sound of a truck heightened as it downshifted into town and the image came hard, fully formed, far-fetched yet so logical it cleared the muddle of events since she'd discovered her necklace was missing: Kat.

34

Her mother had fallen asleep reading on the futon, and the kids were fast asleep in their beds. Cal had taken a sleeping pill, only the second time since they'd married. She wrote a note: *Didn't want to wake you. You need your sleep. Went to Kinko's to get paper for the printer and to check on something.* She propped the note on the bedside table between his lamp and alarm clock, which said ten o'clock at night.

The streets were so empty they felt eerie on the drive to Kat's place. When she pulled into the yard, Kat's Volvo was parked against the fence next to a big truck with rooftop-mounted head-lights. She could assume Kat had company, probably male, and backed the Jeep against the barbed wire fence separating the yard from the marine benchlands. She left the keys in the ignition and walked toward the bungalow, stepped up the uneven porch steps and knocked loudly. No one answered, but a light in the living room went off, signaling visitors weren't welcome. She knocked again.

"It's Olive."

Kat opened the door, disheveled. Her tank top was off her shoulder and her sweatpants hung below her midriff. She was barefoot and the polish on her toenails was chipped. "What do you want?"

"I have to talk to you."

"I have nothing to say to you." She started to close the door, but Olive jammed her boot in the frame and held out the necklace.

"What the fuck is that?"

"My necklace."

Kat stepped outside and closed the door behind her. She smelled like a potpourri of weed and Southern Comfort, and the delicate crust of white powder caked around her left nostril added an element of crazy. When the front curtains moved, Olive assumed whoever had moved them was the person who belonged to the big truck.

"Tell me how my necklace wound up in Cris and Thea's backyard."

Kat tilted her head toward the window, put her finger to her lips and walked past Olive, down the steps and apparently out of earshot. "Shut up," she hissed. "I've known Cris since I was a kid."

"You're not a kid now."

Kat grabbed Olive's wrists and as her nails dug into flesh, Olive asked, "Did Thea know about you and Cris?"

"I don't know, and I don't care."

"Was she jealous of you?"

"She didn't even know me."

That was probably true since, Olive recalled, Thea hadn't recognized Kat when they were at the restaurant.

"Where were you the morning Cris died?"

"I was in Oakland on my way to the market, stranded. You should know that. I called your house to get your husband to come and get his broken-down box truck."

"Why'd you abandon the truck on the side of the highway before he got there? Not even a note, Kat." Olive glanced at the curtain.

Kat released her grip on Olive's wrists. "None of your fucking business."

"Do you know what happened to Cris that night?"

"Shut up."

"Who's behind the curtain? Robert Johnson? You're afraid Johnson will hear? Is that him behind the curtain? I thought you and he broke it off."

"We made up. That's what lovers do."

Which translated as "yes, Robert Johnson is standing behind the curtains listening in."

236

"Does he drive a white van?"

"No."

"Know anyone who drives a white van?"

"Jesus. Lots of white vans in this town. Why?"

"The person who stole Cal's tomatoes drives a white van. Did you tell anyone we were transplanting the starts?"

"How would I have known? You fired me, remember?"

"You knew about the theft."

"Everyone knows."

Olive glanced at the big truck parked along the fence. "Is that Johnson's rig?"

She shrugged.

"Could a jealous corporate ag-man hire someone like Johnson to steal our plants, in your opinion?"

Kat's eyes darted back and forth as if she were scanning a hundred scenes for something that fit. "You mean Gil? He operates in sections, not acres. Your farm is nothing to him."

"Then why is he foreclosing on it?"

"To prove that he's a prick," said Kat. "Maybe, you're not seeing what's in front of you."

"What I see right now is an interloper. While Thea worked, you and Cris got together, I'm guessing, on the morning he died. Were you having an affair with Cris?"

Kat hissed, "shut up," and when she pointed to the window Olive knew she was panicking about the man in the house. "Want him to kill me?"

"Would he kill you for cheating on him?"

Kat had to think about that, biting her lip and nodding. "Maybe."

"Well, that worries me, Kat, and I should probably call the police." She pulled out her cell phone. "I want to know how my necklace ended up in Thea's yard."

Kat tugged Olive farther away from the house, out of hearing range, which affirmed her suspicions that Kat had more to hide than stealing a necklace.

"Did you take the necklace off so it wouldn't get damaged?"

"Why would I take off a necklace for a hot tub?"

"I didn't say anything about a hot tub."

Kat looked up at the dark sky. "Fuck me."

"Does Johnson know about Cris?"

She shrugged.

"Would he be jealous if he did know?"

"What guy doesn't think he owns a woman once he's fucked her."

"Did Cris own you?"

"It wasn't like that with Cris." Her tone of voice shifted an octave higher, and Olive saw her pupils constrict in the moonlight. "How can I get that across to you? I've known Cris since I was a girl. Way before Thea. We were friends and we loved each other."

"To be clear, was this a sexual love?"

"None of your fucking business. He was more mine than hers."

"Why rendezvous at his place and not yours?"

"Convenience. I had to drive the box truck to the market."

"Kat, Cris was married."

"A piece of paper. Not real."

"Thea is pregnant with his child. Is that real enough for you?"

From Kat's shocked expression, Olive guessed it was. "A child who's going to grow up not only without a father but with the stigma that he killed himself even though he knew his child was on the way."

"How do you know it's his?"

"Seriously?"

"He ruined my life by dying," Kat cried, trying to keep her voice down.

"You'll get over it," Olive said. "Can't say the same for his widow and child."

Olive watched rivulets of sadness flow into the cleft of Kat's chin. Her grief appeared genuine. As for Cris, he'd fallen notches from the good guy Olive had assumed he was.

"Do you believe he killed himself?" Olive asked.

Kat wiped her cheeks on her bare forearm and glanced furtively over her shoulder to the window. "That wouldn't say much for our relationship, would it." She shivered. "It's cold. You have to go."

It wasn't that cold and Olive wasn't leaving. Coyotes started to yip. They were close and sounded like a frantic pack. Either two alpha coyotes were mating, or the mates and their young were reacting to Olive and Kat by creating a sound fence around their territory. Kat, too, was establishing—or at least trying to establish—her own defensible space. But she was boxed in between Olive's questions and the man inside the house.

"Who are you protecting?" Olive asked.

"Who does anyone protect? Myself."

"Who's in the house?"

Kat clenched Olive's shoulder and squeezed hard. "I said, you have to go. Get out of here, now."

Olive gave it one more try. "People are concerned about your safety, Kat."

"Have you been talking to Gil?"

"No," Olive said, "but I saw him at the North Coast Café. With Robert." Olive lowered her voice to a whisper. "Having a very serious conversation."

"That's a lie," Kat said. "They don't even know each other."

"I walked up to them and introduced myself. I congratulated Robert on your engagement in front of Gil, who clearly did not like what he heard. My take? He hired Johnson to spy on you and Johnson violated that contract by getting romantically involved with you."

Kat's eyes widened with disbelief and horror. "I don't believe you."

"I took a photo."

"Go." She gripped Olive's hands until they hurt. "Please."

"Think about it. Why was our greenhouse ransacked on the morning Cris died?" She tilted her head toward the window where she was fairly certain Johnson listened.

"I took that fucking necklace off because Robert had given it to me, and I didn't want his karma around my neck while I was with Cris." She turned and, before she stormed up the steps, Olive grabbed her elbow.

239

"Be smart, Kat. Your boyfriend is a dangerous man."

She shook off Olive's grip. "Get the fuck out of here. I can deal with him. Go back to your sweet little life and leave me alone."

Olive followed Kat up the steps and into the living room. A ghostly streak crossed the room. Kat flipped on the light. Johnson. Barefoot, no shirt, white skin overlaid with a galaxy of orange freckles and a doughy beer belly. He stood in the center of the room, holding something in his right hand. A switchblade.

Kat strode up to Johnson and pushed his chest.

"Asshole," Kat said. "What is she talking about seeing you and Gil together at a cafe? I swear it better not be true."

Johnson glared menacingly at Olive as Kat poked his chest with her finger. "I don't hear you denying it. After everything I've done for you." She shoved him again.

"Is it true? Tell me you bastard. Are you spying on me?"

Lobster the Crustacean turned to Olive. "Bitch," he said. "Wasn't losing your kid enough of a warning to keep your fucking snatch out of our business?"

Kat picked up a paperback from the coffee table and threw it at him. "I saw you that night, asshole."

The book hit him squarely in the chest, gearing up his fury.

"Get out," she shrieked. "You're a fucking piece of shit."

Olive punched in her phone pass code, tapped the green icon 9-1-1.

"Don't," Kat pleaded. "I can handle this without the cops."

Olive didn't think so and pressed send as Johnson stepped toward her with the knife at his side. Her call failed. He gave the knife a small toss, flipping the blade once, twice. She turned to leave and saw the men's boots by the front door. She thought better about taking them.

As slowly as she could, Olive walked out of the house, fighting the urge to run. No one but these two—a knife-wielding thug and his hostile woman—knew where in the universe she was right now.

Olive bristled with the sensation that Johnson would overtake her before she got to the Jeep. She fumbled with the door and bumped her head on the frame. Her hand shook as she turned the key, still in the ignition. The gears ground as she jammed the stick into low. She side swiped the metal lawn chair as she tore out of the driveway, tires spinning, dust and loose rock flying.

She made a sharp right onto the street, glanced up and saw only black in the rearview mirror. Ahead, dappled moonlight on an empty, tree-lined road. She checked the mirror, again, and made out two beacons of light on what were probably rooftop-mounted lamps. Johnson. He was coming up fast.

Olive switched off her headlights and the road was black, but she remembered the blind curve ahead and a steep driveway on the left. She flashed on the headlights for just long enough to see the mailbox before she switched them off. Three seconds later, she cranked the wheel sharply left and accelerated up the driveway, then coasted, careful to keep her foot off the brake as she slowed and stopped a few yards in front of a garage. She shoved in the clutch and made a reverse two-point turn. Headlights sped by on the road below. Johnson's truck. Olive coasted cautiously down the driveway. Seeing no sign of a vehicle, she turned right, back the way she'd come, passing Kat's house and reaching what looked like the end of the road. Perpendicular to the dead end, Olive knew, was a notoriously difficult road that descended the bench lands and supposedly emerged onto the Coast Highway. She checked the blackness on all sides and proceeded.

35

The Jeep's steering wheel yanked one way then the other as Olive dipped into the ruts of the dry wash. As she struggled to retain control of the wheel, she thought of Cal. If he woke up and found her note, he'd try to call her and the call would fail because she was in nowhere land where cell service was patchy at best. Then he'd worry. After a while, he'd panic.

She floored the gas pedal and gunned the Jeep up the wash to the top, pausing to catch her breath. KPIG blared "The Road Home" on her radio. The life/death lyrics felt like a bad omen. She turned off the ignition and switched off the radio, rolled down the window. Ocean waves, sounding closer than they were, pounded the distant cliffs, as if berating her initial decision to drive out to Kat's in the first place.

Olive stepped from the car onto the prairie and held up her phone, turning a full circle. Please, please, please, she chanted. Kat's property was visible from where she stood, the porch lights on, the light dirt of the yard glowing in contrast to the surrounding geology. The rooftop lamps of Johnson's truck pulled into the yard.

Olive worried about Kat being alone with her violent boyfriend. Olive felt certain Johnson had killed Chris because Cris had caught him in the act of stealing. Hearing Kat admit she'd seen him at the scene had probably shocked Johnson, and now he was worried about a pissed off girlfriend ratting him out to police.

Headlights flooded the prairie to her left. A searchlight mounted on the driver's side scanned the ground, its light ending close to where Olive stood. Johnson was on the move. Time for Olive to do the same.

The road ahead was clear, until a geo-slash across the dirt forced her to slam on the brakes. A two-foot-wide trench cut across the road directly in front of her. She got out of her car and examined the slash, a result of erosion in wetter years. The rift had been haphazardly filled with branches and two wooden planks placed perpendicular across the pit. A perilous bet.

She decided speed was her ally. She backed up, put the Jeep in low and sped across the trench, boards and branches slamming the undercarriage. She made it to the other side, but her back wheel hung up. She rocked the Jeep and on the third try cleared the trench and raced down a narrow dirt chute of ten-foot walls.

Jagged roots grew out of the embankment and clawed the vehicle's sides. At least Johnson's monster truck couldn't make it through this passage. She floored it, anticipating the Coast Highway around each turn, until she heard a pop, loud as gunshot. The Jeep tipped to one side.

When she saw the slashed right front tire with a small, sharp root sticking out of the wound, her escape seemed futile. The burst of speed had blown a puncture wide open. The last time she'd changed a tire was Driver's Ed in high school. She raised the back door of the Jeep and swept the toys and blankets and shopping bags onto the ground. The spare was under the rug, fastened down with a center screw.

At the sound of a truck, she froze. Johnson. She climbed onto the roof and spotted him still driving across the prairie in her direction. She scrambled down and turned off her headlights. Her cell phone rang. She dug into her back pocket. Cal.

"Where are you?" he asked.

"I'm in trouble ..."

"You said you were going to Kinko's."

She pressed the phone between her ear and chin and used both hands to heft the tire from the well. "And I said I had to check something out. I'm on a dirt road on the west side of city limits with a flat tire. Robert Johnson is chasing me down." She threw the tire onto the ground with a grunt and started looking for the jack and a wrench.

"Where are you?" He sounded angry. "Exactly."

"The abandoned road parallel to the land reserve on the west side of city limits. Past Kat's house. Ariela knows. I'm heading downhill to Highway 1, but the Jeep has a flat and I have to change it."

"I'm on my way," Cal said.

"He's getting closer. He has a knife. He killed Cris. Kat saw him."

"Get away from the car and hide. Put your phone on vibrate. I'm taking the Coast way in and ...." He cut out.

Olive switched to vibrate and stuffed the phone in her back jeans pocket and ran to the nearest oak, crouching behind its trunk. A sweep of light stopped a yard from where she cowered.

36

The jury took one half hour to deliberate. When cheers rose from the room, Gil felt condemned and his shame turned to rage. But he'd gotten what he'd wanted all along. A chance to appeal his case to the higher court. His lawyer leaned over to him, careful not to pat his shoulder. "Game on."

Even so, Gil walked out of the courtroom dulled by public contempt. Yes, he would show them who was really in charge. Not some radical left-wing jury bent on stopping progress. The State of California had absolutely no restrictions that prevented farmers from growing genetically engineered plants, and the state prevailed over local law. The upper courts had become more conservative. By the time his case traveled up the judicial ranks, Gil knew, he would prevail. They'd see. He would appeal to the state's power over local bans and if the state didn't honor his argument, the federal court eventually would. If it made Supreme Court, no question he'd not only prevail but set a precedence. He'd make case law history.

Stupid people. Brussels sprouts, tomatoes, beets. They were all the same. The country needed food, especially sugar. Sugar for coffee. Molasses for cows. There weren't enough conventional beet seeds to supply the national and global demand. GE beets were the solution. Why couldn't they open their myopic eyeballs and see the bigger picture?

He walked across the parking lot and paused before stepping into the crosswalk that spanned four lanes of Ocean Avenue and would take him to the Jury Room bar for a smoky Scotch on the rocks.

The drinks in that bar worked like a mother's womb, dark and safe and abiding. He lost track of time. And now, he was ready. He pulled out his iPhone. Gypsy. He pressed call.

"Hello Gil Souza," she answered.

Couldn't the woman at least pretend to be surprised?

"I've been thinking of you," he said.

"I, as well, have been thinking of you," she said, in that husky voice that went straight to his pecker.

"I'm wondering if you would join me for a drink. I can pick you up so you don't have to drive your cart."

"I like driving my cart at night. The air cools my skin and my lungs thrive on the fresh air."

He imagined those lungs and almost felt human after a grueling day in court. The smell of the courthouse wood and cement cleaned with antiseptic lingered. So did the image of the Water Street parking lot full of green and white sheriff's cars, and that same transient—or maybe a different one—asleep in the bush in clear view of the cops.

"You had a bad day, Gil?"

"I never said that. I'm inviting you out for a drink."

"You sound drunk."

"I've had a few. I'll let you catch up."

Her tone of voice when she said, "I'm sorry," felt like a big rig rolling over his pride.

"I'm watching my grandchildren."

"Oh." He heard his own disappointment. "All I see is that damn courtroom and a despicable jury of judgmental eyes, not that it matters in the long run. I expected to see your daughter in the audience."

"She had some business to attend to today. Mercury in retrograde."

The knot in his throat scared him. He'd lost in the eyes of the jurors and the opinion of the liberal community he'd grown up with, and the millions in fines—he swallowed the last inch of his Scotch in one gulp—in the big picture, he'd become the new model. He slammed down his glass to punctuate his prediction. He had a trick up his sleeve. A new plant gene technique that sidestepped the present definition of transgenics. Oligo-directed mutagenesis, or something like that. He was a little too tipsy to remember the name and if anyone asked, he for sure couldn't pronounce it. Bottom line, well, he didn't care about the bottom line right now.

"Gil?"

"So, Gypsy, what do you say? Help me grieve." Women couldn't resist a vulnerable man.

"I can't now. It's very late even for me to be going out. My daughter hasn't gotten home and my son-in-law has gone out to find her."

His bone ached, and not in the metaphorical sense. "Ruining the chemistry even before our first drink together. C'mon."

The bartender behind the counter approached him with the bottle of Scotch. Gil pointed a finger to his empty rocks glass.

"This is not the voice I use to ruin chemistry," Gypsy said.

He stared at the amber liquid spilling like a delicate waterfall from the bottle's metal spigot, splashing onto the ice cubes. A pleasant sound that reminded him of her bracelets. He imagined those expressive hands waving some spell-casting design as she reveled in rejecting him. Why had he even thought this was a good idea? His swirled the Scotch and raised the glass.

"I tried to call you, Gil, but you didn't pick up."

He slammed down the drink. A twinge of guilt?

"Listen here, Gil Souza. I'm thinking of those cards. That girl on the log. Those two men below. If you're being underhanded acquiring this dream of yours, someone will get hurt and it better not be my daughter."

Gil hung up without saying goodbye and tossed his cell phone on the counter. He waved the bartender over and as he held out his glass, asked for two aspirin.

"Salud." He raised his glass to the bartender, who addressed him as "sir" and told him this was his last drink.

His last drink. No one had ever spoken those words to Gil. The comment felt deeply rude. And off base. In fact, it hurt his feelings, right there in his solar plexus. He touched the spot in the center of his chest where he felt actual physical pain and wondered if this would suffice for that damn Gypsy's ludicrous prophesy. Someone will get hurt.

37

Olive's eyes ached from the strain of looking for Cal's headlights, and her legs cramped as she crouched behind the oak as the fog moved in like the walking dead.

Johnson's truck, on the other hand, lit the prairie. She broke from her hiding place behind the oak and ran across the road to the thickets on the opposite side. When the bank caved underfoot, she stumbled down a gully just as the truck's search light scanned the overhead brush. Her palms felt the stab of oak leaf litter as she scrambled back up the bank and dry-heaved into the dirt to muffle the noise. When she looked up, Johnson was parking his truck perpendicular to the Jeep. He got out and opened the Jeep door, arched his back, taking a piss on her front seat.

The faint whine of sirens. Johnson heard them, too. He hustled to his truck and backed out, tearing across the fragile prairie without headlights toward Kat's. The diminishing roar of his truck brought relief as Olive waited in the brush while the sirens grew louder then stopped and it felt safe to walk out of the woods.

She shouted, "I'm over here."

"Identify yourself," a cop said, his voice amplified.

"Olive Post. I'm on foot walking toward you."

As the cops shone their flashlights, she shielded eyes with her arms, feeling weak. Her legs buckled and she felt the first few feet of her fall. Then nothing.

"I'm here." Cal's arms surrounded her, his voice trying to soothe, and she felt his heart beat a little stronger and faster as he raised her head and the cops asked questions she couldn't understand.

Cal held her more firmly. "Give her a chance to process."

She dug into her front pocket, pulled out the necklace. "Look what I found."

No smile from Cal. Too worried to feign amusement.

"My necklace. I found it half-buried by Thea's hot tub."

"We can talk later." He pushed back her hair. "Can you stand?"

She raised up but the dizziness pushed her back to the ground. "You needed your sleep."

He cradled her head. "That's getting old, babe."

"Ma'am. Can you give us the name of your pursuant?"

She forgot his name.

Cal said, "Robert Johnson."

"Nickname Lobster," Olive added, pushing herself from the ground.

"Make of vehicle?"

"Very large red truck." She remembered the icon on the front grille. "A Chevy. Big tires and rooftop headlamps. High axel for high clearance."

"Take a picture of the tire treads," Olive said, her voice like shattered glass. "I want to see if it's a match to the one I saw the night Cris Villalabos died."

The cops looked blank, except one. "I was there. That was a bad scene."

"Why was he chasing you?" another asked.

"I blew his cover." Now that she was standing, hands on her knees, salivating, she breathed out the nausea. "I think he killed Cris Villalobos."

She couldn't lay out the events of the evening in chronological order, not for want of will, but, rather, a general lack of focus. She heard barking. The coyotes.

"You need to check on Kat Granger," Olive said to the cops. "She's a witness."

"How do you know it was Robert Johnson chasing you?" the taller one asked.

"I recognized the truck and saw him where my Jeep broke down. He got out of his truck, approached my Jeep, opened the door and urinated on the seat. I could hear it."

One of the cops walked away toward the Jeep. She felt Cal give her a squeeze and she knew he was putting this show to rest.

"I need to get my wife home. We've got kids at the house."

"Affirmative on urine in the Jeep," a cop called. "Someone in a heavy vehicle drove off in a hurry. Deep treads. I snapped pix."

The road to the coast highway was mostly straight and without obstacles. They drove in silence. Cal's serious expression changed to something between fatigue and frustration.

"Cris was having an affair with Kat."

"Is that what you want to talk about?"

"Don't clam up on me."

"Not clamming up."

"Then speak."

"Never thought much at all about Cris to tell you the truth."

"And the necklace and being chased with a knife wielding thug and Kat being a witness to Cris's murder?"

"That's three questions. Which one first?"

"The necklace."

"It's just a necklace." He wiped tears from the corners of his eyes. "I almost lost you."

Olive put an arm around his shoulder, expecting him to resist, but he didn't. She lay her head on his shoulder and watched fog envelop them as they moved closer to home.

"I'm so sorry," she said.

"You put yourself in the middle of all that, completely aware of what you were doing. That's crazy."

"I saw blueprints on Gil Souza's den wall," she said, "for an industrial plant by the railroad in that neighborhood we drove through."

He leaned over the steering wheel. "You went to his house? To-night?"

"The other day. I snuck in." She withheld that Ariela was her accomplice.

"Olive, look, why aren't you afraid? You're a mother. We have two small children."

"I am afraid, Cal." And that was true. She hadn't stopped being afraid since she'd found Cris dead on their farm. "But what really scares me is knowing that people are out to take. Us. Down."

"People." He said it as if he'd slung the last pound on a nail head. "What people?"

"Souza. Souza is the one foreclosing on us. I took photos of his documents." She reached for her back pocket to take out her cell phone and show him, but the phone was gone. And with it hope of convincing Cal. "We have to turn around. I lost my phone."

Cal's straightened his arms and leaned back from the steering wheel, distancing himself from the request.

"I'm serious."

"No way." He shook his head in disbelief and glanced at the time on his truck radio. "It's after midnight, and I'm just learning that you broke into Gil Souza's house. When?"

She couldn't think back to count the days. He slowed at the first stoplight into town. They waited out the red light in several seconds of uncomfortable silence before he let out a long whistle.

"Unbelievable." The light was still red, but he drove through it.

"There's more. A quitclaim."

"For what?"

"Our land."

"What about the necklace?"

"Kat said she didn't want her boyfriend's karma—meaning the

necklace—around her neck when she was in the hot tub with Cris, whom she's loved since she was the bat girl on his baseball team. The tattoo artist that was at the memorial insinuated Cris had a roving eye."

"What tattoo artist?"

When she told him about interviewing Cap, Cal shook his head. "You interviewed a tattoo guy?"

"He validated that Cris hadn't killed himself, and, if you can't be more positive, I'm not telling you what he said."

"You interviewed a tattoo guy?"

"Cal, what am I saying?"

"You're saying you haven't been honest with me about anything."

"I'm saying that Cris paid two thousand dollars in advance to get his tattoo colored in, but when I found his body in our beet field the tattoo was gray scale. He had invested in his future, Cal. She was with Cris at his house until it was time to take the box truck to the market. She admitted being in the hot tub with him and taking off her necklace. I think Johnson at Souza's bidding was destroying us by destroying your plants and when Cris caught Johnson in the greenhouse, Johnson killed him. I don't think Johnson knew Kat was there, but she saw him. That makes her a witness to murder. She was protecting Johnson but mostly herself from him all this time. Until tonight when she figured out her father had hired the thug to spy on her. She told him in front of me that she basically saw him kill Cris. She's so angry, she's thrown caution to the wind."

Cal took a deep breath as if he were about to jump in the deep end. "How did Johnson know where we grew the plants?"

"Probably Kat. Pillow talk. No idea that he'd use it against us." An involuntary shudder came over her and Cal put his arm around her.

"The plants are one thing, babe."

Here it comes.

"But you're another. What if Johnson had hurt you?"

"He didn't."

"You think of me and the kids for even a minute?"

"I was doing it for us."

"You were doing it because you're obsessed with this restless meddling and prying until you get to the bottom of this thing. You couldn't tell me where you were going because you felt guilty before you even left the house."

"I wanted Kat's reaction to the necklace. I wanted her explanation."

"It doesn't do any good if you're dead."

She slunk back in her seat. "Am I dead? The answer is no. Do we know a lot more about what's happening to our lives? Yes."

She hadn't expected Johnson to be there.

"Why couldn't you have waited until morning and asked her to meet you at a café?"

"Well, yes, I could've."

"And you could've told me."

"If I had told you, you'd be saying that a necklace isn't worth facing a pathological thief."

"If someone's sick enough to steal your necklace, you're right, who knows what they'll do under pressure."

"I took a risk."

"You told me you were going to Kinko's."

"I intended to go to Kinko's after, and, yes, the day was bad enough without a fight."

"Better a fight than the alternative."

"I think Gil Souza wants to quitclaim our farm to his daughter to win her love." Olive's entire body ached. She remembered putting her phone in her back jeans pocket and crouching behind the oak as Johnson scoured the prairie for her, his headlamps yards from where she hid. "Cal, we really do have to go back for my phone."

Cal jerked the truck left across the dividing line, in a squealing, swerving U-turn of surrender.

38

Another baby sea lion had washed up on shore. Its corpse was curled into a neat apostrophe while a turkey vulture gorged on the entrails. Biting flies swarmed over its eyes and flesh. Sea lions, like this one, were dying at an epidemic rate from a bacterial disease that had marine biologists panicking. As Olive walked past, she kept a safe distance. If that was the cause of the pup's death, he could be contagious, even dead.

She reached the staging area farther down the beach. Offshore, a paramedic on her rescue board worked to disentangle a surfer, who had apparently become tangled in the kelp, possibly drowned. The waves, which came in sets of three, impeded her progress. The first swell broke close to shore, but the second and third sets lifted the paramedic, not breaking, but powerful enough to push her yards away from the surfer. Another paramedic, who'd been standing onshore gripping a flotation device, jogged into the surf and swam out.

Olive scanned the small crowd of first responders who stood at the water's edge. It was a good thing she'd gone back for her cell phone. Cal had helped her search the bank where she'd fallen and it wasn't there. She found it under the oak where she'd crouched to hide from Johnson's search light. Detective Henry Rogers had called early this morning to tell Olive that the Highway Patrol had found Kat Granger's car in the parking lot off Highway One and a body was reported in the surf.

A man ran across the sand, bellowing at the top of his lungs.

Gil Souza, barefoot in the shore break, dressed in khakis and a long-sleeved shirt, jumped into the water. He dove under the first incoming wave, with barely enough time to get a breath before the next wave knocked him down.

An onshore paramedic dressed in his wetsuit bolted into the surf as another wave pummeled Souza, whose arms and legs flailed until the paramedic secured a grip around his chest and pulled him shoreward. Two cops dragged Souza in and sat him down on the wet sand. His chest heaved, head hung between his knees, sobs as loud as the crash of breaking surf.

The paramedic had pulled the victim onto her rescue board. From the shore, the body looked diminutive as the paramedic knee paddled toward shore with the assisting paramedic guiding the nose and negotiating swells between sets until they got onshore.

Remorse filled Olive as she stared at the blond dreadlocks tangled with thin strands of seaweed. It was Kat Granger.

Olive put her phone away for the sake of the paramedics, who loathed bystanders videotaping emergencies on their cell phones and sharing them on Facebook. The trend forced the medics to position themselves at angles that would block facial shots as they tried to save a life.

The paramedic kneeling at Kat's side was tall and broad shouldered with straight, powerful hips. Her wet hair had been pulled back into a tight braid to keep it from interfering with her work. She inserted the dull tips of orange-handled sheers into the neck of Kat's wetsuit and stripped the neoprene to her waist.

A chartreuse tattoo of seaweed vined down from Kat's neck to a jellyfish that covered her chest. Identical to the tattoo Olive had noted on Cris. Except for the color. Kat's was inked in vibrant Mediterranean blues and sunset pinks.

An EMT placed electrode pads on the top of Kat's right chest and to the side of the left breast. If the electrodes detected activity, the defibrillator would discharge a shock to restart the heart. A plastic hook was inserted into her mouth to depress the tongue and keep the airway open. An oxygen mask was adjusted to cover her face and one of the EMT's squeezed the semi-rigid balloon to pump air into her chest.

A sheriff's deputy asked Olive to step back.

"I know her," Olive said, understanding full well that knowing a victim did not give her the right to be present at the scene of an incident.

The paramedic glanced up quickly, then back to her work, cutting the arms of the wetsuit.

"Her name's Kat Granger," Olive said. "I was with her last night. She and her boyfriend were arguing."

"Sarg, did you catch that?"

The man addressed as Sarg was stout, near retirement age, not much taller than Olive. Sgt. Nunne was printed on his name tag. He asked Olive her name, where she lived, the time she witnessed the argument.

Olive told him, "It was roughly ten at night and she was visibly afraid of him, until she went ballistic. The he brandished a switch blade on me."

"Did you see the woman enter the surf?" he asked.

"No. She hates surfing. Doesn't even like the beach." Olive didn't need to offer any more details. She'd made her point.

Nunne took out his notebook and Olive stared at Kat's pale midriff, dotted with small dark moles. Her bony chest rose and fell with the pumped in oxygen. An eternity passed before they removed the shock pads, the mask and tube from her mouth. Olive cried. Sergeant Nunne pulled out a handkerchief and blew his nose. "Never get used to this."

The crew spoke softly as they packed up their equipment. The paramedic who'd pulled Kat out of the water draped a thin, wool blanket over the body.

"What's her boyfriend's name?" asked Nunne.

"Robert Johnson. Nickname Lobster."

Olive spotted Souza seated on the fire truck's rear bumper, a blanket covering his sagging shoulders. A cop stood by.

"That's her father sitting on the bumper," said Olive. "Gil Souza. He'd hired Robert Johnson to spy on Kat. She found out last night."

"The fellow who ran into the water? That's her father?"

"Yes."

Nunne pressed his shoulder mic and spoke code as he walked toward Souza. He was still asking questions when the deputy's neared, carrying the stretcher holding Kat's body up from the sand. When they reached the parking lot, Souza shrugged off the blanket, rose from the bumper and pushed Sergeant Nunne aside.

He bent over his daughter, touching his forehead to hers. Then he spotted Olive. "Why are you here? You're into every goddamn thing that goes wrong.

The cop held him back by the shoulders as he spewed profanities at Olive Purple veins corded on his forehead and spittle clung to his lower lip. "Get out of here."

"Sir, I am so sorry for your loss." Olive meant it. "You need know that I witnessed your daughter last night arguing with Robert Johnson."

The medics lifted the stretcher into the mouth of the van.

"Hold up," Souza ordered. His face was beet red and lips tight as he took out his phone and walked out of earshot, pulling the towel around his neck to muffle his voice. He was on his phone for less than a minute and returned with a vertical vein bulging in the center of his forehead.

Olive watched as Souza lifted a strand of hair from his daughter's face and tucked it behind her ear. A thread of sea grass lay over her cheek. He plucked the grass and wrapped it around his first finger. Brushed coarse sand from her face, cupped her chin in both his palms and kissed her forehead.

"I loved you, baby girl." He turned and walked unsteadily to the parking lot toward the yellow corvette.

Nunne slapped the wagon door, signaling it was clear to leave. They watched the coroner's van turn right toward town and the county morgue. Souza turned left onto the highway. His Corvette kicked up gravel and sped across the southbound lane, heading north toward his house.

To Olive, Nunne said, "I have a daughter her age and I'd never say, 'I loved,' as if it was finished." He sighed. "You never get used to this."

"Did you see signs of foul play?" Olive asked.

"Drowning is a sign of foul play. My girls always wear a rash guard when they surf. That one, Kat, no rash guard."

The breakers broke, creating a deafening boom. "I should have gone back," she said.

"What's that?" Nunne asked.

"If I had gone back to Kat's house last night, she might still be alive."

"You could say that. On the other hand, if you'd gone back, assuming what you said to be true, we might have two dead women on our hands." Maybe so, but his reasoning didn't assuage Olive's guilt.

"Not every day we see a dead body," Nunne said, "specially someone we know. Death plays tricks on us. Be extra cautious on your drive back home."

Olive looked around the parking lot for her Jeep before remembering she'd taken Lyft to get here. "Can you give me a ride to town?"

39

As Gil drove home, he replayed the phone conversation in his head. Son of a bitch.

"My daughter is dead," he'd told Johnson (as if the bastard didn't know), whom he'd called right after the Post woman told him about the argument. "She drowned. They found her up the coast in her wetsuit, tangled in kelp, and they're bringing her up the beach right now." He tried to control his voice. The Post woman had watched him while he listened to Johnson think up infuriating lies: I can't believe it, man. Holy shit. What was she doing in the water? The fakery stoked a rage that Gil couldn't control.

"You know anything about that?" Gil had asked.

Johnson's reaction was bogus—that's awful, no shit, what happened—which confirmed Gil's suspicion.

"I'm going to put a gun to my head if you don't get me something to take away the pain." Gil wasn't exaggerating.

"Go to urgent care, man. I don't know what to say, man. I'm in shock."

"I can't drive. I can't even see straight. Neon lights, tunnel vision. I need a drug. Oxycodone, whatever. I feel like I'm going to die."

Pause. "I feel for you, man, but I'm hung up here."

Prick. "My daughter is dead, goddamn it. I … need … your help." He'd softened his voice, sighed. "There's a bonus in it for you."

The bribe seemed to break down Johnson's resistance. He agreed to bring him drugs. After Gil stuffed the phone into his windbreaker, his eyes felt about to roll back in his head. The bait he'd thrown out to Johnson was true. He felt like he was going to die. He breathed deeply, watching the paramedics approach the parking lot with his daughter. One coil of her hair hung over the edge of the stretcher. Part of him was leaving with her, unraveling like a rope around runaway horse.

The All-Clad saucepan hanging from the stainless-steel pot rack above the stove would do just fine. And the skillet beside it, too. He poured a jar of Barilla Marinara into the saucepan. Into the skillet, a generous amount of olive oil. He selected his sharpest paring knife. From the overhead cupboard a box of linguine and from the freezer a Tupperware containing amanita the little boy Byrd had discovered on their hike up the mountain, which felt like another lifetime.

As he slid the blade of his knife under the pieces of mushroom, he almost laughed reimagining that woman sliding down the rock on that ample rear end.

The door chimed. Gil wasn't ready for Johnson—moreover, the meal wasn't ready—and reluctantly he turned off the flame under the skillet, the pleasant musky sweetness of sautéing mushroom rising. When he opened the front door, the Gypsy stood there with a hand on her hip, brazen as usual, and dressed in a low-cut silk blouse worn belted over a long turquoise skirt and scuffed, round-toed leather boots. He liked the boots, but her look of empathy put him on guard. He knew this about women—sympathy was designed to control. But he wouldn't fall prey. He had to stay mean to avenge his daughter.

"I know what happened, Gilbert." She put a booted foot in the doorway and for a moment he worried she might try to hug him. "My daughter told me, and I am so sorry."

"What's up?" He sounded rude, even to himself, but not rude enough. She continued to stand there like a she-wolf waiting to be invited in. No, ma'am. He had to get rid of her. If Johnson showed up when she was here, he'd have to call off his plan. That wasn't going to happen. She stepped over the threshold, brushing him slightly and smelling like roses. "Wait," he said, as she headed straight to the kitchen and took his seat at the breakfast nook where she began pulling things out of her satchel and setting them on the table.

"You're cooking?" she asked.

"I have to eat."

"It smells good."

He nodded. "So do you."

"You look like the walking dead. Take off the apron, put down the potholder, sit and talk to me. You're in crisis."

He picked up a Ziploc bag of what looked like some kind of herb and dropped it back into her satchel. "This is not a good time. You have to leave."

She stared at his feet and worked up to his eyes, searching, he gathered, for some understanding of what she'd interrupted. "You're really a mess. Your aura is black and your eyes are reptilian."

What the fuck did this woman expect? His daughter was dead and he was planning a murder.

In frustration, he opened the freezer and yanked a fifth of Stolichnaya from the shelf. The container storing the amanita fell onto the linoleum floor, skull and crossbones side up. He threw the container back in freezer and slammed the door shut. Ariela had a shocked expression on her face, but he wasn't inclined to explain, not even a lie.

The ice maker made a hostile sound when he pressed the highball glass against the ice lever. He set the glass on the counter, filled a second glass, poured the vodka, very robotic, worried Johnson would come to the door any minute with the drugs Gil had ordered as a pretext to lure him.

He pushed one of the vodkas-on-the-rocks toward her.

"Do you have green olives?"

He almost laughed at her audacity. He was pretty sure a couple of jars sat in the cupboard but bringing them down would only prolong the torture. "No olives." He remained standing as he took a large swallow of the drink. The breath-stopping sting transcended his emotional pain. He took another.

The Gypsy picked up her drink, swirled the liquor over the ice, bracelets jangling, creating a cacophony that she'd told him before was designed to scare off bad spirits. She was grating every cell of every involuntary muscle. He felt like screaming but finished the drink and set the glass in his stainless-steel sink.

"Kat's here," she said.

Reflexively, he glanced toward the kitchen doorway expecting to see her walk through. She pointed to the ceiling above the stove, where the sautéed amanita spores steeped in olive oil.

"Up there. She wants to communicate something."

Gil slammed his fist on the table. "Stop the hocus pocus. I'm expecting company. For god's sakes, my daughter is dead. I have things to do."

He pushed her shoulders to move her and smelled her rose perfume. The vodka had given him a buzz. He bent at the waist and kissed her hard on the mouth.

She flopped back in the seat. "That was an angry kiss." She wiped something from his cheek and smeared it on her silk blouse, leaving a wet blotch the size of a dime. A tear. "A sad, passionate, grieving, angry kiss."

The kiss aroused him, but he was tired of playing games and pulled her up. "I appreciate your concern, but I have work to do. You really do have to go." Murderous little bubbles gently broke the surface of the marinara he'd neglected to turn off.

"What company are you expecting?" She looked like woman who'd just realized a guy is two-timing her. At least that got her to standing. Now, pick up your satchel. As if she'd heard him and refused, she walked over to the stove and picked up the wooden spoon he'd left in the saucepan. She stirred slowly as if it were her fucking magic cauldron.

"No," Gil said. "You may not do that."

She lifted the spoon to her nose and sniffed. He snatched the spoon and raised it in the air out of her reach splattering oil on the cupboard. "What is wrong with you?"

She cringed but not in a frightened way. More like mockery. "What are you up to Gilbert?"

"The funeral director. He's coming over to counsel me. I'm fixing him supper for driving all the way out here."

She squinted, and he knew she didn't buy his lie because the only thing a woman would believe at this point was an admission of cavorting with another woman. Or the truth. She'd believe that he was plotting to poison his daughter's killer. He could tell her but that could deflate his intention and he could not allow that. She started to dip her finger into the limp mushrooms and warm olive oil. Horrified, he slapped her hand away. She glared at him and for a moment Gil was sure she knew his plan. He grabbed her elbow. "That's it." He marched her firmly down the hallway as if she were a disobedient child.

At the front door she turned to him and once again Gil feared she would try to smother him with a hug. "I'm leaving you to your company and spaghetti sauce but I'm returning tomorrow to check on you. You are not well and understandably so. I'll bring a strong tea to chase those demons and ease the broken heart. Something that will help you relax."

Little did she know he had plenty of potions on the way—the pharmaceutical variety which would be far more effective than her concoctions. He stared at her, feeling an odd transcendence, miles away from the person in front of him. Maybe this was the feeling you had when planning suicide and no one has a clue. Right now, she was offering sympathy to a man who was plotting murder. Tomorrow, he'd be a murderer.

She walked (not fast enough from Gil's perspective) to her absurd cart and swung surprisingly gracefully into the driver's seat. How in the hell she even got that thing up here to his house was a fucking mystery. He remained at the front door until she was out of sight, hoping she wouldn't pass Johnson on her way back down the mountain.

40

Robert Johnson placed two brown plastic prescription bottles on the table. Gil turned the bottles so he could read the labels. Oxycodone and Ativan. That should do it. He hadn't intended to actually take the drugs, but their promise of numbing his pain was speaking to him.

Johnson looked way too comfortable sitting in the exact spot the Gypsy had occupied less than twenty minutes ago. That might be a problem. She'd figured in her irritating way that he'd been expecting company, making her a potential witness to a crime he hadn't yet committed.

"Did you pass anyone on the way up the hill?" Gil asked.

"No, unless you count a doe and two fawns."

At least he didn't have to worry that the Gypsy had seen Johnson. As he placed two bowls of pasta on the table, a sense of power came over him.

"Pesto or tomato sauce?" Gil gripped the two stainless steel spaghetti scoops and held them in the air out of reach while Johnson decided, betting his last pair of socks that Johnson was not a pesto guy.

"Pesto."

Gil disguised his disappointment as he ladled the basil and garlic laden pasta onto his victim's plate, thinking if there was a god, it was working against him. Gil reconsidered. Maybe god was protecting him from a rage that would switch his rails for the rest of his life. Maybe he wasn't meant to kill a man, even if that man had drowned his only daughter.

"What about a glass of wine?" Gil stepped away from the table and walked a half dozen steps to the kitchen counter, opened the utilities drawer and fished out his best corkscrew. He perused the bottles in his wine rack on top of the refrigerator. Took down a Pinot Noir and decided he needed something bolder. Chose the bottle next to it, a vintage Zinfandel from Napa that had cost a small fortune. But hell, what better way to mark this sudden shift of plan by some mysterious work of providence. He peeled off the red seal from the bottle's slim neck and inserted the opener's pointed tip into the cork. He bent into the chore, twisting the tip through the spongey plug of Quercus suber, lifting it slowly and fully from the neck until it popped. He smelled the cork—spicy and rich—and poured two Schott Zweisel Air Bordeaux wine glasses a third full. He swirled the wine and took a dutiful sip before turning around.

Johnson had finished the pesto and was helping himself to the red sauce ala amanita.

Oh, well. Gil placed the glasses on the table and picked up the fresh wedge of parmesan with one hand and the grater with the other. "Cheese?"

"Sure," said Johnson.

The parmesan fell like snow over the glistening red sauce until it was so thick the red couldn't percolate up. Johnson, mesmerized by the grating, was about to devour a painful death.

"It's strange how someone is here one day and gone the next. That's the thing I can't accept. My daughter gone. I know it's true, but it doesn't feel true. I'm numb, then sad, then angry. I want to kill someone." He glanced at Johnson who shook his head, lifting his napkin to wipe his mouth. "I hope the meds help. She was an awesome girl. I miss her. I'm sorry man."

"You have no idea." Gil enjoyed a certain pleasure in watching Johnson, his head down, sucking up the noodles, splashing bits of the red sauce on his T-shirt, confirming he was not fit to live. "You're helping me more than you know."

As Johnson slurped up the noodles, red sauce speckled the table, and Gil had to control his impulse to wipe it clean. He didn't want to distract his prey or spread the evidence.

270

"I know you loved my daughter."

"What's not to love?" Johnson looked hungover, his eyes red and puffy, his face a deeper red than normal.

"I didn't intend for you to get involved in that way, though. I was thinking stewardship not, you know, relations."

"She was persistent. And hard to resist. A sexy chick."

Gil cringed. "I told you that she could never know I hired you."

"Not my fault. That Post bitch screwed it up."

No, dickwad, you screwed my daughter. "Robert, I don't have any extra work for you, and you'll just remind me of her."

"Not a problem. I got no reason to stick around. Going back to SoCal, maybe visit my bros down there. Check in with my surf sponsor. I need to process this whole thing."

Gil felt like puking, watching Johnson twist the linguini around his fork and shove it into his ugly mug, sucking up the hanging noodles with a slurp that made Gil want to lunge across the table and choke the pig. He chewed while he talked and Gil watched in disgust, aching to put end to this piece of shit. Soon enough. He needed some details. More lies from Johnson to justify his end.

"What was she doing in that surf?"

"That's what puzzles me. I told her not to surf alone."

"I thought you said she was afraid of the water?"

"I pulled her through that phobia."

"Something else has been bothering me."

"Yeah?" He looked up, still chewing.

"That little girl at the farmers market. Did you snatch her up and put her in the outhouse?"

Johnson's eyes opened wide as he put down his fork, and Gil knew the answer before the dumbshit spoke.

Gil continued, "The cops say someone put a note inside the baby's diaper. See how easy to lose what you love."

The silence translated to another yes.

"That Post bitch, as you like to call the baby's mother, identified the note as my handwriting. The cops came to my door asking questions."

"That cunt was snooping around where she shouldn't be. You saw her at the café with that elitist attitude."

Gil grabbed the pepper shaker and squeezed. "You're an idiot."

"I didn't hurt the kid."

"Like you didn't hurt my daughter?"

"What do you mean?"

Gil remained silent to see where Johnson would go with the question.

"You mean breaking the engagement? She got over that."

Gil watched Johnson clean his hands on his pants, rubbing back and forth, searching for a defense.

"I don't know why she went surfing by herself, man. I told her not to."

Gil noted the telltale flinch in Johnson's right eye. Then a hitch in his shoulder.

"I hired you to look out for her. You let me down." Gil scooped another helping of linguini and held it over Johnson's platter. "There are consequences in life, Robert. Consequences for loving too much. Consequences for thinking you've outsmarted the law." The noodles hung like tentacles and Gil thought of his daughter. "Consequences for letting me down." He lowered the noodles into a neat coil. "Did you know my daughter got herself a tattoo?"

"Yeah. It was cool."

Gil ladled tomato sauce around the pasta.

"You aren't eating," Johnson said.

"It was a huge tattoo." Gil imagined it covering most of her torso. "I can't eat." He wasn't lying.

Johnson leaned back from his plate, picking up his wine glass and pointing to the prescription bottles on the table. "Oxy for pain. Ativan for panic. They're yours man. No charge. My parting gift."

"Ah, parting gift." Gil studied the bottles in silence. "More than you know. My daughter was always mad at me. You know why?"

"She had a righteous temper, that's for sure."

"Did she ever say anything about me?" Gil waited. He wanted an answer.

"I don't think she fully appreciated you, the way you gave her money whenever she needed it. Even though she never wanted to see you, you were always there. At some unconscious level she knew that."

Johnson almost sounded intelligent.

"But if she knew what you were up to with that farm and those tomatoes, she would've turned both of us in. In a heartbeat."

The poison had by now entered Johnson's bloodstream and should be reaching his liver. Knowing this assuaged some of the pain Gil felt hearing Johnson's analysis. "How are those tomatoes?"

"Going well. The dude seems pretty sure he'll save enough seed for next year."

Next year. The concept crushed his nuts. There'd be no next year for the ruddy-faced asshole sitting across from him. And Gil had no idea how he'd get through to next year without his daughter, spiteful as she was. "Did she ever talk about me?"

"I'm going to be honest with you, Gil. You copped her power and snuffed her true self whenever you could. That's what she said."

"She said that?" He wondered how many other people had heard his daughter bad-mouth him. Everyone she met, probably, in her peanut gallery of brainwashed lefty friends.

"Sorry, man. You know as well as I do, her tongue could slice stale bread."

"What I can't understand is why."

"Why what?"

"She drowned. That puts her in the water when it was dark outside."

"She was pretty upset about me working for you. Maybe she killed herself."

"Like that wood carver they found in the field." Gil forked his cold linguini, raised it above his plate and watched the pesto sauce drip back to his plate like a leaky faucet. Another lie. Johnson had never told Gil he'd killed Cris Villalobos, and Gil purposely had never asked. But he knew, was pretty sure Johnson had been caught in the act of carrying out his orders to steal those stinkingly famous tomato starts. "How did you like my linguini?"

"Good."

"The sauce?"

"Nice job, man." He nodded, shifting in his seat.

"The mushrooms? You like their flavor?"

"Not a mushroom fan to be honest. But I ate it, didn't I?"

"Like a pig." Gil went to the freezer and pulled out the duct-taped plastic container. Johnson looked slightly stunned. "My turn to be honest."

Gil felt a tangible satisfaction watching the confusion on Johnson's dumb face.

"What's with the skull and crossbones?" he asked.

"I'm a fungus forager and an opportunist. That's how I got where I am and that's why you're where you are." Gil shook the container. "Amanita gathered from my own property. It's local and organic." Gil laughed at the irony.

"I'm not going to poison someone for you," Johnson said, "if that's what you're asking."

"Not asking you to poison someone. I can do that myself. That mushroom sauce ala these amanita…" He thrust the container in Johnson's face … "has entered your intestinal walls. By now, your gastrointestinal track has absorbed enough spore to kill a horse. It should be hitting your kidneys and liver within the next half hour. Quick to suffer, but a slow, agonizing death."

Johnson pushed back his chair, stuck his finger down his throat and gagged. Red and green vomit slapped the floor of Gil's kitchen.

Gil took a deep breath. "Too late for that."

Johnson stuck his finger down his throat, again.

"You might want to call emergency while you can. A little charcoal carbonate to protect those organs. Maybe they'll put you on the liver transplant list, which, personally, would be a waste of time. A wicked plant. That's what killed my hound. Renal failure. Maybe you'll be luckier than my dog. But I doubt it." Gil put his hand on Johnson's shoulder. "I loved that hound. Can't say as much for you."

Gil watched Robert Johnson ram the electric gate with his big truck and roar off down the mountain.

He opened the prescription bottles and shook out two from each and climbed the stairs to his bedroom. He lay down on the leather chaise in front of the plate glass windows and stared at the view of the forest. In that drugged first stage of spreading relaxation and improved mental focus before oblivion, he noticed for the first time that the latch on the sliding glass door was unlocked.

41

Olive studied Cap's reaction as her words soaked in. His nano-second of shock was earnest. "She was found dead this morning. Drowned. In a wetsuit, tangled in kelp."

Cap took a puff on his vape.

"She was your client."

"How do you know she's my client?"

"Her tattoo. A jellyfish, exactly like Cris's but with color."

"Anyone could do that." He shook his head, slowly. "Was she high or what?"

"Trapped in rough surf and drowned. The police aren't saying if they suspect violence, but she didn't like to surf, much less on a cold morning, and she would never go alone."

"Her boyfriend who was always skulking around have any-thing to do with it?"

"Her fiancé?"

"She never said he was her fiancé."

"She came in on Cris's tailwind," Cap said. "Everyone in the shop knew she had a thing for him, although I don't think it was as reciprocal as she'd like. That made it even hotter for her, my guess. Some women are like that, addicted to the unavailable guy. It's familiar and, from what I gathered, her father was a jerk. Let's check out her last and next appointments. Surly, find out when Kat Granger's next appointment is scheduled."

Surly checked the computer. "Next appointment is this week. She already advanced a thousand."

"She's dead, man."

"Should I scratch her off the calendar and call our cancellation list?"

Cap shook his head apologetically. "Inappropriate, Surly."

Olive was short on time. She had to pick up Byrd from preschool and take him to a playdate at the park and relieve her mother from watching Gus. "Can you tell me what you know about Kat? I'm trying to put the pieces together."

Cap put his vape aside and crossed his arms so the intricate dragonhead on his one bicep bulged. "Father issues. Whenever the father word came up, she had bad stuff to say. Sounded like a rich corporate dick who tried to control her with money. She'd sit in the chair and go deep about the bad things his business does. She was passionately anti-Frankenfood, and it sounded like her pop was a head honcho in that scene. I'd just listen while I worked on her."

"What about her fiancé, Robert Johnson?"

"That dude skulked. He'd drop in and ask if she'd been by. We couldn't tell him because we respect our clients' privacy. It didn't seem like love on his end or hers. More like a power trip." Cap scratched his nose. "She was basically a good girl. She'd just given me an advance to start on her back. Don't know what to do with her deposit. You got a second? I want to show you something."

Cap produced a sheet of white art paper and set it on the table in front of her. A sketch of a nude woman sat with her back to the viewer. A tattoo of tomato vines spanned the lower back. The small red tomatoes were delicate, and he'd colored the vines so exactly green that she could smell the acrid scent she craved this time of year.

"That's really pretty," she said, flatly, "but I'm here about Kat. Are you going to tell the cops about Cris and Kat and the down payments?"

"Some of my clients are cops, but I'm not going to invite them in. That's asking for trouble. Now, what do you think of the sketch? I designed it for you.

She felt uneasy as Cap chipped at her boundaries. "I'm here on serious business. A woman who was having an affair with my dead neighbor is also dead. And the dead woman's father is foreclosing on my farm. That's more than I want to tell you, but you need to know I have a personal stake in this."

Cap leaned back and tossed the sketch onto his desktop as if he were drawing a finishing stroke. "I wouldn't mess with those dudes—not the fiancé, not the father."

42

The Oaxacans worked skillfully and efficiently. At their pace, the tomato vines would be tied by the end of the week, which was still pushing it. Cal needed more labor.

He stood in the field among the tomato plants instructing a small group of inexperienced young adults on how to stake and string the vines. The process of staking and tying was time consuming and repetitive but essential. Though the Oaxacan crew was skilled, there weren't enough of them.

Olive smiled as she watched Cal demonstrate to what he called his "auxiliary crew" how to tie the string high enough on the vine and tight enough between the stakes to prevent sagging when the plants grew fuller and taller and the fruit heavier. The crew consisted of four university graduates and Brody. The graduates needed extra summer work to survive the cost of living in Santa Cruz. Brody had showed up for the extra money but, mostly, to support Cal. They listened intently as Cal instructed them. Meanwhile, the Oaxacan crew were already halfway down the rows.

Brody was a quick study, and, apparently, he wanted to prove his worth to Cal. He was already a farmer, and his work ethic growing up on a ranch gave him confidence and a bit of healthy attitude. He waited until one of the Oaxacans started a new row before beginning his own. He worked diligently and quietly. Every few minutes, he glanced up and measured the progress of his competition in the next row. Before he was halfway down the row, he took the lead.

Olive worried Brody might have sacrificed tightness for speed. If the string were loose, it wouldn't hold the vines' weight once the tomatoes fruited, and the entire row would have to be restrung. Cal was on the same wavelength as he walked down the row checking the work. He wouldn't make a big deal out of the quality of Brody's work, either way. If it were taut, he might say a couple of words of affirmation. If it were loose, he would talk to Brody, no criticism, just the facts, and Brody would have to restring. Olive watched, tension mounting. Brody didn't glance up or pause in his routine as Cal examined the string.

Nice work is all Cal said. Brody's shoulders relaxed. He hadn't heard about Kat until this morning when Olive told him that she had drowned. He was shocked. Olive recalled their chemistry at the farmers market that day Brody had been trying out his "wife of a farmer" routine.

She was about to hug Brody, but he stepped back and held up his gloved hands. "I saw so much potential in that girl." He walked away, slipping off a glove so he could wipe his eyes, then spit into the dirt. Brody would have been a better match for Kat than Johnson, Olive thought. Those two might have made something of their lives.

Byrd waved a metal stake in the air and she ordered him to put it down. An impaled child was the last thing she needed. When Gus cried from the playpen, she lay down her hammer and covered her with a blanket and rubbed her back until she closed her eyes and fell back to sleep.

Ariela drove down the road. Her long turquoise skirt billowed from the cart, exposing boots and bare thighs, and she'd wrapped a scarf around her head to keep her hair in place. Clearly, Olive thought, she was going somewhere important, looking straight ahead without slowing down even when Johnny Pogonip appeared out of nowhere and stood squarely in the middle of the road.

She blared the horn as Johnny waved his arms for her to stop. She slowed down to a creep and nudged him to the side of the road with the front end of her cart as if he were a cow, and then drove past, leaving him shaking his fist and shouting words Olive couldn't understand.

And now, he strode toward Olive, who picked up her hammer and a stake as Johnny closed in. He seemed more distraught than he had been the morning she'd found Cris in their beet field.

"M'lady is in danger." Johnny's breath was labored, and he held his hand on his chest. "The lay lady lay is in so much danger."

Johnny's small eyes were surprisingly bright blue and another canine was missing so that his top lip caved slightly inward.

"I saw something, miss, while standing outside in the moonlight of death. I confess. I saw them."

"Who did you see, Johnny? You have to be specific." She had to be firm or he'd drift into a stream of dialogue that Olive didn't have patience for.

"The two of them in the waters of the Nile, alligators and poisonous snakes dripping from the quintessential hanging fruit. Put down your weapons and I'll tell."

Olive let her hammer and stake drop onto the chunky dirt. She crossed her arms.

"When said woman goes to the said man's house, she's all fucked up." He waved his arms. "The wood carver and trustilocks."

"Who? Ariela?"

"No. Trustilocks. The girl who walks the tightrope above the pond of Venus flytraps," Johnny shook his arms wildly and Olive had no choice but to assure him she understood.

Cal, at the opposite end of the tomato field, was engrossed in work when she shouted for him. Once she caught his attention, she waved him over and told Johnny she wanted him to repeat what he'd said to Cal and they'd decide what to do.

"Can't do that," said Johnny. "The words come and leave and a new string appears. They ran from the woods like Adam and Eve's first fight from paradise into the mouth of the snake."

"Everything okay here?" Cal, wanting to work, hung his head as Olive told the short version of what Johnny had said. "I think he saw Cris and Kat in the hot tub the night Cris was murdered."

"No." Johnny shook his head. "That's wrong. I saw the white devil kill him, and the Fairy Queen is next."

"Let's call the cops," Cal said.

"Don't you know what those cops'd do with a peeper? They'd drill me so bad I'd be Swiss cheese." Johnny stared at Olive. "Something bad is about to happen."

Olive nodded. "Johnny, do you know where Ariela is going?"

He shook his head. "Full speed to the devil."

Cal put a hand on Johnny's shoulder and scanned the field "Why should we believe you saw someone on the night Cris died?"

"It wasn't night. It was like a shade, man."

"Do you know who?"

"I told you. The albino." Johnny put a finger to his head. "You got a light in there."

"We're calling the police."

"I said no cops. They'll kill me."

Olive recalled Johnson's ghostly skin at Kat's house. This explained Johnny's albino reference. Her cell phone rang. Detective Rogers's name showed up on her screen.

She tapped speaker and they hovered over the phone as Rogers reported that Robert Johnson was in the ICU with renal failure.

"Check Johnson's phone and find out if Souza called him yesterday morning. I watched Souza make a call at the scene of Kat's death, and he was raging."

"I need a warrant to check the phone."

"Can't you get one?" Olive watched Johnny retreat into the woods. "And we have a tip." Cal nodded for her to continue. "Someone else witnessed Cris's murder."

"Go on."

She told Rogers what Johnny had said and her interpretation of what he'd said. "I'm pretty sure my mother is heading to Souza's."

The silence on Rogers's end was ambiguous. So were his parting words. "Don't go out there on your own and let me know if you hear anything else."

"I'll drive out there." Cal started to walk toward the washing shed where he'd parked the F150. "You stay with the kids."

Brody's legs straddled the dirt. Watching Cal leave, his crossed arms resting on a stake. Once Cal disappeared, he resumed work.

43

The chimes reduced Gil's brain to shards as he rose from bed and shuffled to the door. The last person he wanted to see stood in the entry, a basket on her cocked hip.

"You have a bad habit of busting in without calling first." He rubbed the grit from his eyes. "It's rude, especially considering I've just lost a daughter."

The Gypsy reached her arm across the threshold and patted his cheek before pushing past him, leaving a wake of patchouli and turquoise as she went to the kitchen.

"I would've brought food, but the last time I was here I saw you're able to cook. How did that go? With the friend you were making dinner for."

"He backed out at the last minute." Gil followed her into his kitchen where she stood before the stove.

"And you have the leftovers to prove it. Two plates, in fact." She scanned the counters, claiming the bench seat where Johnson had sat and she before that.

"I'm in a bad mood. Do whatever it is you have to do and leave me alone."

"I wouldn't expect otherwise, Gil. I'm here to set your soul at ease."

He'd be damned if he was going to acquiesce to her woo-woo shit. His body ached and he was hung over from the drugs, the closest to depression he'd ever felt. The pots and pans scattered across the counters magnified the chaos he wished would suck him down the mudflats of extinction. Then he remembered. He'd actually sat in his lounge chair, sometime between drugged sleeps, with a loaded shotgun on his lap. He told her, "I thought of killing myself last night. Just a thought, kinda like fish swimming across my mind."

Her face was expressionless as he shoved down the chill that wanted to race up his spine.

"How?" she asked.

"Shotgun. It's still loaded."

"Then it was more than a thought." Gypsy lifted a baggie of dried twigs from her basket. "Much more. I'll fix some tea."

The smell of marinara with amanita had intensified from sitting out on the stovetop—onion, garlic, basil, wine, oregano and a hint of sweet earthiness that had to be the mushroom. "I'd be grateful," he said, "but I'm sick, and I can hardly stand on my own two legs." He put his head in his hands and groaned. It was real, this feeling so bad that death was an option.

She lifted sticks from the baggie. "The tea will take the edge off, not the sadness. You will feel, but feelings can't kill you."

The hell they can't. He didn't want help. She had ulterior motives. She saw his weakness as an opportunity to control him. "I need to lie down. Alone."

"Look where alone's getting you." She filled the teapot and turned on the burner as if she owned the place.

"You like being stronger than the man, don't you?"

"It's not a matter of 'like,'" she said.

The rustle of her skirt as she followed him upstairs reminded him of that damn lawyer walking down the aisle. As he lay himself down, he heard himself groan from fatigue for the third time that morning. He let her take off his socks and put a pillow under his knees and he instinctively placed his hands over the crotch of his pants.

She sat cross-legged at the end of the bed, took out a bottle of something that smelled like pumpkin pie from her satchel. When she pressed the ball of his foot between her thumb and first finger, he jumped and she didn't seem the least bit surprised.

"When's the last time something beside a sock or a rug touched your feet?"

He tried to come up with a sarcastic reply, but the words wouldn't come because her thumbs on the ball of his foot depleted all resistance. She pressed until he yelped.

"Your points are responding. That's good." Her fingers dug into the arch of his foot. "This spot releases grief and may make you cry. Know that you're safe with me."

He was confused and wanted to kick her in the chest, but the tears running down his temple itched.

To his relief, the kettle screamed from the downstairs kitchen and she climbed off the bed and left the room. He felt himself drift.

"Sit up."

His eyes opened. "Jesus Christ. I was asleep."

She held his head as he sipped her tea. "Good," she cooed.

He waved her off. "Don't mother me."

She reassembled herself at the end of the bed, the mattress bounced and her ample ass moving so close to his face that he might have spanked it if he had the energy. She faced him and refocused her energy on the ball of his other foot.

"Does this feel good?" she asked.

"Kind of."

"It's okay to admit pleasure."

"While you think up the next bit of torture."

Something wet sprinkled his face. She'd doused him with the tea sticks.

"This will keep the bad energy at bay."

A little late for that.

Swiftly and surprisingly gracefully, she stood on the bed above him. He covered his face with one arm and held up a hand to steady her as she climbed to the head of the bed and placed his head on her lap. Her fingers went to work on his temples.

"Breathe," she said.

"I am breathing."

"Close your eyes and concentrate on your breath. It will block your dark thoughts and help you relax. Inhale. Keep inhaling. Hold. Breathe out through your mouth."

Looney tunes, he thought, and reached up to scratch his ear. When she pushed his hand away, he grabbed her wrist.

A strength came to him. His grief turned to anger. He pulled her down and flipped her onto her back, scooted down and buried his face in those skirts, smelling her. No underpants. He was hard, and she moaned when his breath warmed that spot. "How's this for breathing?"

Her hands pressed his head like a vise and she moaned as he knew she would. He pulled himself up and kissed her mouth as he eased himself into her and felt her warm, rippling flesh all around him, begging him to cum. He climaxed in a loud, elongated shout and collapsed into her massive hair as a sob rose from his chest.

She smoothed his head, pausing at the spot she'd clipped. When he got off her, she turned and wiped tears from his face. What had just happened? Then, he remembered his daughter was dead. A chill shot up his spine. Kat's tattoo and her face strewn with sea grass shot into his brain and the shame burned every cell of his body for hiring a treacherous bum to spy on his own daughter.

He rolled away, feeling her against him, warm and fleshy. When he woke up, she lay beside him, dressed in his white undershirt, breasts spilling out the sides.

His stomach hurt.

"Are you okay?"

"My stomach." He went to the bathroom. In the middle of a

noisy cramp, he heard the Gypsy shout that she was going downstairs to give him privacy.

A lifetime passed before he felt he might live. He showered and climbed back in bed. The Gypsy entered the bedroom, this time wearing his jeans and flannel shirt, and carrying a mug of something steamy.

"This will help your stomach. Camomile, catnip, ginger, peppermint and orange peel." She held it to his mouth, so he had to drink. "I'll give it ten minutes. After that, I'm on top."

He closed his eyes. "You are a beautiful woman, and I don't say that to just anyone."

"And you're a good cook," she said, her head thrust back.

He bolted upright. "What did you say?"

"I like your spaghetti sauce, even old."

"Goddamn it, woman. I told you not to clean up the kitchen."

"Why? What's wrong?"

Something I can't fix.

44

The gate to Gil Souza's estate was wide open. Her mother's golf car had been parked neatly in the circular driveway near the front porch and Cal's Ford was parked on the lawn. She drove up parallel to Cal's truck and left the keys in the ignition. As soon as she reached the front porch, she heard an explosion.

Gunshot. It reverberated on all sides up to the treetops. A man ran from the side of the house into the woods, his bathrobe flying behind him. Souza, unquestionably.

Olive rushed inside as Cal collapsed at the base of the staircase and hit his head on the stone foyer. Blood gushed from his left shoulder. She ripped off her shirt and pressed it onto the wound to slow the bleeding.

"What are you doing here?" he asked, staring up at her. "You were supposed to stay with the kids."

"Brody's watching the kids." She punched 911 when Ariela appeared at the top of the stairs. No visible blood on her. "Are you hurt?" Olive shouted.

"I'm fine."

"An ambulance is on the way."

In the half hour it took the Davenport paramedic engine to arrive, Cal had lost a lot of blood. The paramedics gently pushed Olive aside and applied compression bandages, took his vitals and hooked up an IV. His blood pressure had dropped, his heartbeat was slow. Fuck.

More sirens screamed up the driveway, then abruptly stopped.

The only sounds were a raven's caw and patrol cars closing in. Olive relayed everything she knew to the sheriff deputies. In minutes, the firefighters had secured Cal in a gurney and rolled it to the ambulance.

"I know where he went." Ariela looked ill, most likely in shock, and Olive assumed that she and Souza had been in bed (if the bathrobe were an indication) when Cal had showed up.

"Did he hurt you?" Olive asked.

"Not on purpose." Her words were lethargic.

Other waved another paramedic over. "My mother needs attention."

As the EMTs secured Cal and two additional paramedics checked Ariela, Olive decided she should stay with her mother.

"I'll be fine, Love," Ariela insisted. "I took an antidote."

"An antidote for what?"

"Amanita, Love."

"There is no antidote for amanita."

"Love, believe me. I've been preparing for this moment." She grasped Olive's forearm. "Now find Gil and do not hurt him."

45

Olive was out of her mind about Cal as the ambulance raced off to the nearest medivac landing and she waited impatiently for the second ambulance to arrive. She watched, shaking her head, as the EMTs loaded up her protesting mother, who insisted she was fine and didn't need medical attention. Ariela lifted her head from the prone position she'd been coaxed into and pointed to the mountain top. The van's back doors closed.

"And don't kill him," she rasped.

Olive watched the ambulance taillights flashing red as it descended the road. The mountain fell quiet, no more shots fired. She had the Jeep in drive, ready to follow the ambulance when Detective Rogers drove through the gate. He leaned an elbow out the window of his sedan. "I need to talk to you," he said.

"Cal's been shot. I have to get to the hospital."

"Turn off the car."

She froze at his tone, dreading bad news about Cal.

"He's critical but it could be worse. The shots missed his heart. You need to calm down. If you can't, you'll be wasting your time."

He pulled out his radio and asked for a check on Cal Post. She overheard the voice on the other end. Critical. Loss of blood. Blood pressure low but holding. Ambulance five minutes out from the medivac. Helicopter is waiting for transport.

"Transport where?" Rogers asked, his voice calm and firm.

Olive's mind raced. "His blood type is O."

"Stanford," he relayed to Olive.

Santa Cruz County's two hospitals lacked a trauma center. Victims of gunshot were flown over the mountain range to Stanford Hospital near Silicon Valley.

"The wife reports victim is type O."

"Is he going to live?" She gripped Rogers's sleeve.

"They're doing everything they can." He ended his call. "I'm going to ask you to tell me what happened here, from the beginning." When she filled him in, he asked if they'd found Souza.

"You're the cop. You should have more information that I do."

"At ease. I'm assessing your lucidity."

"I know where he is." At least, based on her mother's vague directions. She turned from the patrol car and walked toward the only path she could see that headed up mountain.

46

Gil stumbled forward with his shotgun until he reached the peak. He raised his arms and held his gun overhead, robe flapping from a gentle onshore breeze. He almost felt good. On top of the world. The sky was big, the ocean big. Humans were small and absurd.

Someone called his name. The voice came from the trail. The damn Post woman. She was telling him to surrender. He didn't have the energy to argue with one more pushy woman. He turned the shotgun and aimed, almost laughing at how ridiculous she looked with a gun pointed at her chest.

"Gil, if someone hurt my daughter, I'd want to do the same."

"He did hurt your daughter." He only saw what was in his center vision. The rest was flashing neon. He couldn't feel his feet and his tongue and hands tingled. He was having a fucking heart attack. "This is your fault." His tongue felt thick and the words were slurred.

"Why us?" he heard her say.

He raised the shotgun and smelled gun metal as he stuck the muzzle hard under his chin.

"Don't," Olive shouted.

Like she cared.

Rogers, his revolver drawn, ordered Olive to stay back. She ignored the order and called Souza by first name.

"It's over, Gil." Olive inched closer and watched Souza strain to focus.

When he jammed the shotgun's muzzle hard under his chin, she grabbed a handful of dirt and threw it at Souza's eyes. He dropped the gun and stepped backward off the cliff, creating a soft thud when he landed twenty feet down, sprawled on his back in a dense thicket of manzanita.

Upstairs, on the second floor of Dominican Hospital, Gil Souza lay in ICU with a broken neck. Downstairs, in the ER, doctors and nurses administered to Ariela activated charcoal with an IV of silibin, the antidote that had recently saved an entire family of mushroom foragers. Her blood count was normal, her kidneys and liver functioning. No signs of amanita poisoning.

One of the nurses congratulated Ariela on her speedy recovery.

"I didn't recover because I was never poisoned." Ariela described her routine of daily ingestion of milk thistle as soon as she had packed up for California. Then she turned in her hospital bed and asked Olive how her "outlaw-son-in-law" was doing.

Olive shook her head. "He's in critical condition, tubes everywhere, collarbone shattered and he's lost a lot of blood. "The nurses didn't let me stay long and the kids cried the entire time."

Ariela's arm with its own share of tubes grabbed Olive's hand. "Widow is not your story."

47

Could it be worse? Always.

Summer's heat had developed complexity in Cal's tomatoes. Their customers raved over their tart sweetness held by sturdy skins. Mateo stood in the aisle of the farmers market and held out a slim fork with a tomato wedge. One at a time, passersby held out their palms as if receiving holy communion. They walked away but, as the flavor registered, invariably made a U-turn back to the tables stocked with boxes of firm, red fruit, the last of the season. The last of their cash crop. And they were broke.

Dead broke.

But it could be worse. They could have lost the farm to Gil Souza. But they took him to court, and court had decided in Cal and Olive's favor. Souza showed up in court with a square metal cage around his head. He'd broken his spine in two places from his fall off Pico Verde. The doctors weren't sure if the manzanita had broken his fall or his back, but nonetheless, the metal halo was dramatic, albeit ironic, and it did nothing to sufficiently raise the jury's empathy. Their unanimous decision found Souza guilty of foreclosure fraud, coupled with willful and malicious destruction of crops on the night Cris Villalobos had died. Gil admitted sending his employee Robert Johnson to do the dirty work and he admitted his motives: a final attempt to win back his daughter by gifting her an organic farm. The court dismissed the charges against Robert Johnson: A dead man is beyond the reach of human criminal law. But his murder was another story. Souza faced charges and his trial was set for January.

Meanwhile, Gil's appeal to the ninth federal district court fizzled. Likewise, his GE sugar beet processing plant and dreams of reaching the pinnacle of biotech collapsed in the dump of bad ideas.

Olive knew, however, if one grower had almost gotten away with violating the county's GMO ban, others were doing the same. Bad behavior was never unique, especially when it promised money. So, even though Gil Souza had lost his generations-old business, his child and his reputation, his fate would not deter those intent in following his footsteps.

"Do you have any more tomatoes?" A woman wearing large horn-rimmed sunglasses and a wide brimmed straw hat held a canvas shopping bag that overflowed with carrot tops from the farm down the aisle. Olive cheerfully explained, as she had many times today, this was their last harvest for the year.

"That's too bad." The disappointment was unmistakable.

Olive apologized while she watched her mother dropping a tip into the musicians' basket. She handed some change to Byrd and gestured for him to do the same. Ariela walked the perimeter of the market, checking out produce with Byrd in tow, and didn't stop until she reached Brody's stall. Apparently, she made one of her blunt comments, judging from the way Brody laced both palms on his chest in a What? Me? gesture.

Ariela appeared in a huff, not especially out of the ordinary, and interrupted Olive's money exchange.

"I can't stand it," Ariela said, "when people wear offensive T-shirts to get a rise." She tossed her head defiantly, as Olive concentrated on adding up her next customer's produce. "Two carrots for three dollars a bunch, onions for three a pound, butter lettuce at five a pound ... "

"That Brody is wearing a Jefferson State T-shirt."

Olive concentrated on her customer, ignoring her mother.

"It's such dark energy," Ariela said. "I think he trying to get a rise out everybody."

"Looks like he succeeded." Olive counted change back from a twenty into her customer's hand. She'd only heard about the Jefferson Staters, who resurfaced after Hillary Clinton took California by a landslide. The first time she saw one of their green and white billboards was on a road trip through the northerly farmlands on her way to the Shakespeare Festival in Ashland, Oregon. This fringe movement of white, anti-immigration folks mostly lived in California's rural reaches up to the Oregon border and beyond. Their objection to being politically overshadowed by the loathsome liberal Central Coast had spurred their mission of independent statehood and rejoining the Union as Jefferson State.

"Maybe he's being ironic," Olive said.

She put the twenty under the cash tray, remembering the so-called dark energy her mother had invited into their lives when Olive was growing up, mostly in the form of men. She waited until her customer walked out from under the canopy toward the next stand. "How can you be so judgmental of a T-shirt? You just involved yourself sexually in relationship with a man who not only tried to steal our farm, but also hired a murderer to spy on his daughter, then poisoned him."

Her mother had a retort, Olive sensed, from the way she clenched both hands to her hips, raised her eyebrows and inhaled long and deep. Let it rip, Olive thought. I've said what I needed to say.

"Let me point out, dearest daughter, that if it were not for my manipulation of that man, including the sex, we would never have found out what he was capable of." Now she wagged her finger at Olive as if she were a naughty girl.

"You wouldn't have had sex with him if you weren't attracted." Olive had to admit, her mother did cinch the case against Gil Souza. The forensic match between the contents of Ariela's stomach and Robert Johnson's was positive for amanita. It was a wonder she was alive standing beside her in full Ariela form.

"Where are the tomatoes?" A man holding up a fresh bunch of basil was clearly disappointed.

"I'm sorry. It was a small crop this year." She forced another smile, this one even wider. "I appreciate your asking."

"That's a shame." The man started to turn. "There's only one other farm that sells a similar tomato."

Olive's curiosity rose. Despite organic farmers sharing deeply held values, they were still in competition for markets and customers. She asked which farm.

"A farm in the mountains. I live in Morgan Hill."

Morgan Hill was a sweet rural community nestled at the southern foot of the Coastal Range near the Salinas Valley. She kept her voice even. "Do you remember the name?"

He tried but failed. "The farmer only charged three bucks per pound. That I remember." His eyes widened to underscore Cal's four-fifty per pound.

She watched the customer leave, stop, and turn sharply.

"Jefferson Farms," he said, triumphant his memory hadn't failed. "The guy who sold them is over there." The customer pointed across the market, and Olive knew who he was pointing at without looking. A panicky feeling came over her and she kept her head down.

"The pumpkin stall," the man said.

Across the food court's tables and chairs with people sitting to eat and chatting was Brody, talking on his cell, staring at customers as they passed his stall, not stopping, because his produce was meager—potatoes and squashes—and uninteresting. Except for the pumpkins. All shapes and colors. He felt Olive staring, glanced up. In a few seconds he put his phone in his back pocket and turned away. Ariela, beside her, eyes closed, was already chanting under her breath.

"Mom, we're leaving. I'm breaking down the stall. You round up the kids and get them in the truck. Hurry."

She paced herself to appear unrushed but turned down the last-minute shoppers who wanted a good deal. Packed the unsold onions, lettuces, chicory, string beans, beets into black plastic crates and stacked them in the back of the box truck. Next, she stacked the unsold flats of strawberries. Whipped off the flowered tablecloths and stashed them in a corner of the truck. Now, the tables. She hefted the first of five onto its side, threw the rings and kicked the legs to collapse it, carried it to the back of the truck and shoved it along the wall.

She picked up the weighing scales and discreetly glanced sideways at Brody as he lowered his single umbrella. There was a quality about Brody that she had noticed but didn't make much of, until now. The way he looked out at the near distance while he worked, as if he were anticipating someone or something. Even now, as he carried the umbrella to his truck, he looked to his right, as if watching for oncoming traffic where there was none. On his return to the stall, he scanned the emptying market lot, then saw Olive. He didn't smile like he normally would. Instead, he looked through her and beyond her as if she weren't there. She averted her eyes and sped things up, taking down the white board and the CCOF sign, assuring the produce was certified organic. She unhooked the Shell Bean Farm banner. Unlocked each leg of the easy up. Lowered the canopy and pushed in the corners tight enough that she could tie a strap around the middle. She looked up at Brody, who had just put up his tailgate, scanning the market as he did. She finished just as he climbed into his flatbed.

Olive swung into the cab while Brody idled at the exit from the market parking lot, about to turn left. She waited until he turned onto the road to follow him.

"Not too close, Love. Guilty men know when they're being followed."

As Olive drove south on Highway One, she realized she had no idea where Brody farmed. His truck turned off on the Old San Jose Road ramp, which led up mountain to patches of fertile land surrounded by redwoods. Olive tailed him up the winding road and lost sight of him on the succession of tight curves until she spotted his flatbed on the far side of a rickety wooden bridge that spanned the creek. He appeared to be waiting for something, probably, Olive guessed, confirmation that he was being followed.

Ariela slunk down in her seat. "Duck."

Ducking wouldn't hide the large block letters on the side of the box truck. Shell Bean Farm. She kept driving to the summit.

"We're turning around up here."

"Why, Love? Why don't we just confront him?"

"I need to tell Cal."

At home, she made gnocchi out of Brody's potatoes. They sat aside as she plucked stems from overripe Augusta Girl tomatoes, pushed her finger in the brown to break the skins and dropped them in a pot to simmer. As the gnocchi sunk in the broth, she skimmed the tomato skins. When the gnocchi popped to the surface, signing they were done, she scooped them with a slotted spoon to dry before braising them in olive oil. She had a plan.

Cal emerged from the shower, his wounded left arm in a freshly laundered sling. He sat down at the head of the table with the kids and Ariela. Olive stood beside Cal and ladled the sauce into a soup bowl, then spooned the steaming gnocchi on top.

Cal was famished and promise of hot food made him happy. Sadly, his mood would be short-lived.

"You made these? Really good."

"They're from Brody's russets. I steamed them, riced them and mixed them with a little flour and herbs."

"For goddess sakes." Ariela said. "Stop with the passive aggressive. Tell him or I will."

Cal looked up from his second helping of gnocchi, confused. "Tell me what?"

"Just say it, Love. That charming young man is a wolf in sheep's clothing. I never did buy his gentleman ways. Who stands when a lady leaves the dinner table except a guilty man?"

Cal, fork mid-air, looked bewildered. "What is she talking about?"

"You tell it, Love, or I will."

"We followed Brody up Old San Jose Road. He's up to something."

"I'm confused."

"A man at the market said he bought tomatoes as good as ours at the Morgan Hill farmers market, sold by Jefferson Farms. He pointed across the food court to Brody and said he was the guy who sold them."

"Brody doesn't grow tomatoes," Cal said.

"No," said Ariela. "He steals them."

Cal appeared even more confused until Olive laid out the events.

"Remember," she said, "when you told him at dinner exactly when we were transplanting the tomatoes. We think it was Brody in the white van checking out the plants. And then you taught him how to stake and tie the vines." She cringed when she recalled how she had trusted him to watch Byrd and Gus.

"You followed him to Old San Jose in the box truck?" Cal was starting to see the picture Olive was drawing.

"Three-quarters of the way. He crossed a bridge and waited to see if we were following. Basically, he busted us. I wanted to tell you … "

"A bridge?" Cal was out of his chair, headed to the front door. "I know that property," he said, grabbing the golf club from the umbrella vase on his way out. "Olive, aren't you coming?"

Of course she was coming. She turned to her mother, and though she didn't need to ask, she did need to make eye contact to make sure Ariela realized this wasn't about watching the kids to the best of her ability. It was about taking good care of the kids while she and Cal got to the bottom of things.

48

The pumpkins that grew in the surprisingly open meadow boasted fuzzy, gray-green leaves as large as plates. Cal walked through the patch toward a thick curtain of tall corn, his stride long and purposeful beside Heriberto and Mateo. They formed a phalange of machete-armed men, cutting through the stalks, Olive slightly behind because a pumpkin vine had tangled around her ankle. As she followed their blazed path, careful not to step on the felled husks, the bristly leaves stung her bare forearms.

Ahead of them a two-foot hedgerow of Sudan grass had been planted to keep down the dust, signaling even to Olive that a vehicle road was on the other side. Cal slashed through the grass. Heriberto and Mateo, already on the other side, shouting. She noted the dirt road, fresh tire tracks, and no sign of a vehicle. Then, she saw them, the dark green tomato vines, bent with red tomatoes.

The three men were examining the plants when Olive walked up to them. Cal showed her the vine's lobed leaf, his voice tense with excitement. At first glance, Olive validated the lobed leaf Cal held out patiently for her replicated their Augusta Girl's unique genetic signature. That sealed it for both of them. No words were needed. Brody was the thief. Brody had stolen their seedling trays, and from the time they had disappeared from their stacks at the end of the farm's rows five months ago, they had not only survived but matured into these healthy vibrant plants, laden with luscious fruit in want of harvesting.

Mateo spun at a noise. A ground squirrel. It ran down the bank and disappeared in a thicket of wild berries. She caught the glimmer of water. A creek, maybe. Then she saw something that did not belong, something manmade, and she shouted until the men saw it, too. They and their machetes took the lead along a deer trail through the brambles where, under the limbs of an old giant maple, someone had erected a yurt.

Cal unzipped the front of the yurt and they stepped inside while Heriberto and Mateo scouted the perimeter. Inside, the yurt looked more spacious than Olive had initially perceived. The thick plastic floor was clear of clothing and bedding. All that remained was random trash and a few utensils scattered about.

"He cleared out fast," Cal said, appearing far more relieved than Olive expected, considering he'd just discovered his tomatoes—tens of thousands of dollars-worth of tomatoes—growing in someone else's field. Stolen by someone he'd trusted.

Olive picked up a receipt from the thick plastic floor. Redwood Market. Eleven dollars and twenty-two cents with yesterday's date. They might remember Brody.

She held up her phone. "No service." One more time, notifying Detective Henry Rogers would have to wait. She scanned the redwoods that rimmed the acreage, reaching clear to the dusky blue sky. The creek's underground murmur and an occasional car downshifting on the mountain road sounded a little like home. But the tomato vines' acrid release of the day's heat smelled exactly like their farm.

Heriberto shouted from upstream. Olive and Cal walked up the muddy, mostly dry creek. In the brush, a white van.

49

As Cal stood in the middle of their office, eyeing the south-facing wall, Olive knew what he was thinking. Punch out the wall and put in French doors. Her mother would appreciate the added light—anyone would—but especially now that they'd invited her to stay with them and live on their farm. She was getting older, Olive told herself. She lived alone. If she had an accident, no one would be around to help her. And she was her children's grandmother.

The new living space would leave them without an office. But they'd create an alcove in the dining room.

Olive felt a hand clamp down on her shoulder.

Her mother. "Hello, my love and son-in-law." She hadn't called him outlaw.

"What do you think?" Cal asked. "A couple of French doors opening onto a small patio?"

Ariela winced. Olive expected a different reaction. A criticism or a suggestion.

"I've made up my mind." There was a sheepishness in her voice that Olive had seen only once before when she discovered years ago that Ariela had been sleeping with the principal of Olive's high school. Then, she noticed the oblong, black cardboard suitcase by the office door.

"You're leaving."

"Now, guess where I'm going?"

Tuolumne County came out of Olive's mouth before she registered the thought.

"You know how you knew that?"

It was a rhetorical question, so Olive didn't answer.

"You read my mind." Ariela emitted that glow her skin saved for men. "He's lost so much."

He. Olive, only a little surprised, knew what was coming next.

"He'll be in the prison up there for years. Decades." Ariela pressed her hands in the universal prayer gesture. "You don't need me anymore. His poor misguided soul does."

Her mother's departing words *you don't need me anymore* sounded, to Olive, like a cliché but an ironic one. She had an urge to reply she hadn't needed her mother from the time she'd showed up on their doorstep uninvited. That would be mean. And it wasn't wholly true. At least when she looked at it from Ariela's side of things: she had been Olive's only constant sidekick when Olive had begun tracking down the truth. Ariela was her co-conspirator when she'd broken into Gil Souza's home. Who else would back her in such an outrageous "stunt," as Cal called it? She'd helped Thea come to terms with Cris's death. She'd watched the kids. Moreover, Ariela believed without qualification in Olive's instincts, she was sure of this, even defending her tenacity and self-reliance to an angry son-in-law.

Olive put out her hand and touched her mother's arm. A familiar sensation raked her gut. She never could get used to that mixed feeling of guarded love.

"I'm going to reopen my psychic bookstore in Jamestown," Ariela said.

Olive remembered well this small Gold Rush town that had escaped development, largely because most investments in the depressed foothill town ended in vacant store fronts. But a tangible degree of old-world charm survived. And it was roughly ten minutes from the state prison where Gil Souza was incarcerated.

"A larger metaphysical community than you'd imagine. And I'll lobby the prison to let me serve the spiritual needs of the inmates."

Cal had remained quiet through most of Ariela's announcement. He knew something about prison work, having led a gardening program for inmates in San Quentin to reduce recidivism.

In fact, that was how he had met Olive, when she showed up as a crime reporter covering the story.

"Just don't make any promises you can't keep," Cal said. "And remember at all times that you're trying to help a convicted murderer."

"The man was avenging his daughter's killer." Ariela's bracelets jangled with passion as she spoke. "I would, too, if someone hurt my girl." She pressed her hands to Olive's cheeks and kissed her nose. Then, she turned to Cal. "Outlaw, I don't want my departure to stop these remodeling plans. You may need me again and your futon is hard on the back." She picked up the black cardboard suitcase and left.

50

Olive took two sticks of butter from the freezer and chopped them into cubes. She sang the chorus to Marvin Gaye's "Save the Children" while cutting the frozen cubes into the flour with a pair of kitchen knives. She kept the pie butter chunky to produce a flakey crust, divided the dough into two equal balls, wrapped them in wax paper, flattened each with her rolling pin into one-inch-thick rounds and stored them on the middle shelf of the refrigerator.

While the dough set up, she peeled and thinly sliced four Jonagolds and five Pippins. On the stove top, melting butter waited for brown sugar and flour that would create a bubbling syrup.

Olive placed the chilled rounds of pie dough on her floured board and rolled out the dough until its circumference was more than enough to cover the rim of the glass pie dish. Her fingers danced among the apple slices as she piled them into the dish.

Cal had promised to be home early. Tonight, Thea was coming over with the baby. She'd named him Oliver Cristobal Villalobos. They were going to celebrate his naming along with Shell Bean Farm's survival. Cal and Olive had broken even from their rescued tomatoes. They held a u-pick harvest right in the field. It was an unexpected windfall that allowed them to catch up on their mortgage and pay their crew back wages—with bonuses for sticking it out. Enough profit to lease the barren land next door to the farm—newly planted in organic strawberries—and enough in reserve for next year's seed money.

Olive drizzled warm syrup over the slices and unrolled the top crust over the hill of crisp, buttery sweetness. Rather than trim the excess dough, she pressed the crusts together to form a thick trim so that, as the pie baked, the crust would start to droop from the weight of fat and crisp into an asymmetrically scalloped crust.

Her home smelled sweet and buttery when Byrd burst in the kitchen door after spending a day on the farm with his dad, and she could hear Cal kick the dirt off his boots, one, then the other. He was whistling and breathed in deeply when he walked into her kitchen, the fresh air clinging to his clothes.

Olive pulled on black quilted potholders and turned her face away from the rush of heat as she bent down to open the oven door. She pulled out the rack and lifted the apple pie from the baking sheet. As she carried the hot pie through the swinging kitchen door to the dining room table, thick glistening juice bubbled from its vents and trickled down the crust in rivulets of transient perfection. She thought about her dream of one day harvesting her own apples, next year, if all went well. You never could be sure in farming.

"Byrd, look up," *his mother said. "At the cloud. What do you see?"*
Byrd looked up, filling her with hope.
"A fluffy dog," he said. "I want a puppy."

Acknowledgments

Writing a book is hard. Publishing the book even harder. My GLOW writing circle sustained me through this effort: Enid Brock, Paula Mahoney, Simi Monheit, Sarah Savasky and Becky Wecks. Sylvie Drescher at Bookshop Santa Cruz Publishing Services took my manuscript and turned it into a lovely book. My sister Marti Somers designed the book's cover and nourished my soul. Denise Silva, my writing partner and editor-divine provided incisive critique and encouraging praise through several drafts of this manuscript. Thank you KT Taggart for editing and urging me to keeping moving forward. Coastal Cruisers chapter of Sisters in Crime provided a community of authors, mostly women, who demonstrated that publishing our books is not something we dream about. It's something we do. To Kat Helmer for writing sessions at The Abbey. Also, to Laura Davis, whose writing groups and retreats provided the initial vehicle for putting down the words. To Amber Sumrall for providing a venue to read the first chapter in public. To my therapist Joyce Kutcher for breaking a decades-old spell and nudging me through the portal. Thank you to Capt. Dara Herrick of the Santa Cruz Fire Department for her details on water rescue. Praise to my son Joe Schirmer, an organic farmer and leader in the organic and sustainable food movement, and Miranda Schirmer, my daughter-in-law who models charm and the quest for order in all she does. My grandkids—Alex, Colin, Charlie, Calvin, Pearl—and foster grandkids, who offered a candy store of irresistable lines and behaviors. To my precious daughter Jennifer Dunn for putting the manuscript into its first book form. To my Havanese Buster, who sleeps under the table as I write and takes me on walks. To Jose and Yadi Camarillo for their input on the Spanish dialogue of the novel. To Kevin Gallagher (rest in peace) who was the catalyst of this book and dwells in the margins of every page. And to my husband Dennis Schirmer, who brings me coffee in bed, fixes everything that breaks and makes sure I have a safe place to write.

CPSIA information can be obtained
at www.ICGtesting.com
Printed in the USA
FSHW011950081020
74646FS